SHATTERED

A BILLIONAIRE ROMANCE

MICHELLE LOVE

CONTENTS

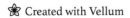

KLAPPENTEXT

Looking back over their sensual and tumultuous relationship, Lila searches for clues as to why Richard might want her dead but cannot reconcile their love with what has happened. While Richard languishes in jail awaiting trial, an exhausting and draining recovery keeps Lila at her lowest point until she meets handsome doctor Noah Applebaum. Despite her loyalty to Richard, Lila cannot help the feelings he stirs in her. Everything changes though, when a tragedy hits the Carnegie's and Lila has to reevaluate her life. But growing ever more paranoid and when secrets are revealed, she must try to keep her sanity as well as her life...

A beautiful artist is the victim of a savage attack just two days before her lavish Upper East Side wedding. Lila Tierney is stabbed and left for dead and her handsome billionaire fiancé arrested for her attempted murder. Can Lila recover from her terrible injuries in time to save her betrothed from a life in prison? Lila fights for her life while everything falls apart and she is left wondering who to trust – and who to love...

SHATTER ME: SHATTERED BILLIONAIRE PART 1

Now...Upper East Side, Manhattan

L ila stepped out of the dress, smiling as the assistant gathered the fabric up and stood, her eyes questioning. Lila nodded. 'It's perfect, thank you. I'm sorry you had to make those alterations, but Richard's mother is a lot slimmer than I am.'

The assistant, Tess – they'd become good friends in the months since they'd met – rolled her eyes. 'Oh stop. I'd kill for your curves.'

Lila flushed and thanked her as Tess turned to go. Lila looked in the long mirror at her reflection. This was *really* happening. Lila Tierney, artist, orphan, native of Seattle, Washington was marrying into one of the oldest, wealthiest of New York families. She who had spent many a night sleeping in her car because she couldn't make rent or making a bag of rice last for a week. Stealing apples from neighbor's trees with her best friend Charlie when they were kids in the children's home.

Eighteen months since Richard's proposal and she couldn't quite believe the whirlwind that had overtaken her life. Now here she was, in the most exclusive bridal boutique in Seattle – one that was by invitation *only* – trying on dresses for their wedding. Thankfully Delphine – Richard's effortlessly chic mother – had offered her own wedding dress, and although Lila had been skeptical, it was perfect, simple, light, comfortable but classic.

Lila shook her head. Jeez, what on Earth had happened to her? She wasn't the type for tradition – or even marriage – but the joy she had seen in Richard's eyes when she had agreed to marry him...his happiness made her glad. And his family – far from the Upper East Side snobs she'd expected – were welcoming, warm, especially Delphine who had taken the shy Lila under her wing and made her feel a part of their family. Delphine, the mother to five, didn't play favorites with her children but did with their partners; Lila was her buddy, her pal and Lila was very fond of the older woman.

Her cell phone beeped. A text from her best friend, Charlie. *How's it going?*

She called him back, her chest warming when she heard his deep, loving voice. 'Delphine's dress...it's perfect, not over the top, but just...me.'

'I'm glad to hear you're not going too Upper East Side for me.'

She smiled down the phone at her old friend. 'Hey, West Coast, Best Coast, always.'

'Glad to hear it. Look, I might come and meet you, take you for lunch. I could be there in five minutes.'

She gave him the address. 'I'm starving, so hurry.'

'When are you not hungry, Fatty?'

She blew a raspberry down the phone and hung up, grinning to herself.

She dressed hurriedly, snagging her hairbrush and dragging it through her tangled, shoulder-length dark hair. Her simple cotton dress was pink and made her golden skin glow, her big violet eyes wide and shining. She smiled at her reflection. Lately, her face always seemed flushed and excited, and Lila decided it suited her.

She finished tidying herself up, grabbed her purse and pushed the curtain of the dressing room aside. She started as she saw a man, a ski mask covering his face, standing directly outside the cubicle then as he clamped a hand over her mouth and pushed her against the wall of the fitting room, she saw it. His knife. Without hesitation, her attacker drove the blade into her belly again and again.

Pain. Unimaginable pain.

Even if she could have, Lila had no time to scream.

1

NOW...

Blink.
Pain. Someone screaming. She could smell blood.
Blink.

Someone talking to her. Lila? Sweetheart, can you hear me? Charlie. Help me.

Blink.

She's losing too much blood; we have to get her to the theater now. Urgent, urgent.

Blink.

Who would do this?

Blink. 'We're putting you under now, Lila, just relax.'

Who did do this?

Blink.

Who would?

Who?

Eyes closing now, darkness.

Who?

...and why?

2

THREE YEARS EARLIER...EAST VILLAGE, MANHATTAN

Lila wiped down the bar as Mikey, the bar owner, locked the doors. It was a Saturday night - actually, it was Sunday now, Lila thought, glancing at the clock. Three a.m. and she had one last chore to do and then her bed was calling her. Mikey smiled gratefully at her.

'Seriously, Lila, if you hadn't volunteered to stay and help me clean up, I'd be here until Tuesday. What a night.'

'Well if you will offer half-price beer...'

'Wait...what?'

She grinned at him. 'Kidding. Dude, I have Machiavellian reasons...Charlie and I were thinking about going to Seattle for a week. See the old stomping ground. Any chance I could get a week off soon?'

Mikey considered. 'As long as we arrange cover, I don't see why not. I'll even throw in a week's vacation pay in advance.'

Lila goggled at him, her large violet eyes wide. 'Seriously?'

Mikey grinned as he stacked chairs on tables. 'Of course, you think I'm a tyrant?'

'I do not; I think you're the best, thank you.'

'You're welcome. So tell me again...why aren't you and Charlie a thing? Apart from him being the scariest mofo this side of the Hudson.'

Lila rolled her eyes. Since she'd started here a year ago, juggling bar work with her studies at the School of Visual Arts, she'd fallen in love with New York and the constant activity of it. Her best friend Charlie, the boy to whom she'd grown up closest to in the children's home, now a police detective sergeant, had transferred with her from Seattle, much to her surprise and gratitude. They'd shared an apartment for a few weeks before Lila decided she wanted to see if she could strike out alone. Charlie had been understanding, had even helped her move out, and she was glad that their friendship was as strong as ever.

Charlie, a few years older than her at thirty-four, was a hard read for anyone who didn't know him as well as Lila did. A serious, intense man, he nevertheless had no lack of female attention with his brooding, almost dangerous looks. His last girlfriend had reluctantly broken up with him when she realized he was never going to propose to her and since then he was the king of the one-night stand. Most nights, though, he would hang out with Lila, happy to watch TV. while she studied; he even cooked for her.

Lila adored Charlie, had done so since they were young and lived at the children's home in Seattle. He had been fourteen; she had been a toddler when he took her under his wing. When she was nineteen, she helped him celebrate his thirtieth birthday by drinking (illegally) way too much tequila – it was the one and only time their relationship had turned sexual. Lila lost her virginity to Charlie that night, and while it was a wonderful, sensual night, they had never repeated it. Too much history and Lila was afraid of souring their friendship.

So, now, as she smiled at her boss, she shook her head. 'Friend zone 101. And he's not scary, he just keeps to himself. Admittedly,' she laughed to herself, 'he is the king of *Resting Bitch Face*. But, Mikey, if you knew him...he's the kindest, warmest person ever.'

Mikey harrumphed. 'I'll take your word for it.'

There was a knock at the door that surprised them both. Mikey glanced out of the window and chuckled. 'Speak of the devil...'

Charlie nodded as Mikey opened the door for him. 'Thanks, man.' His face softened when he saw Lila. 'Hey, Snooks. On a night shift so thought I'd come give you a ride home.'

'She could do with one,' Mikey muttered, with meaning and Lila, flushing swiped at him then went to hug Charlie. 'You're a lifesaver.'

Outside, Charlie's partner, Riley Kinsayle, a cheerful blonde detective grinned at her. 'Hey, gorgeous. Still single?' Riley, who had an enormous crush on Lila, never let the chance to flirt with her go by. He was the absolute antithesis of Charlie – open, gregarious, cute as all hell, with his messy blonde beard and a wide grin. *If he hadn't been Charlie's partner then,* Lila told herself, *I would absolutely date Riley,* but it was that 'you don't date your best friend's friends' thing. Occasionally, alone at night, Riley would creep into her fantasies – and sometimes, she grinned to herself, Riley *and* his twin brother, Woods – who admittedly was gorgeous but a real piece of work as well.

She pushed that thought away now as she climbed into the back of the car. Riley turned around. 'Hey, you wanna ride up here? On my lap?'

She laughed and kissed his cheek. 'Raincheck?'

'You better bet 'raincheck.''

Charlie got into the driver's seat and grinned at them both. *See? Not scary,* Lila thought fondly.

'You want me to book this guy for harassment?' He said to Lila, his voice a deep, slightly flat tone.

She grinned. 'No way. If he stops, *then* you can book him for non-harassment.'

Riley laughed and high-fived her as Charlie gave a grunt. 'That's not a thing, you know.'

He pulled the car out onto – for New York – a quiet street and turned the car towards the Brooklyn Bridge. They chatted casually until suddenly Charlie slammed the brakes on and was out of the car, weapon drawn. Riley opened the car door. 'Stay here, beautiful.'

Lila sat up, alarmed. Charlie and Riley ran to an alleyway where she could see a group of men gathered around someone on the floor.

She watched as the two detectives approached, then as the group hurriedly disbanded, Charlie giving chase while Riley helped whoever it was to their feet. As Riley brought the figure nearer, she saw it was a young man, covered in blood, barely able to stand up. Lila opened the door and got out.

'Jesus...here, Riley, put him in the back seat, and I'll take care of him. Go help Charlie.'

Riley, grim-faced, nodded, although clearly not happy about leaving her alone with the injured man. He slotted him into the back seat of the car and Lila got in next to him, pulling off her over-shirt and using it to wipe some of the blood from the man's eyes. He was obviously dazed, blood pouring from wounds on his face and jawline. He winced as he gently touched his face.

'I think you've broken your cheekbone,' she said gently, 'not that I'm an expert. We'll get you to the hospital, I promise, as soon as the guys come back.'

She dabbed the blood as best she could without hurting him. After a while, she saw he was staring at her and smiled at him.

'You're really beautiful,' he said in a cracked voice, and she chuckled.

'And we'll get you checked for concussion too,' she joked, although concussion was a very real possibility in this case.

He smiled. He was good-looking, even with a messed up face, dark wavy short hair, and deep chocolate brown eyes, so full of pain at this moment that she couldn't help smiling back and her heart began to thump just a fraction faster. 'What's your name, angel?' His voice, still broken, was rich and warm.

'Lila,' she said, 'Lila Tierney. And who are you?'

The man raised his hand and gently cupped her cheek. 'Lila...I'm very, very pleased to meet you...I'm Richard...'

3

NOW...LENOX HILL HOSPITAL, MANHATTAN

'Lila? Lila, dear, I'd like you to wake up now...it's okay, just open your eyes.'

The woman had a soothing voice, and Lila wanted to do as she asked, but she was afraid. What would she see? Was she dead or alive?

Pain. Oh god, there it was, the wracking, searing agony she'd first felt when that knife had sliced mercilessly into her flesh. Instantly, she was back in the dressing room, smiling as she pulled the curtain back, then the shock, the breath being wrenched from her body as she was stabbed. Her attacker – her killer? – grunting as he attacked her, vicious, cruel blows. *Him. A man. God help me...*

'Lila, it's okay, it's Doctor Honeychurch, please open your eyes if you can.'

A doctor, not an angel. Lila opened her eyes, wincing from the light, waking to a new horror. A tube down her throat and strangers around her.

No. Not all strangers. Charlie's face was even more serious than usual, wracked with worry and pain, and was standing at the end of her bed. She lifted her hand and reached for him. Charlie glanced at the doctor who smiled at him encouragingly.

'Please, take her hand. This is really good progress...she's been in a coma for a month; this means she recognizes you.'

A month. *Oh Jesus, no...* A tear rolled down her face and Charlie moved quickly then, taking her hand and bending down to kiss her cheek, kissing the tear away. It was such a loving, tender thing to do... but it felt so wrong. As much as she adored Charlie, it should be Richard here, holding her hand, kissing her tears away. She grabbed Charlie's hand, opening it to his palm. The doctor hovered in her peripheral vision.

'Lila, please don't over exert yourself.' But she ignored her and with her finger, traced letters on Charlie's palm.

Why here?

Charlie's eyes were haunted. 'You were stabbed, sweetheart.' So she *was* remembering it right. *God.*

Why?

Stunned, she saw his eyes fill with water, and he looked away. 'We don't know, Lila. Not yet.'

How long?

'A month, baby.'

Where's Richard?

She saw him glance at the doctor and hesitate. The doctor gave a little shake of her head. Charlie gave Lila a smile – a forced one. 'He'll be here later, sweetheart.'

Lila, exhausted, let her hand drop. The doctor stepped in then, checking her reflexes, shining a light in her eyes. 'Are you in pain, Lila?'

She tried to nod and the doctor, an African American woman with a kind, soothing face smiled at her. 'Alright, I'll get you some morphine. Try not to do too much, we've had to operate a bunch of times so your wounds are still raw. You kept trying to leave us, Lila, honey, but every time you changed your mind and came back. That's my girl.'

She smoothed a warm hand onto Lila's forehead. 'You're a little warm, so we'll try and get your temperature down before we take that tube out, okay?'

Lila sighed. She felt bound up, the heavy bandaging on her belly and, weirdly, on her chest too – she didn't remember being stabbed in the chest, but maybe it had been after she passed out. The thought made her want to vomit. Who could hate her that much?

She felt fatigue flood over her, and she closed her eyes again. As she sank back into sleep, she heard another voice, familiar, warm. Delphine.

'How is she?'

'Still too early to tell,' Lila heard the doctor tell her would-be-mother-in-law, her friend. 'She woke up and recognized Mr. Sherman, so that's positive.'

There was a pause.

'Does she know? Did you tell her?' Lila was shocked at the pain in Delphine's voice, and then Charlie cleared his throat.

'No, we thought it wise not to upset her. We'll tell her when she's stronger.'

Tell me what? What the hell is going on? Who stabbed me?

And where the hell is Richard...?

THEN... LENOX HILL HOSPITAL, MANHATTAN

Lila stood at the elevator and hesitated. She had been determined to go visit Richard in the hospital after Charlie told her they were keeping him in with a head injury, but now, as she stood waiting, she felt dumb, awkward. He probably won't even recognize me, she told herself, and I'll make it uncomfortable. She hadn't told Charlie her plan to visit the injured man, and now she didn't know why. She just felt...something. A connection. She couldn't get him out of her head. True, that night, after Richard had told her his name, he had collapsed into her arms, unconscious so by the time Charlie and Riley had returned to the car empty-handed, she was begging them to get to the hospital *now* and not wait for the paramedics. At the hospital, Richard had been borne away quickly into the labyrinth of the E.R. and Charlie had taken her home, still covered in Richard's blood. The sudden silence of her tiny apartment seemed claustrophobic, and she'd been too keyed to sleep. Charlie had apologetically had to leave to file a report on the incident so Lila had simply decided to clean her whole apartment in a bid to exhaust herself into sleep. Luckily, Sunday was her one day off from all work and study commitments, so by the time nine o'clock came around, she showered then fell into bed and slept until three o'clock when Charlie knocked on her door with Chinese food.

THE ELEVATOR DOORS OPENED, and before she could change her mind, she stepped onto it. To hell with it, she wanted to see if he was okay. *Yeah, right, so nothing to do with his gorgeous brown eyes, then?* 'Shut up,' she muttered to herself, ignoring the amused look a nurse gave her.

She found the floor he was on easily then again got cold feet. By the nurses' station, she could see an elegant older woman with white hair, tall, talking to a doctor. She hovered near them, trying to hear if they mentioned anyone. Jackpot.

'So Richard's facilities remain as they were?' The white-haired woman, spectacles pushed onto her nose, was ticking off items on a notepad. Lila saw the doctor repress a smile.

'Mrs. Carnegie, as I said, Richard has a mild concussion and cuts and bruises. He was very lucky, given the severity of the injuries he might have received. Now I know he looks battered, and it'll take some time for the swelling to go down but from the tests I've performed, there's no brain damage. Your son's ribs are understandably badly bruised but again, they'll heal just fine.'

The woman – Mrs. Carnegie – Richard's mother – thanked the doctor who escaped with a look of relief. He nodded to Lila on the way past. Lila took a deep breath in and went up to the woman. 'Excuse me?'

Mrs. Carnegie glanced at her over her glasses; severe at first then she smiled. 'Yes, dear?'

Lila realized her own hands were sweating and wiped them on her jeans. 'I couldn't help but overhear – are you Richard's mother?'

Her other woman smiled. 'Yes, I am Delphine Carnegie...can I help you?'

'Um...' Lila got tongued-tied. 'My name is Lila Tierney and I...'

'Lila? You're Lila?' Suddenly the woman's face changed, her eyes widened. 'Oh, my dear!'

She threw her arms around an astonished Lila and burst into

tears. Lila hugged her back awkwardly and then as Delphine's sobs subsided, she took Lila's face in her hands and kissed both cheeks. 'Thank you, my dear, for looking after my son so well. He says you saved his life.'

Lila rocked back. 'No, no, it wasn't me it was the two cops with me – one is my friend, I wasn't under arrest – they pulled the attackers off. I just...I just...'

Delphine wiped her eyes with a lace handkerchief and then tucked her arm under Lila's. 'Nonsense. You took care of him, in the car. He told me everything...now, when I last checked he was sleeping but let's go see if he's awake now.'

She was steering Lila inexorably towards a private room and Lila had no time to think before Delphine pushed the door open.

Richard Carnegie was reading, but as he looked up and saw her, a wide smile split his face – which made him wince as the movement pulled on some stitches. Still, his smile made Lila's stomach warm.

'Here she is,' Delphine said, beaming at them both. 'Look who's here to see you.'

'Lila...wow, it's so good to see you, thank you for coming.'

Delphine maneuvered Lila into the chair next to his bed. 'I'll just go see where your father is,' she said pointedly, with a grin and closed the door after her. Lila blushed furiously as Richard grinned at her.

'I just wanted to see how you were,' she said, hating that her voice trembled. The fact his face bruised and stitched didn't detract from how handsome he was, how his eyes twinkled at her, his mouth seemingly set in a permanent smile.

'I'm very well, actually, although I'm milking it a little for the Jello they keep bringing,' he chuckled as she laughed.

'I'm glad to hear it...unless it's a disgusting flavor.'

'It's mostly orange, maybe a strawberry now and again.'

'Nice. I like lime too.'

'I had one once. They're like gold dust apparently. We have to swap packs of cigarettes for those.'

She giggled. 'Oh, you do?'

Richard nodded, looking comically smug. 'I'm a favorite of Big Bernard's.'

Lila snickered. 'You mean you're his bitch?'

'Something like that,' Richard laughed. He reached over and took her hand, winding his fingers between hers. 'Seriously, though, Lila... thank you for coming. It gives me the chance to both say how much I appreciated your help that night...and to ask if I can see you again when they let me out of here?'

Her stomach flipped, and she flushed with pleasure. 'I would like that...but I really didn't do anything.'

He drew her hand to his lips and kissed her fingers. 'Yes, you did. If I had died that night, at least your lovely face would have been the last thing I ever saw. I'm okay with that.'

His compliment was lovely, but she couldn't help the grin that crossed her face. 'Dude...'

Richard laughed sheepishly. 'Too cheeseball?'

'A little but I'm okay with it.'

Richard leaned forward and tentatively brushed her lips with his. 'So, can I see you again?' God, he *was* a cheeseball but so, so adorable with it...

Lila leaned her forehead gently against his. 'Yes, Richard Carnegie...you can...'

5

THEN...FRIEDMAN'S LUNCH ON 9TH, NEW YORK CITY

Charlie Sherman sat at his desk, staring into space. He didn't hear when his partner Riley called him the first two times so when Riley threw a ball of paper at him, he looked up, annoyed. 'What?'

Riley grinned easily at him. 'I said, we going to this place for lunch or what? I'm starving over here.'

THEY WALKED the two blocks to the sandwich place. Riley ordered a Reuben's while Charlie just stuck with black coffee. Riley smiled at his partner. 'What's with you? You've been quiet for days. Not that you're not always quiet. But heck, you're freaking me out. What gives?'

Charlie grinned suddenly at his friend. 'Who needs to talk when you're around, buddy?'

'Fair point.' Riley took a huge bite of his sandwich. 'How's my girlfriend?'

'Lila?' Charlie laughed and shook his head. 'Dude, you wish. Anyway, she's good. I think she's gone to see Richard Carnegie today.'

Riley's eyebrows shot up. 'Really?' Then he laughed. 'Knowing Lila, she has no idea who the Carnegie's are.'

Charlie looked confused, and Riley sighed. 'If you hadn't landed me with the paperwork, you would know that the Carnegies are old money – *serious* New York old money. Richard Carnegie Senior is Bill Gates times a million. Absolute genius. Richard Junior, same thing. Harvard grad, brilliant, loaded and good-looking. And right now, probably hitting on my girlfriend.' Riley suddenly looked crestfallen, and Charlie chuckled.

'Yep, try and compete with that, buddy.'

Riley studied him. 'Can I ask you something?'

'Go for it.'

'I'm serious now...if I had the 'in' you have with a woman like Lila...there's no way I'd let her go. Let some other schmuck graze on that pasture. No way.'

Charlie laughed. ''Graze on that pasture'? Dude, that's gross.'

Riley shrugged. 'I thought it was poetic.'

'This,' Charlie said, stealing a French fry and pointing at Riley, 'this is why you're single. Anyway, Lila has the hots for Woods, she told me.'

'Oh ha ha,' Riley scowled at his partner. 'Don't invoke the Evil W.'

Riley and Woods Kinsayle's sibling rivalry was the stuff of legend. Riley blamed his overly competitive father, always pitting the twins against each other from birth but the glee with which Woods, his older brother by five minutes, carried on the 'feud' into adulthood was annoying. Woods, a sports agent, crowed over his 'lowly' cop brother all the time, and it didn't help that his gung-ho father loved his college football more than life. Both of them dismissed Riley's career as if it were nothing. Thankfully, Riley was old enough to ignore the petty childishness of it – and lately, Woods had seemed more supportive.

'Yo, kids. '

Charlie looked up at the precinct's desk sergeant, Joseph Deacon, a large dyed-in-the-wood New Yorker with the accent to prove it. 'Hey, Joe, you want something to eat?'

Joe looked regretful. 'Nah, Claudia's got me on a diet.'

Riley snorted. 'Bummer. Joe, you really are a character from those old cop shows, aren't you?'

Joe grinned good-naturedly. 'You got it, kid. Anyway, I was sent to find you. Deke pulled in one of the guys from that assault a few nights ago. The Carnegie kid.'

Charlie and Riley got up and went back to the station. Deke Holmes, a detective from another precinct, greeted them. 'Thought you might want this one.'

They thanked him and soon they were facing the arrested man. Charlie studied him; dirty, edgy, continually sniffing. Stereotypical junkie, who he'd expect to find out on the streets at that time of night. They interviewed him, but he didn't tell them anything they didn't know.

Afterward, back at their desks, Charlie finally confessed to why he'd been distracted earlier, and Riley nodded along as Charlie said aloud what they'd both been thinking.

What the hell was a guy like Richard Carnegie doing on the mean streets of New York at three am.?

6

NOW… LENOX HILL HOSPITAL, MANHATTAN

ust five minutes, Lila thought, *five minutes without pain, that's all I ask.* It was searing, agony shooting through her with every movement. *He really sliced and diced me,* she thought now, with a humorless snort of laughter. *Whoever you are, I hope you rot in hell.*

She'd woken up in the worst mood a few hours ago and couldn't go back to sleep. The repetitive bleep-bleep of the machines keeping her alive was getting on her nerves as was the tube down her throat. With any luck, they'd take it out, now she was doing better.

Was she doing better? She didn't know. The doctors and nurses talked in hushed tones, just outside her room – it made her paranoid. Not as much, however, as when Charlie and Delphine did the same thing. There were no words for how pissed she was at two of the people she loved most in the world. No-one was telling her anything.

And where the fuck was Richard? He was the person she was the angriest at. She knew she was wallowing in self-pity, but she'd been stabbed, for Christ's sake. Shouldn't he be here, holding her hand? She entertained a thought of him rending his clothes at the sorry sight of her…*now you* are *being a drama queen,* she thought. But it was breaking her heart not knowing where he was...*oh God*. The thought hit her like a sledgehammer.

Was Richard dead? Did whoever stab her almost to death kill Richard too? *No, no*...She couldn't stop the hot tears then, and she started to sob, choking on the tube down her throat. *Oh god*...that's why they weren't telling her anything...now she couldn't breathe, the panic attack overwhelming her. No oxygen, no oxygen...the machines beside went crazy, nurses rushing in, garbled voices, a prick as a needle pierced her arm and then...

Darkness.

'WE HAD TO SEDATE HER, I'm afraid, she had a panic attack. When she woke, she was calmer. She indicated that she wanted the tube out so we've asked for Dr. Honeychurch to come see if we can do that for her. We think Lila's suffering from depression...she's very down. Why don't you go sit with her?'

Charlie nodded, his face set. Delphine sighed, looking exhausted and patted his back. 'You go in. I want to phone home, see if someone can come sit with her. Maybe Cora.'

'I thought you said Cora was too fragile to see Lila like this?'

Delphine, suddenly looking every one of her seventy years, shrugged helplessly. 'I think Lila's need is more pressing. You should get some rest too, Charles, you've been here practically every day.'

'I do what I need to do for her,' he said gruffly, then impulsively kissed Delphine's cheek. 'I should check in at work, though, see if there's...' He trailed off, but Delphine understood.

'I'm going to call Cora now.'

Charlie waited until the woman had moved away then knocked softly on Lila's door. His friend was staring out of the window, dark shadows under her eyes, her cheekbones – never prominent before in her softly rounded face – were sticking out. Her whole demeanor screamed hopelessness.

'Lila,' he said softly, and she looked at him with dead, flat eyes. The startling violet had dimmed to a dingy purple, and the depths of pain in them were hard to look at. The hated tube down her throat was obviously uncomfortable. Lila pointed to the pad and pencil on the table next to her, and he handed them to her.

I hate this.

Charlie took her hand. 'I know, sweetheart, I know. But, please, you have to get better. For me. For the people who love you.'

She stared at him, her expression was hard, and when she wrote again, she pressed down on the paper so hard the paper ripped slightly.

I'm so fucking pissed at whoever did this.

'Me too, darling, believe me. I can't believe anyone would do this to you, of all people.' He stroked her cheek, and she leaned into his touch, her eyes filling with tears.

She hesitated before writing again and when she did, her tears splashed on the paper.

Is Richard dead?

Charlie read the note and looked up in shock. 'No, no, God, no he's fine, he's...*Jesus*...' He looked away from her. Lila scratched out another note and tapped him furiously on the arm until he looked at it.

Then why the FUCK isn't he here?! What the hell is going on, Charlie, and don't fob me off, or I'll rip this tube out of my own throat and stick it down yours!

Charlie half-smiled. 'Don't do that...just, breathe deep and I'll tell you. Promise?'

She nodded, never taking her eyes from him. Charlie blew out his cheeks.

'Okay...Lila, sweetheart, Richard isn't here because he's not allowed to come. He can't come. He's in jail.

Her eyes nearly boggled out of her head. *Why? Does he know who tried to kill me? Did he go after them?*

Charlie shook his head slowly and met her gaze. For a second they just stared at each other then he saw realization dawn on her face. She shook her head.

No. No. I won't believe it.

Charlie took her hand again, but she shook him away.

Say it, Charlie. Say the words out loud or I won't believe it.

Charlie reached over to cup her cheek. 'I'm so sorry, baby... Richard has been arraigned. He's been charged with soliciting your murder. Honey...Richard was the one who tried to have you killed...'

Lila's breath was coming in short gasps, and she was trembling violently and even with the tube in her throat, the scream that came from the very core of her was a keening, howling sound of unutterable grief.

Charlie would never forget it.

7

THEN...DINER, EAST VILLAGE, MANHATTAN

'I cannot believe you're a grown man, and you still like PB&J. Are you five? And with French fries and pickle? So gross.' Lila grinned at Richard as they sat in the midnight diner. Richard laughed.

'Hey, don't knock it until you've tried it. You must have a weird food thing, everyone does,' he waved a French fry in front of her until she snapped at it, clenching it between her teeth and he chuckled.

'Oh, okay, let me think...while stealing more of your French fries...' Lila shoved another one in her mouth and chewed. 'Okay... how about pretzels dipped in Nutella?'

'That's not weird. Come on, you're not even trying...'

'Pineapple on pizza.'

'That's gross but pretty mainstream. Ante up, Tierney.'

She grinned at him. This was their third date since he had gotten out of the hospital and she had to admit, every single one of them had been fun, playful teasing and getting to know each other. Tonight, he'd come to meet her after work, surprising her but she had felt such joy when she saw his boyish grin, that she forgot all her rules about not mixing work and pleasure and introduced him to her friends there. Tinsley, the new girl from Australia, had nudged her when Richard was talking to Mikey.

'Girl, you get on that as soon as you can.'

Lila had flushed. Although she hated to admit it, she *couldn't* think of anything but his hands on her when they were together. So far, he'd kissed her cheek, brushed her lips lightly with his but hadn't tried anything and God, she wanted him. She looked at him now in his t-shirt and blue jeans and wondered what it would be like to slide her hands under that shirt and...

'Lila?'

She shook herself and grinned ruefully. 'Sorry, miles away. Um...I really can't think of anything.

Richard - *Rich*, he said, *Richard is my father* – shook his head, disappointed. 'You failed me.'

'I'm sorry.'

'You'll have to make it up to me.' And there it was, the look he'd given her that first night, the one that could burn her clothes from her body, inflame the desire deep inside her. Lila couldn't look away from those dark, dark eyes...

'I can certainly try,' she said in a quiet voice. Without looking away from her, Richard raised his hand. 'Check, please,' he said calmly.

IN HIS CAR, he took her hand but made no other move to touch her. Lila's heart was beating out of her chest, her breath coming in ragged gasps. Even in the elevator, he didn't touch her, prolonging the agony although she could see his erection pressing hard against the denim of his jeans. His eyes ranged slowly all over her body until, as the elevator, stopped, he met her gaze again. He held out his hand to her, and she took it, feeling the jolt as his skin touched hers.

He led her into his penthouse, but she barely registered her surroundings. They moved straight to his bedroom and when she stepped into the room, he turned and took her in his arms, his mouth on hers. *God, that kiss*...she felt it in every cell of her body. His hands slid gently under her t-shirt, and she raised her arms so he could slide it from her, dropping it to the floor.

As if the fabric hitting the floor was a starter gun, suddenly they were tearing each other's clothes off, gasping, breathless in their desperation and when they fell onto the bed, naked, Lila knew this was right, this was what she wanted. She curled her legs around his waist as he kissed her, his cock hard against her thigh and *Jesus,* but she wanted him inside her, urged him to hurry. Richard groped in his nightstand for a condom, and she rolled it onto his quivering, hard cock as he smiled down at her.

'So beautiful,' he said and gathered her to him. His cock teased her sex sliding up and down in her slick crevice before at last, he thrust deep into her cunt. Lila gasped as he filled her, rocking against him, spreading her legs wider to accommodate his size. Richard's pace quickened as he slammed into her harder and harder, his hands locked either side of her head, his eyes on hers. Lila arched her back, her belly touching his and he groaned. 'God, yes...*Lila...*'

Her fingernails dug into his back, clawing at him, wanting him deeper and deeper, his sac hard against her butt as his cock drilled into her. She bit down on his shoulder and heard him give a short laugh. 'I'm going to rip you in half, little girl,' he growled, and she came as he drove himself into her. Richard's orgasm came in a rush then, shuddering and moaning, and they collapsed together, still connected. She loved the feel of his cock inside her, even as his erection faded and Richard made no move to pull away. He lay on top of her, smoothing the damp hair away from her face. 'I never want to be anywhere but buried in your delicious cunt,' he murmured, and she grinned, thrilled by his coarseness, her sex again beginning to swell around his cock. Her clit felt like it might explode when his fingers found it, and she moaned softly, and he began to rub and tease it. His lips were at her ear. 'Sweet, sweet Lila, I'm going to fuck that sweetness out of you, keep you all to myself, take you in every way you've ever dreamed of.' He moved down the bed and caught each of her nipples in his mouth, sucking and teasing then biting gently down on the nub, looking up at her with those soulful, wicked brown eyes of his. 'I could eat you whole,' he whispered and ran his tongue down her stomach until it dipped into the hollow of her navel. She shivered as he moved down and then his mouth was on her, his tongue lashing around the hyper-sensitive clit.

Lila moaned as waves and waves of pleasure crashed over her as Richard went down on her, his fingers clamped onto her hips, his tongue lapping and driving her towards an unbelievable orgasm. No sooner had she come, crying his name, then he launched his diamond-hard cock back into her, and Lila thought she might lose her mind. Richard, above her, looked victorious, and he made her come over and over.

Finally spent, they wrapped their arms around each other, studying the other's face as they caught their breath. Richard rubbed his nose gently against hers, his dark eyes shining.

'That was incredible,' Lila was still breathless, her whole body on fire, every nerve-ending vibrating with pleasure.

'You are incredible,' Richard said, running his hand down the length of her body. 'So sexy, so soft...Lila Tierney, you make my brain go to mush...'

She grinned. 'So, no change there then.'

Richard laughed. '*And* you bust my balls...so to speak.' They both laughed, and Lila sighed happily.

'If only a beat down wasn't the reason we met.'

Richard kissed her gently. 'Totally worth it.'

Lila cupped his cheek in her palm. 'You never did tell me what happened that night. Charlie told me you weren't pressing charges.'

Richard looked uncomfortable. 'Do we have to talk about it now? It was a just a mugging. I'd rather it wasn't made public, is all.'

Lila shrugged. 'That's fair, I was just wondering. Charlie's been...'

'Charlie's been what?' His response was snapped at her, and she rocked back.

'Nothing.'

Richard looked immediately contrite. 'Sorry, baby, I didn't mean to snap. It's just that guy pushes my buttons.'

'Who, Charlie?' It was Lila's turn to look uncomfortable. 'He can be too serious, sometimes. It's just his way; he doesn't mean anything by it.'

Richard looked at her, half-smiling. 'He's around you too much, and he's just too darn tall plus he's got that Neanderthal like machismo going on.'

Lila chuckled. 'He does come across like that, I'll admit. You jealous?'

Richard looked as if he was about to protest then grinned good-naturedly. 'A little. I hate that you're around him all the time.'

'He's my family,' she said quietly, and he kissed.

'I know. Ignore my pathetic male ego. Anyway, I really don't want to talk about Charlie Sherman when you're lying naked in my bed.' He pulled her on top of him and kissed her. 'How about we forget about everyone else and just do this all night?'

She grinned down at him. 'Now that, Mr. Carnegie, is a very good idea...'

NOW...

Every time he closed his eyes, he relived that moment. The moment his knife plunged deep into Lila's abdomen, her wide, shocked eyes, the slight catch of the fabric of her dress as the knife cleaved it then sank all the way into her soft belly. *God, the feeling.* He had stabbed her quickly, but he recalled every second, ripping the blade out then plunging it back into her body. And *God,* at that moment, she was more beautiful than ever.

The first six blows then she passed out, and he lowered her to the floor, crouching to stab her again, her blood soaking the thin cotton, making it stick to her skin. He stabbed the knife into the deep hollow of her navel again and again as his cock stiffened, blood-lust in his veins. He finally stopped, breathless, and stood, not able to tear his eyes away from her. Her dark red blood was pooling around her, her breathing labored.

I love you so much, he thought, *so very much, my beautiful Lila...* He gripped the knife and knelt to slide it between her ribs into her heart, to finish it, but then he stopped, froze.

He heard the saleswoman's voice and regretfully – and with a last look back at the dying woman on the floor, darted out of the fire exit door through which he had made his entrance. As he made his getaway, he heard the scream of the saleswoman as she found Lila's body and smiled to himself.

There was no way she would survive that attack. *No way.*

EXCEPT NOW HE KNEW – she had. Was lying in a hospital bed, alive. Which meant that once again, he would have to plan things carefully. It wouldn't be so easy this time; she would be protected, cared for, on the look-out for danger. So, he would be careful, vigilant, organized.

Because when he stabbed her the next time, he would make certain she was dead...

NOW…LENOX HILL HOSPITAL

L ila took the cup of ice chips the nurse held out and scarfed some down gratefully.

'Pace yourself,' the nurse chided. 'Just because you've had that damn tube out doesn't mean you're not still very sick. Your temp's up and the doc won't be happy about that. You still in pain, hun?'

Her mouth full of ice, Lila nodded. She wasn't making it up either; the hated tube was out, but her whole torso felt like it was on fire. The doctor told her it was to be expected. 'The knife shredded your intestines, Lila; it's a miracle you haven't had a major infection up to now. Plus your muscles, your damaged liver…it's going to take time. It's a marathon, not a sprint.'

Worse than the belly pain, though, was the fact she could barely feel her legs. She could wiggle her toes, but the pins and needle would not abate, and more than once she had woken up screaming from the cramp.

Lila tried to stay positive, but it was difficult. Worse now she knew the police thought Richard was involved. *No way,* she thought, *there's no way.* As soon as the tube had come out, she wanted to ask for a telephone but knew they wouldn't let her speak to him. Charlie would be furious. He and Richard had never seen eye-to-eye, but this was beyond a jealous spat. Delphine, in tears, had told her that Charlie had apologized to her for arresting Richard but the only lead they had was him and that Charlie told her he couldn't tell her why. Apparently, Richard had gone with the police without protest, telling his mother in a dead voice. 'I knew they were going to come for me, Mom. I didn't do this, but I know why they think I did. Tell Lila I love her, please.'

And Delphine kept her word, and Lila had squeezed the distressed woman's hand, trying to comfort her the best she could. She wrote 'I believe him, Delphine. No way was it, Richard.'

Delphine had smiled at her through her tears. We all love you so much, Lila Belle,' she used the nickname that she had given Lila almost as soon as she met her, 'we all do but no-one more than Richard. You are his life.'

I know. I know I am.. A small part of her spoke up. *If Richard wants me dead, then maybe I should be*...but she pushed that thought away. *Stop wallowing in self-pity. Get better. Do what the doctors say. Go fight for Richard.*

But suddenly being dead didn't seem the worst thing in the world. *I will save you, Richard Carnegie, if it's the last thing I do.*

There was a small tap on the door, and a small red-haired girl peeked around it. Lila felt herself relax and smile. 'Cora, darling...'

Richard's youngest sister, Cora, slid into the room and over to her side. Her large green eyes were wide and wary. 'Can I hug you?' Her voice wavered.

Lila reached out her arms, and Cora went into them. Lila hid a wince of pain as Cora hugged her tightly. 'I've been so worried, L-Belle,' the younger woman said finally, dragging a chair over to Lila's side.

'Don't be scared, C-Belle,' Lila grinned. Almost as soon as they had met, she and Cora had connected, a deep, binding connection almost as strong as her relationship with Richard. Cora – 'Cora Belle' to her Mom hence the nicknames – was nineteen now, a slim, petite redhead with a thousand watt smile and an adorable lisp when she talked. Fragile physically and mentally, she hero-worshipped Lila as her sister. Her two older half-sisters were neither warm nor loving – Delphine, the mother of them all, called her two eldest children 'The Foundlings' behind their backs. 'I cannot fathom how two such cold creatures came from my womb,' she would often say about Judith and Flora, 'they must take after their father.'

Delphine's first husband had died three years after they were married, a sudden heart attack. 'Brought on by sheer bile,' Delphine would mutter, almost gleefully.

Judith and Flora barely tolerated their younger siblings: Richard, another son Harry who lived in Australia, and then the surprise baby of the family, Cora, who had been born when Delphine was fifty.

Cora and Lila had become like sisters almost straight away – Judith, and especially Flora couldn't stand Lila, her artistic skills, her rebellious nature, her independence all at odds with their Victorian attitudes. On the few occasions she had met them – and caught them bullying Cora – she'd called them out to their faces, not standing on ceremony at all. She apologized afterward to Delphine, but Delphine had cackled wildly. 'Don't apologize, it was almost regal.'

This, *this* was why she loved the Carnegies. Richard Carnegie Sr. was the most serene, calm, intelligent man she'd ever met and she, like his children, doted on him.

'When I look at you and Richard,' Lila told Delphine, 'that's what I want. A partnership, a great friendship as well as passion.'

And she had that with Richard... *used to have it,* she amended with a pang. *Lately...not so much.* She smiled at Cora now.

'You look good, birdie. How's college?'

Cora smiled. Like Lila, she was a passionate artist and was enrolled at the same art college as Lila. 'Everyone asks after you,' she said now, 'they all send their love. I miss you, L-Belle, at home, we all do. I...' She trailed off and looked away. Lila guessed what she was thinking.

'I miss you too. And Richard...I miss him terribly. He didn't do this, you know. He couldn't, he wouldn't. As soon as I get out of here, I'll be making sure they know that.'

Cora was chewing her lip. 'Are you sure?'

Lila squeezed her hand. 'You bet,' she smiled to try and alleviate the tension. 'I'll be Erin Brockovich until they let him out.'

'No,' Cora hesitated, and her lip wobbled, '...are you sure it wasn't Richard who did this?'

Lila stared at her in shock. Cora was Richard's biggest fan; her adored infallible older brother. *No...no, this wasn't right.*

'Cora, you must never say that again, do you understand? To anyone! Of course, I'm sure...Richard would never do this to me, not ever – '

'He was screwing somebody else.'

It was like a wrecking ball to the chest hearing it said out loud, and Lila had to gasp for air. Tears poured from Cora's face. 'I'm so sorry, Lila, I couldn't not tell you after all of this. I only found out a few days ago, and I haven't been able to get it out of my head.'

'He wouldn't...' *You know he was, you know it, don't deny it...* Lila squeezed her eyes shut, felt a wave of dizziness, of nausea and pressed her hand to her chest. Another panic attack on its way... *breathe...breathe...*

Cora stood and grabbed the call button, and instantly a nurse came through the door. Lila could hear her saying something and Cora saying 'She can't breathe...' She heard a deeper voice...Charlie?

I'm alright, I'm okay, she wanted to scream at them, but nothing would come out, and now her lungs were burning, but all she could think about was *how she used to believe that Richard would never, ever cheat on her...*

...and how, now, she knew without a doubt that he had.

10

NOW...LENOX HILL HOSPITAL

Charlie took Cora by the upper arm as he caught her at the door of the hospital and steered her to a quiet place. 'Why the hell did you tell her that?' He kept his voice low, but Cora could see how angry he was.

'I'm sorry, Charlie...she was just sitting there defending him, all those tubes stuck in her arm and I couldn't bear it.'

Charlie's face softened as he looked down at the young woman, so broken-hearted and vulnerable. He ran a hand through his hair. 'I'm sorry, Cora...I didn't mean to scare you. It's just...I care about her, you know, I hate seeing her like this.'

Cora nodded. 'I know. God, Charlie, every night I go to bed and lay there awake trying to figure out who would do this. And the only answer, the only motive belongs to my brother.' She looked at Charlie's set face. 'I know you are on both sides of this, wanting to find who did it and having to arrest my brother. I'm so sorry, Charlie. I want you to know none of us blame you for Rich's arrest.'

'I want to know who did this Lila. That's all.'

Cora sighed. 'Look, you go back in, I'm going to go home and talk to my mom. I want to be there for Lila...especially after all she's done for me.'

Charlie nodded. 'Okay, pickle.'

Cora gave him a smile. 'You know you're the only person who calls me that. Lila says you never call anyone by a nickname except me.'

Charlie smiled back at her. 'Can't help feeling like you're my little sister too.'

CORA DROVE HOME to the vast family mansion in Westchester. Once a home of love and laughter, now it rang with sadness and hurt. Her father had disappeared into his work; her mother had canceled all of her committees and social events. Cora knew everyone in their circle was talking about them. The prodigal son in jail for the brutal stabbing of his beautiful bride-to-be. It was unthinkable. She had tried going back to school – had lasted a day before the whispers and loaded glances got too much. She'd almost broken her sobriety, found someone who had connections in the college dorms... she had resisted. Just. The thought that kept her going wasn't that she would spiral down immediately had she taken something but the hell and the pain her family – and Lila - would go through if she did.

Because Lila and Richard were the ones who had gotten her straight in the first place. Both of them had risked their reputations, their position, and their lives to help her get free of that life and she would not betray them by falling back into addiction.

Never again...

THEN... MICKEY'S BAR, MANHATTAN

L ate night, Friday night, Mickey's Bar was busy. Lila, not working for once, was sitting in a booth with Charlie watching Richard and Riley, Charlie's partner, howling with laughter at the bar with Mickey. Tinsley, the Australian waitress who'd been there for a month and was already Lila's good friend, winked at them as she moved around the bar. Lila noticed she colored a little as she looked at Charlie then looked away when she saw his set face. Lila nudged Charlie, sitting stone-faced next to her. 'You are *scaring* people again. Quit scowling.'

He shrugged. 'Wasn't aware I was, sorry. Just thinking about work.'

'Bullshit,' Lila hissed under her breath, and he turned to her, his full attention on her now.

'Huh?'

She looked at him, her violet eyes flashing with annoyance. 'You hate Richard. Just be honest about it, Charlie, you hate him and always have.' She grabbed her glass and got up, intending to go over to her boyfriend and Riley, who were playing pool. Charlie reached out and grabbed her wrist.

'No, don't go, I'm sorry.'

Lila sat back down with a sigh. 'At least, tell me why you don't like him.'

Charlie rolled his shoulders. 'I don't dislike him...I just don't trust him.'

Lila looked at him coolly. 'Because?'

'Something's hinky. What the hell was he doing on that street at three am.? Dude's loaded, seriously loaded, and yet he's on skid row getting a beat down by known junkies? Nah, hinky.'

Lila sighed and rubbed her eyes. 'So what? I can tell you – he's not on drugs. Even you can't see any signs.'

Charlie nodded. 'I admit that freely...he's not using so the only explanation is that he was dealing.'

Lila slammed her glass down on the table and did get up that time and Charlie didn't stop her, but she could feel him watching her as she crossed to the bar.

'Another Grey Goose please, Michael. Straight up.'

Her boss squinted at her. 'Not like you, Lila, but hey, it's your night off and more profit for me so...' He grinned as he poured her a drink then frowned as she downed it in one. 'You're pissed about something.'

'Just...' she sighed, 'Don't worry about it. Thanks, Mikey.'

She went over to Richard who was bemoaning his loss at the pool table to a gleeful Riley. She kissed Richard's cheek. 'Can we go?'

Richard didn't hesitate. 'Of course, baby.' He stuck his hand out to Riley who, grinning, shook it. 'Rematch, dude? You gotta let me try and win my money back.'

'Absolutely, man, you just let me know when I can whip your ass again, and I'll be there,' Riley's handsome face was split with the biggest grin and Lila was grateful that at least one of her friends liked Richard. They said goodbye to Riley and waved to Mikey. Richard stopped her as she reached the door.

'Hey, you wanna say goodbye to Charlie?'

Lila hesitated and glanced over to her friend. He was deep in conversation with a blushing Tinsley. 'No, it's okay, don't wanna be the third wheel.'

. . .

OUTSIDE THE EVENING WAS COOL, and as they got into Richard's car, he looked over at her and smiled. 'Want to go for a drive?'

She grinned back at him, her eyes soft. 'Sure.'

'We can go parking, like in yesteryear.' He pulled a face.

She laughed. 'Yep, the days of yore. I'll probably do some modern day stuff to you, though.'

'Such a dirty girl, I can't wait.'

They drove around the city for a while trying to find somewhere they could park the car and as Richard put it, 'make out like teenagers' but in the end, they got so fed up and horny, they drove back to her place.

Lila loved that, in the month they had been dating, Richard had spent as much time here hanging out with her as they did in his penthouse apartment. He teased her about her books, piled high, some of them even serving as an improptu coffee table. He spent hours looking at her artwork and talking about art with her. They would turn all the lights off except the string of twinkle lights along her bookshelf, drink wine, listen to music.

He had no pretensions, none that she would have expected but then again, when she'd met Delphine and Richard Sr., she realized where his every-man charm came from.

Now, on her single bed, they stripped off, tumbling together onto the hard mattress (the only thing he complained about) and made love, completely absorbed in each other as they moved together.

Afterward, famished, they ordered pizza and ate it in bed, chatting about school and work and what to do the next night. There was never any question that they spend their free time together – they were still in that heady, love-struck phase.

'So when do you finish school for the summer?'

'A couple of months. I do love it, but I'm looking forward to a break. Why?'

Richard smiled, hooking a lock of her hair over her ear. 'Because I thought we could take a trip together...Paris, London, wherever you want. My treat, of course.'

Lila picked at her pizza, feeling uncomfortable. 'Rich...'

'I know what you're going to say. But it's a gift from me to you; a thank you gift if you like.'

She shook her head, half-smiling. 'You can't get around it like that.'

Richard sighed. 'Look, Lila, let's talk about the elephant in the room. Yes, I have money. I've been very lucky both with my family and in business. That's just reality. But I'm also just a guy who wants to go on a vacation with his girlfriend. Do I not get to do that because I'm rich?'

She touched his face. 'But I don't want to be...kept.'

Richard laughed out loud. 'You are nothing of the sort. Look, we can even do a budget, backpacking thing if you like, if that's what makes you feel better.'

Lila was surprised. 'Really? You'd do that?'

Richard stroked her cheek. 'Of course. For you, anything.'

Lila wound her arms around his neck. 'In that case...yes, I'd love to travel with you, Richard.'

He kissed her thoroughly then looked at her with a wicked look on his face. 'Can I make one suggestion...as a compromise?'

She squinted at him in amusement. 'What?'

'Paris...that's luxury and all on me.' He studied her face and she shook her head, laughing.

'Oh if you must...'

He grinned and pushed her down onto the bed, covering her body with his. 'Thank you, Lila...now, let me show you just how thankful for you I am...'

AFTERWARD, Rich slept as Lila lay awake, unable to sleep. She was chewing over the idea of Rich's offer. She'd love nothing more than to travel with him – and she was touched by his understanding of her financial situation. She knew, if she let him, he would pay for...well, her entire life, really but she would not let that happen. They had to have some kind of parity.

Something else was bothering her too...Charlie. Despite her annoyance with him, she had to admit he had a point; what *had* Rich been doing on that street that night? She couldn't believe he was dealing – why the hell would he need to? He was a billionaire, several times over. She turned on her side and gazed at him...she had no experience with drugs except the odd joint now and again so she didn't know what a high-functioning junkie would look like. Was he using? He didn't have track marks, that much was obvious, so whatever it was, it was going up his nose...

Stop it, don't think like that. Charlie's just being over-protective as usual.

She closed her eyes and willed sleep to come but couldn't get the thought out of her mind. *Just ask him.* She sighed. *Later, another time.* After all, was it any of her business?

She had a lot to learn about Richard, she knew, it was just...she had already fallen hard for him, and Lila didn't want anything to break this blissful bubble she was in...

12

NOW...LENOX HILL HOSPITAL

D r. Honeychurch wrote down Lila's latest vitals then frowned at her. 'You're not doing as well as I would hope by this point,' she said gently. 'We've handled the risk of infection, and your wounds are healing well. But I'm worried, Lila. I think we need to set up a session with a serious neuro specialist because your nerves are obviously badly damaged, and I'm concerned your spinal injuries will affect your range of movement.'

She moved to the foot of Lila's bed and raised the covers. 'Can you feel this?' She drew her finger up both of Lila's feet.

Lila nodded. 'I can feel it, but the pins and needles are still there. I have been walking, but it's like walking on someone else's legs.'

'Right. And how's the pain?'

Lila sighed and shrugged. 'Pretty bad but it is what it is.'

Dr. Honeychurch pursed her lips. 'I think I'll change up your meds. You really shouldn't be in this much discomfort still.'

Lila looked at her. 'Do you think it could be psychosomatic? I'm all for finding out.'

Dr. Honeychurch smiled. 'I don't know, but that's the right attitude. How's the counseling going?'

'Good. Slow but good, although I just wish I knew...' She trailed off as Delphine Carnegie knocked and poked her head around the door

'Is this okay? I can come back.'

The doctor looked as if she was about to agree to that but Lila shook her head. 'No, please, come in.' She smiled at the doctor. 'Delphine and I have no secrets; she was to be my mother-in-law after all.'

Delphine's eyes widened, but she said nothing, sitting in the chair in the corner so not to get in the way.

'Well, look, I'm going to go see if I can make an appointment with the neuro gods. Just happens we have a superstar attending neurosurgeon visiting for a week. He's from your old haunt, actually,' the doctor was scribbling on her notes, 'Seattle-born boy. Nice fella too.' She leaned in conspiratorially. 'Has already won every surgical award going and he's not even forty yet. That's who you want on your case.'

With a smile, she left Lila and Delphine alone. It was the first time Delphine had been to see her since Charlie had told Lila about Richard's arrest and Lila could see the upset, the wariness in the older woman's eyes. She reached out a hand to Delphine, and she could see Delphine relax slightly. 'Come sit with me,' Lila said and when Delphine was settled, Lila fixed her with a steady look. 'Richard did not do this. I believe that with everything I have, with every cell in my body. He did not do this, Delphine.'

Delphine promptly burst into tears. 'Oh my little darling, I'm so sorry. Thank you for saying that...I've been so worried. I know my son, and he simply isn't capable.'

Lila tried to smile through her own tears. 'I know. He's flawed, and spoilt,' – she grinned playfully at Delphine at that – 'and sometimes the biggest pain in the ass but a murderer he is not. I will not believe it until Richard himself tells me it's true.'

Her smiled faded. 'Delphine...Cora told me that...' She couldn't get the words out and choked a little, breathing deeply. 'He cheated on me.' She said the words in a rush to help soften the blow, but her own heart clenched with sadness. 'Now that...sadly I *can* believe.'

Delphine was staring at her in horror. 'Sweetheart...no. He loves you. Deeply.'

Lila nodded. 'Oh, I know that, I do. But Delphine...he's done it before.'

Delphine got up, shaking her head. 'He wouldn't, Lila. He just – '

'He told me.' Lila said in a small voice. 'He confessed it to me. I just didn't listen at the time, blocked it out. But hearing Cora say the words...I assume the police think that's the motive for the stabbing. Which is why I know he didn't do this – *or rather* – it's another reason I know he wouldn't do this. He confessed once – in a rather round-about way – so why wouldn't he just say, *'Lila, I don't want to marry you, I have someone else,'* rather than sticking a knife in my gut?'

Delphine flinched, her eyes dropping to the bandaging around Lila's abdomen. 'Do you remember anything about that day?'

Lila nodded. 'Whoever stabbed me wanted me *dead;* he was merciless, brutal. The level of violence is something I'll never forget. Richard isn't capable of that kind of...' She stopped as Delphine looked away from her. 'What? What is it, Delphine?'

'No, nothing,' the older woman said hurriedly. 'I agree with you.' She was silent for a long time, then, in a voice broken by fear and distress, she looked at Lila and spoke quietly.

'Would you go see him? When you're well, I mean? Talk to him?'

Lila picked up her hand and squeezed it. 'Of course. As soon as I'm able. I want to see him, see if we can't sort this mess out.'

Delphine clutched her hand. 'Whatever you decide, you will always be my family, Lila Belle.'

Lila smiled at her but couldn't help feeling sorry for her. Caught in the middle.

'Who would, then?'

Lila blinked. 'Would what?'

'Want you, of all people, dead? Everyone adores you.'

Lila laughed softly. 'Not everyone. But, to answer your question, I really don't know.'

She hoped to God that she wouldn't be proved wrong.

13

NOW...LENOX HILL HOSPITAL

Noah Applebaum flicked through his notes from the surgery he'd just completed. Thanks to him, the seventeen-year-old being wheeled into recovery *would* play football at college next year. Noah knew he was good at his job – hell, that's why Lenox Hill invited him to the table – but he would go through the surgery in his mind, noting anything that went wrong, felt wrong, anything new he'd learned from the other people in the room. Noah had always listened to his nurses, his anesthesiologists, every one of the theater staff because they were the people in the trenches, as he called it. His collaborative methods and lack of arrogance made him one of the most popular surgeons back home in Seattle and his reputation was known around the country.

Even though he'd deny it, it didn't hurt that at six-five and built like an athlete, with a face carved by Greek Gods, his physical presence was like catnip to others.

They'd laugh if they knew how shy he really was, that his last girlfriend had been a few months ago. She, Lauren, had been fun at first until he realized she had found out about his family. His very wealthy, very private family. Not that she wasn't rich in her own right – her father owned one of the biggest PR firms in the world. Then she'd been constantly on his back to get engaged and after one too many 'false' pregnancy scares, he'd simply shut her down. Her vitriol and spite when he had broken things off with her had made him wary of getting too involved with anyone since then, his sex life being a series of one night stands. To most of them, he hadn't even given them his real name.

Work was his reason for getting up in the morning; he loved it more than anything except his family. Now as he made his way to the attending lounge to grab some coffee, he thought how nice it would be to have a break from Seattle – as much as he loved it. He'd been impressed by the staff here – more than impressed, inspired. One of his favorites, Delia Honeychurch, was in the lounge when he came in, and she grinned, raised her coffee mug in greeting.

'Just who I wanted to see,' she said, chuckling. Noah hid a smile, instead giving a moan.

'God, what fresh hell is this?' He winked at her and went to the coffee machine (not as good as the one in Seattle, but hey, he couldn't have everything.)

Delia drained her own cup and held it out for a refill. 'Actually, I think you might be interested. A young woman, mid-twenties, was admitted six weeks ago with multiple stab wounds to the abdomen. Really nasty.'

Noah frowned. 'Yes, I heard about that...wasn't she attacked in a wedding dress store?'

'Like I said, real nasty. Anyway, her wounds are healing, internal organs are responding well, but she's experiencing paraesthesia in both feet and lower legs, sciatica, inflammation of the joints in her legs.'

Noah nodded. 'Not uncommon when the nerves have been damaged. How's her spine?'

'Structurally fine but like I said, it was a nasty, vicious stabbing – the knife nicked vertebrae, sliced through nerves. Lila's young, like I said. Nice girl too. She was supposed to marry Richard Carnegie.'

His eyebrows shot up. 'The Carnegies? *Those* Carnegies?'

'Yup. Richard Carnegie Jr is – or was – her fiancé. He's been charged with her attempted murder.'

'Son-of-a-bitch.' There was nothing, that got under Noah Applebaum's skin more than violence against woman. Something to do with all the times his father whaled on his late, beloved mom... another reason he'd gone into medicine.

Delia Honeychurch waved her hand. 'Don't be too quick to judge,' she said, taking the coffee mug he offered, 'Lila swears blind Carnegie wouldn't do that to her. And it does seem the evidence is flimsy at best.' Delia's tone lowered, turned gossipy. 'Lila's stunning, I mean, a real beauty. Her best friend is a cop, and he was the one who arrested Carnegie. Seriously, it's like a soap opera around here.' Her face changed, and she looked ashamed. 'Ignore me. I'm getting jaded. But back to my original purpose – would you take a look at Lila?'

Noah sat down opposite her. 'Of course. When...?'

Delia grinned. 'How about after we finish this coffee?'

'Slave driver.'

'You bet your ass.'

14

NOW...LENOX HILL HOSPITAL

L ila lay down and tried to turn onto her side, to get comfortable, but nothing helped. Every time she moved, her stomach muscles screamed in protest, but she just hated sleeping on her back. Eventually, she managed to prop up her sore belly with a pillow and get a little comfortable. She closed her eyes, but her mind whirled.

She still remembered the day Richard had tried to confess his infidelity to her. He had picked her up from work, and at first, she hadn't noticed how quiet he was. She had been getting excited all day because tomorrow, *finally,* they were getting on a plane to London. She was beyond excited and so, when Richard met her at college, she was hyperactive, grinning from ear-to-ear and babbling on.

It was only when they got back to his place, she noticed his blank expression, the flatness of his usually expressive eyes. 'What is it, love?' She asked softly, going to him as he sat on the couch. He pulled her onto his lap and buried his face in her neck, pressing his lips against her throat.

She smoothed his hair, frowned at his desolate expression. 'Rich...tell me.'

He looked up at her with a deep sorrow in his eyes. 'Why are you with me?'

The question shocked her. 'Because I love you, silly.'

'And I love you.'

'Then why are you asking?'

He seemed to struggle to get his words out. 'You deserve everything, Lila, *everything*. I'm not good enough for you.'

Lila's heart began to beat faster. 'What the hell are you talking about?'

He looked away from her gaze. 'You deserve better.'

Lila got up. 'Whatever's on your mind, Richard, just say it.'

He sighed and put his head in his hands. 'I saw Camilla today.'

And she'd known exactly what he was trying to tell her. Camilla, his stunning society ex-girlfriend. Camilla of the debutante societies, Camilla who attended cotillions and flaunted her beauty at polo matches. The anti-Lila. Camilla, who'd been introduced to Lila by Delphine and who had immediately gone out of her way to make Lila feel like the outsider she was. That Camilla. *Bitch*.

Lila stared at Richard. 'So?'

He looked up, not understanding. 'What?'

'So you saw your ex? So what? We both have past lovers, no big deal.' She was being deliberately obtuse, but she was also damned if she'd let that bitch win. As long as she didn't allow Richard to say the words out loud, she could cope with his...

Cheating. That's what it was, plain and simple. But Lila, still only very young, was also wise to the world. Ex-sex was a thing, and Richard had made a mistake. *It was okay*, Lila told herself, trying to quell the pain in her heart. She turned away from him, gathering her thoughts, her feelings, getting up and going to the window.

'Don't worry about it, honestly, Rich. Let's focus on the future.'

'Lila...'

'Rich, please,' her voice cracked. 'If you're truly sorry, let me deal with this how I need to.'

He got up and came to her, and she let him take her in his arms.

'Okay then,' he whispered, 'but just know, I love you so much, and I'm truly sorry.'

She leaned into him. 'Don't do it again.'

'I swear.'

WHETHER LILA ADMITTED it or not, it *had* marred the trip. Although they had great fun traveling – their adventures were fun and light-hearted – every time they would dissolve into laughter, Lila would be hit with a jolt of reality. *He cheated. He cheated.* This man in front of her, being silly with her, teasing her, loving her, also cheated on her.

Paris was at the end of their trip and true to his word; Richard had gone all out – a luxurious suite at the George V, a balcony looking out over Paris to the Eiffel Tower. Lila was overwhelmed by it all, and although she loved every minute she had to admit, it was so far out of her realm of experience, this opulent life, she felt out of place. It made her question whether she and Richard should really try to merge their vastly different lifestyles or whether, by being with him, everything she brought to the relationship was somehow diminished.

On their last night in Paris, she was sitting out on the terrace. Richard had taken a business call – with an apologetic look at her – and so she snagged a glass of wine and went out onto the balcony, propping up her legs on a spare chair. She had so many questions, so many things she wanted to talk to Richard about, but she wanted to get things straight in her own head first.

When he came out, phone call over, he pulled up a chair next to her and kissed her cheek.

'Have you had a good time, my love?'

She smiled and nodded. 'I have, Rich, it's been so much fun.'

He studied her. 'But?' He smiled ruefully. 'I know you've been thinking things over, it's been obvious. So, look, let's get our cards on the table, here, now. Then when we go home, we can start with a clean plate.'

She tapped her glass to his. 'I'll drink to that.'

They both sipped their wine then Rich nodded. 'So, you first. Ask me anything. I assume you'll want to know about why Camilla and – '

'No,' she said, cutting him off. 'Not yet. I want to go back further than that. The night we met...'

She could see the shutters come down in his expression. 'Rich... you said I could ask you anything. Why were you on that street, with those people? Are you using? There's no judgment here, I just want the truth.'

Richard sighed. 'No, I'm not using, I swear to God. But...god... Cora was. My sixteen-year-old sister was and hardcore stuff too. Cora's always been vulnerable, easily depressed. She got hooked on cocaine and then graduated to heroin. I went there that night to pay off her dealer; he was threatening her. I also promised her that I would never tell anyone. We pretended she was going on vacation for a month before school started; instead, she went to rehab. She's doing really well too but if the press were to get hold of it...'

'Oh God...poor Cora,' Lila was shocked – she'd had no idea that the tiny redhead, so bubbly and exuberant, had been on drugs. The few times she'd met Cora, she had liked her very much, and the feeling was mutual.

Lila looked at Richard with a new respect, a new fondness. 'You did that for her? You're the perfect big brother.'

He laughed and rolled his eyes. 'Lila, I am far from perfect but what else could I do? Mom and Dad don't know; they would for sure blame themselves.'

She took his hand and kissed his palm. 'You have a wonderful family.'

'Thank you.' He sighed and cupped her cheek with his hand. 'As for the other thing, God, Lila, I cannot begin to tell you how sorry I am. I know we've only been dating for a few months, but there's no excuse for my behavior. I don't know what I was thinking.'

Lila just nodded, a lump in her throat. Richard studied her. 'Are you mad?'

She nodded but smiled, and he stroked his thumb across her face.

'I'm mad at me too. What a douchebag.' He grinned then and she chuckled, despite herself.

'Complete tool.'

'Numbnuts.'

'Dill-hole.'

Both of them laughed then. 'I'm sorry,' he said again, and she leaned her forehead against his.

'You're forgiven.'

He smiled gratefully then moved onto his knees before her, his fingers on the buttons of her dress. He undid them all slowly then moved the fabric apart to reveal her breasts, her belly, and her underwear. He pulled one of the lacy cups of her bra down and took her nipple into his mouth. Lila sighed and relaxed back as he worked, his tongue flicking, teasing, and the gentle sucking of his mouth making her nipple hard and sensitive. As he tongued both breasts, his fingers slid into her underwear and began to massage her clit before his long forefinger slipped inside of her, finding the g-spot and rubbing it until she was gasping and shuddering.

'I'm going to fuck you senseless, beautiful girl,' he murmured, his mouth against hers and Lila moaned. He tugged down her underwear then pulled her towards him. His mouth found her sex and with an expert tongue, he brought her to a shattering orgasm that made her body buck and writhe. He gave her no time to recover before sweeping her down to the balcony floor and launched his cock into her. He was so hard that when he thrust inside her, it was almost painful, but Lila wrapped her legs around his hips and urged him on, deeper, harder, *please...*

They fucked late into the night, moving from room to room in the suite, taking each other harder each time. Lila barely had time to catch her breath before Rich was pressing her against the wall and thrusting his cock deep into her cunt from behind or pinning her to the bed, ramming his hips against hers then coming in great, thick white spurts onto her belly.

Dawn was beginning to break over Paris before they finally fell asleep in each other's arms and Lila began to finally believe that everything would be okay...

15

NOW...LENOX HILL HOSPITAL

Noah Applebaum knocked once at Lila Tierney's door and went in. 'Hey there,' he said cheerfully then stopped. *God...* she was beautiful, even with tubes sticking out of her arms and dark shadows under her violet eyes. She smiled at him, and Noah felt something shift inside him – a yearning, a need. He cleared his throat, trying to regain his composure.

'I'm Dr. Applebaum, you're Miss Tierney?'

'Lila, please.' Her voice was low, slightly gruff as if her throat was dry. He automatically got up to pour her some fresh water, and she took the glass with a smile. 'Thank you. So, Dr. Applebaum, you're the neuro god Dr. Honeychurch tells me about?'

'Ha,' he grinned, 'She exaggerates – well, I pay her to exaggerate my abilities. But, seriously, Lila, yes I'm here to see if we can't help you with some of the issues from your, um, stabbing.' *Who the fuck would want to kill this gorgeous woman?* He tried not to run his eyes over her body; even in a hospital gown, he could see she had killer curves...*ouch, probably not the best description*, he said to himself. He felt like a teenager with a crush. *Get a grip, man.*

'So, I just wanted to come see you, introduce myself and do a couple of quick tests. Then we can come up with a treatment plan. How does that sound?'

'Sounds great, doc. What do you need to me to do?'

'Let's do a quick exam...do you want me to get a nurse to chaperone?'

She shook her head. 'No, it's fine.'

He checked her neck, sliding his fingers around to the back of her neck and asking her to move her head from side to side. Being so close wasn't helping his composure; he could smell her shampoo, her soap. 'Could you lay on your stomach if it's not too painful; I need to check your spine.'

His fingers moved over the bumps of her spine, checking each vertebra. Her skin was so soft, he wanted to stroke it. Finally, he pressed two fingers against her sacrum. 'Does this hurt?'

'Yes,' she said, 'Quite a lot.'

'Okay, I'm sorry, let me help you up. '

Awkwardly he helped her into a sitting position, noticing her wincing. 'I'm sorry to cause you pain, Lila.'

'It's okay,' she gasped slightly, holding her belly. 'I think my muscles are just getting used to moving again.'

He studied her. 'Do you think you could try walking with me? I'll hold onto you, of course.'

'Okay.'

He held her hands as she stood, gingerly, then guiding her, she managed to walk across the room. 'How does that feel?'

'Okay,' she said, wobbling slightly, 'Except my feet feel like they belong to someone else. Pins and needles.'

'Gotcha. Okay, well, you're doing really well – '

As soon as the words came out of his mouth, Lila stumbled, and he caught her in his arms. She looked up at him to smile sheepishly, and their eyes met and held. A beat, then she laughed softly, and the mood was broken.

'Doc, I should tell you, I'm an artist so am prone to attacks of the 'vapors' like that.'

He laughed and helped her back into bed. 'You did well, Lila, really. But I do think you would vastly benefit from a program designed specifically for your injuries. It'll be tough, and there will be times when you'll want to give up, or pound on me for making you do it but, I promise, it'll be worth it. What do you say?'

'I say, let's go for it.'

'Good girl,' he smiled at her, noticing the way her dark hair tumbled in soft curls around her face. *Adorable.* His eyes dropped to her mouth, dark red, full lips. He swallowed. 'Well, if you're willing, and Doc Honeychurch gives the go-ahead, I say we start soon.'

'Aren't you supposed to go back to Seattle soon?' she asked the flushed Doctor. 'Dr. Honeychurch told me about you. I come from Seattle too.'

'You do? Which part?'

'Puget Ridge. You?'

'Medina.'

'Nice,' she grinned, 'you're obviously from the same kind of family as my fiancé.'

Oh yeah, the fiancé. Currently sitting in jail for this gorgeous girl's attempted murder. Noah tried to smile. 'So just general questions... how're you feeling? Physically and emotionally?'

'Physically better, although I wish the pain would abate.'

He frowned. 'Do you mind if I take a look at your wounds? You shouldn't be in this much pain still.'

Lila shook her head and pulled her gown up. Noah lifted her dressings, noting some blood on them. He tried not to look shocked when he saw the pattern of scars on her belly. Nasty, vicious, brutal slices across her olive skin. Noah cursed whoever had done this; he couldn't imagine the pain, the terror she must have felt. He touched her skin gently, pressing lightly, asking her where it hurt. When he pressed against the worst of her scars, the one that bisected her navel, she winced. He gently replaced her dressing. 'You might have a little infection going on. It's still very bruised and I'm concerned you may have a small internal bleed too. We'll get that checked out. We're going to do anything we can to help, Lila, I promise.'

· · ·

HE FOUND Delia Honeychurch updating charts at the nurses' station and told her what they'd decided. 'I'm going to stay on for a few more weeks to help Miss Tierney through the worst of it.'

Delia looked impressed. 'Wow, that's great...weren't you supposed to be on sabbatical after your visit here, though?'

'Which is why I can stay...look, that young woman could use all the help we can give her.'

Delia smiled at him knowingly. 'Noah Applebaum, are you crushing on my patient?'

He grinned. 'Now that wouldn't be professional, would it?'

She laughed, nudging him. 'Whatever, thanks for doing this. She's a sweet girl.'

LATER, Noah swung round to see Lila again, but she was asleep. Feeling intrusive, he nevertheless stood at the door for a few seconds, studying her. She really was something else. *Who would hurt you?* He shook his head and then walked away. *Whoever it was, Lila Tierney, I promise you, he won't hurt you again...*

16

THEN...GREENWICH VILLAGE, MANHATTAN

Charlie Sherman sat back in his chair and stared at her. 'Huh.' Lila scowled at him.

'This is to go no further than you two,' she said to him and his partner, Riley, who was sitting beside him. 'It's to protect Cora, and I won't see her hurt because you two have got sticks up your asses about Richard.'

'Hey,' Riley held his hands up, 'Sounds legit to me. You have my word, funny face.'

Lila smiled at him gratefully then looked at Charlie. 'Chuckles?'

A small smile spread across his face. 'You know I hate that.'

She grinned. 'Yes, yes I do. Seriously, though, we good? Can we all get along now?'

'Can I reserve judgment?'

'No.'

Charlie shrugged. 'Okay then, if that's his story.'

'Argh!' Lila threw her hands and Charlie chuckled.

'Kidding, you sap. I'm with Riley; that does make sense, and his blood came back clean, so...'

Lila was startled, and Riley rolled his eyes. 'So much for keeping that a secret, dude.'

'You did a drug test on him?'

Charlie sat forward. 'He volunteered one.'

'When?'

'A few weeks ago.'

'And none of you thought to tell me?'

'You're not the only one with secrets, Lila. He didn't want you to be mad at me, so he decided to prove he wasn't a junkie. Never mentioned the sister, though.'

Lila sighed and put her head in her hands. 'You boys drive me crazy.'

Riley squeezed her arm. 'We're all good now, though, Lila, right?'

Lila looked away from Charlie's gaze. 'Right.'

Later, Charlie gave Lila a ride home. Richard was in Washington at a conference, and so Lila invited Charlie in to hang out.

She handed him a cold beer from the fridge. 'What's been happening with you?'

Charlie grinned. 'Nice of you to ask. I've been seeing someone.'

The bottle stopped halfway to Lila's mouth. 'No way, really? Who?'

Charlie made a big deal of taking a drink before he answered her. 'Tinsley.'

Lila smiled. 'Oh, Charlie, that's great, how long?'

'Couple of weeks. She's a good girl.'

'And drop dead gorgeous. Oh, I'm so happy for you.' She clinked her glass against his. 'To love.'

'To *really* great and long overdue sex,' Charlie shot back, and Lila laughed.

'Definitely.'

She felt so much better now; for the last couple of months, Charlie, and their friendship seemed to be slipping, his distrust of Richard marring their time together. She sighed happily now.

'Chuck, my old friend, I have this feeling things are going to be great for both of us.'

17

THEN...WOODS, CARNEGIE COMPOUND, WESTCHESTER

I t didn't last, of course. A few months later, just as Richard and Lila were celebrating a year of being together, Cora, to whom Lila had been growing closer, had a meltdown and smoked a joint at a local music festival. A paparazzo bored out of his brain at the gathering, got a few shots of her, and that was that. Front page news. The daughter of tech scion, Richard Carnegie Sr. was a junkie – they managed to find out everything, even confidential files from the place she had attended rehab.

Cora was destroyed, and Richard was losing his mind from worry. Lila, at first, didn't know how to help, but then, when she was alone with Cora one day, Cora asked her a simple question.

'How did you...I mean, what was it like growing up without a family?'

Lila looked surprised. They were walking in the woods near the Carnegie mansion in Westchester, with Richard Sr.'s beloved spaniels racing ahead of them. The day was warm for fall, and Cora was throwing tennis balls for the dogs to chase. Lila considered her question.

'It's strange; I never knew family life at all so it's hard for me to say or make a comparison. I can tell you what it was like being in a children's home; sometimes fun, sometimes awful.'

Cora nodded. 'Same with family. Sometimes I love them all to distraction; other times...I wish I were alone, without all the weight of expectation, responsibility. Without being judged.' She looked away from Lila's gaze.

Lila suddenly understood. 'Is it Judith again?'

Cora nodded. 'She won't leave me alone. Keeps telling me I'm destroying Mom, that I'm reckless and selfish – and I know I am but it's almost a daily thing now. Texts, phone calls.'

Lila stopped her with a hand on her arm. 'You mean, she's waging a campaign? Seriously, C-Belle, that isn't right. What's her problem?'

Cora smiled sadly. 'I'm an easy target. She hates Richard too, but she knows he'll fight back. I'm not good at that.'

Lila shook her head. 'I don't understand what she gets out of behaving like that.'

'She hates us, plain and simple, and by bullying me, she gets a cheap thrill. She hates that she's not in Daddy's will – why would she be? Mom told them when she married him that his money was his money. Mom's not even in his will – at her own insistence. He doesn't like it, but that's what she wanted. She's not exactly poor herself, and they agreed that she would provide for Judith and Flora out of her own money. But then the crash happened, and Mom lost a lot of money. Judith doesn't earn her own money – she believes she can gad around, doing her 'self-improvement' and Mom will keep on funding it.'

'I do hope one of her self-improvement courses deals with how not to be an absolute fucking bitch,' Lila was angry now. She hugged Cora. 'Cora Belle, I will deal with Judith, I promise you that. You just concentrate on recovery.'

Cora hugged her tightly. 'You've been more like a sister to me than they've ever been, Lila Belle.'

. . .

LILA KEPT HER PROMISE. So incensed was she, she didn't tell Richard, or Delphine what she was going to do. She confronted Judith at her holistic spa – a front for Judith's catty friends to gather and bitch about how unfulfilled and empty their lives were and how their husbands didn't understand them.

Lila walked straight past reception, ignoring the woman who called to her and marched straight to Judith's office. She didn't bother to knock. Judith looked up shocked as the door slammed open. The woman sitting opposite her looked vaguely scared. Lila pointed at her. 'You. Out. *Now.*'

The woman cast a quick look at Judith and fled, Lila slamming the door behind her and leaning back against it. She stared Judith down.

'What the fuck do you think you're doing, Lila?' Judith's voice was pure ice, and she stood up and walked around the other side of her desk to show Lila she wasn't scared of her. Judith was a tall woman, dwarfing Lila, but the smaller woman didn't back down.

'I've come to tell you, Judith, that you will stop your harassment of Cora this minute. That if you ever, ever try to bully her again, I will personally see to it that you are punished.'

Judith threw her head back and laughed. 'This is about the little junkie? Oh, for goodness sake, what has she told you? Are you so stupid you don't realize you can't trust a drug addict?'

Lila stepped towards her and to her satisfaction; a flicker of fear came into Judith's eyes. 'I've been in situations you wouldn't dream of, Judith. Unlike you, I grew up in children's homes and when I was sixteen, on the streets. You have no idea who you're dealing with, or what I know, and I'm telling you, leave Cora alone. Do you understand?'

'Who the hell do you think you are? Just because you're fucking Richard does not mean you are a part of this family. The Carnegie's don't need a whoring little gold-digger like you, Tierney.'

Lila's smile was cold. 'Like I said, you don't know who you're dealing with, and you forget Judith, you're not a Carnegie.'

'Get the fuck out of my office, you little tramp, or I'll have security throw you out.'

Lila snorted. 'I'd like to see you try. Anyway, I've said what I came to say. Leave Cora alone.'

She walked out of Judith's office, slamming the door behind her, and smiled grimly to herself. She knew she had gotten to Judith, she had seen it in her eyes.

She walked to the nearest subway station and rode the rail back to the Village. Her cellphone rang. Delphine. Well, Judith had run to Mommy fast. Steeling herself, she answered the call.

At first, she thought the older woman was crying, all she could hear was gasps and squeaks but then, she realized, Delphine was laughing. 'Oh, Lila Belle, I just keep thinking of you and your tiny fists waving in Judith's face.'

Lila chuckled. 'I'm sorry, Delphine, I had to do something.'

'Oh don't apologize...how stupid of Judith to tell me...now, of course, I know the whole story. I hope you don't mind, Lila, but I double-downed on your threat. If Judith doesn't leave Cora alone, then she's going to find her life very difficult. Honestly, I think the thought of having to get a job frightens her more than anything.'

'I'm glad. Bullying doesn't sit well with me.'

Delphine sighed. 'Cora doesn't really have any girlfriends, so I am so grateful you and she have bonded. Come over for dinner tonight, you and Richard, and we'll thank you properly.'

THE DINNER WAS A RIOT, and Cora really did seem better. Judith had sent her a huge bunch of flowers with a simple note apologizing – in a roundabout way. Lila had rolled her eyes, but Cora laughed. 'For Judith, that's practically rubbing gravel in her hair.'

Richard had taken Lila in his arms when he heard. 'I can't thank you enough, but I think I may have come up with a way. Tell you about it later.'

She laughed, thinking he meant sex. 'If that's what you're offering, I'll take it.'

He just grinned, and when they were at dinner, he tapped his wine glass for his attention. 'Hey folks, I have a couple of things I want to say. First off, I'd like to propose a toast to my sister, Cora – Cora Belle, I love you so much, we all do, and I can't tell you how proud we are that you're battling your demons and winning. Everyone falls sometimes, but not everyone has the courage to pick themselves up.'

'Hear, hear!' Lila said, and they all raised their glasses to the blushing Cora.

'Thank you,' she said and smiled gratefully at her brother. A look passed between then, and he gave her a small nod that the others couldn't decipher. She grinned excitedly.

Richard cleared his throat. 'And to my Lila...my little warrior woman. To have stood in front of my sister like that, to go up against Judith, who, quite frankly, terrifies four-star generals...Lila, you amaze me. Thank you from the bottom of our hearts. You might not think it was much because I know you, but to us, to Cora, it proved one thing. You are our family and we, yours.'

It was Lila's turn to color, and she waved their thanks away. 'My pleasure, really, it was nothing.'

Richard hadn't finished. He walked around to Lila and offered her his hand. She took it and stood, slightly confused about what was happening. Next moment, no more confusion.

Richard dropped to one knee, and Lila wobbled. He grinned up at her. 'Lila, you are the love of my life. I know I'm not worthy of you... yet. But I want to spend my life trying to be. Lila...would you, please marry me?'

18

NOW...LENOX HILL HOSPITAL

'Okay, two more minutes and then rest. I don't want you pushing yourself too hard.' Noah fixed her with a look that meant business. 'Lila Belle, I mean it.' He'd picked up Delphine's nickname for her; it suited her.

Lila grumbled but grinned at him. During the six weeks of her rehabilitation, she and Noah Applebaum had become good friends; their friendship flirtatious and teasing. The doctor was thorough, he pushed her, but lately, as she had improved, she had been eager to push herself...and he was worried that she might hurt herself.

'Make your mind up, Noah,' she chided him now, somewhat breathlessly, as she pounded on the treadmill. Her leg movement had improved, the pain diminishing as her muscle tone got better. She had admitted to him that she ached after their sessions but that it was 'a good ache, rather than a searing ache.'

He admired her commitment, never questioning his methods. 'Right, now, as you slow, I want you to concentrate on your abdominal muscles, feel for any pain.' He put his splayed hand on her belly as she ran, trying not to think of her warm skin under his fingers. 'Move my hand to where you feel the most pain.'

Lila was flushed but seemed to color an even darker scarlet when he touched her. He couldn't take his eyes off her mouth, her pink, bee-stung lips. She slowed her pace then tentatively moved his hand to where she felt the most pain – her right side. Noah swallowed as he felt the muscles contracting under his skin. 'The good news is that it's more than likely a side-stitch from cramping.'

He went to move his hand away, but Lila grabbed it and held it against her belly again. 'I'm getting better...can you feel?' Her voice was soft and their gazes held and locked. One beat. Two. He couldn't help but let his fingers stroke her soft skin and Lila gave a little gasp of pleasure, closing her eyes.

You are a professional...Noah reluctantly took his hand away and went to his notes, willing his erection to go down. *God,* he wanted her so badly, but she was his patient...and she was engaged to be married.

'Noah?'

'Yes?'

'They're discharging me on Monday.'

He nodded. 'I know. That's good news, right?'

'Right.' A silence where they couldn't take their eyes from each other then Lila gave a small smile.

'I'll miss you.'

Oh god. 'Lila, I will miss you too...but if I don't get back to Seattle, they'll get rid of me. You're doing great, the aftercare service is phenomenal.' *No, no, stop it, stop pretending that the last six weeks with her haven't been the best of your life, that she isn't the first person you think of in the morning when you wake, the last at night.*

Lila wiped down her arms with a towel and stepped from the treadmill. She went to the door and locked it, pulling down the shade.

'Richard cheated on me,' she said, 'A few times.'

'He's a fool.'

She nodded. 'I'm telling you this because I finally know how he felt when he was with those other women. The love I have for him has changed, become friendly rather than romantic and I believe with all my heart that he wasn't the one who tried to kill me. But these last six weeks...I can't get you out of my head, Noah. Every time you touch me, my entire body screams out for you...I hate that I feel this way, and I know what you're going to say, that it's not uncommon for patients to get crushes on their doctors. This isn't that.'

So many thoughts ran through Noah's head at that moment but instead he went to her and took her face in his hands. 'I've tried so hard to be professional about you,' he murmured, 'but you drive me crazy, Lila. I can't get involved with a patient...but...'

'You're going back to Seattle,' she said, softly, 'and I'm engaged to Richard. And I truly am not a slut. But right here, right now...'

She didn't get to finish as Noah pulled her lips to his and kissed her thoroughly, his hands tangling in her hair, his mouth hard against hers. Lila kissed him back, moaning with excitement as he slid his hands under her t-shirt. Soon they were pulling each other's clothes off, desperate to get at each other. Noah stroked her naked body, marveling over the soft, lush curves of her. 'If you feel any pain...'

She grinned up at him. 'Stop being a doctor, Noah...'

He laughed and gathered her to him, kissing her passionately as he lowered her to the floor. He kissed her full breasts, down her stomach and kissed each one of her still bright pink scars. 'No-one sane would do this to you,' he murmured as he lifted her leg and buried his face in her sex. Lila moaned softly as he licked and tasted her, as his tongue teased and made her clit harden. As he climbed on her body to kiss her mouth again, she could feel his huge, rock-hard cock against her thigh and reached down to guide it into her. Noah thrust into her, still careful, but she urged him on, wrapping her legs around his waist.

They moved together as if their bodies had always been made for each other, their gazes locked. 'Noah...,' she whispered, looking up at him in wonder. Noah felt his heart burst as he saw the love, the tenderness in her eyes. *You are all I have ever wanted,* he wanted to tell her, but he said nothing.

After they'd come, Noah's cock shooting deep into her leaving them both shuddering and gasping, they dressed, stopping to kiss every minute. She placed her hand against Noah's cheek. 'You're wonderful,' she said softly, 'I will never, ever forget you. You gave me back my life...in so many ways.'

As soon as she had left the room, Noah Applebaum knew he was in big trouble. Not from the hospital – there was no way they could find out unless either of them said anything and he trusted Lila with his life -, not from Richard Carnegie, or his family but from his own heart. They might have had a silent agreement that this was a one-time thing but his emotions right now...

Calm. Breathe. Relish the moment...and let her go...

19

THEN...UPPER EAST SIDE, MANHATTAN

L ila looked down at the ring on her finger. At her request, it wasn't the huge bauble Richard at first had suggested, more a simple, classic solitaire diamond, but it still felt wrong on her hand. It was a symbol of ownership to her mind. At work and college, she had a good excuse not to wear it, but everywhere else, she had none.

The night he had proposed, Lila had been shocked – and more disconcerted than delighted. Her heart had warmed at his words and the love in his eyes, but the way the rest of his family had looked at her – she had felt obliged to say yes and perform the role of a delighted fiancé.

And the thing was...she loved Richard, with all her heart, she loved him, but something still didn't fit right. She couldn't pinpoint it either. They liked the same music, books, their intellect was pretty much on a level, but she couldn't shake the feeling that something was waiting around the corner, something that would hit them full-force, that they wouldn't recover from.

She tried to talk to him about it, but Richard would think she was referring to his infidelity and shut the subject down - pleasantly but with finality.

It was Delphine who noticed she was quieter than normal and the older woman, taking Lila out to lunch in a high-end restaurant in Manhattan, asked her directly.

'Lila, do you want to marry Richard? No recriminations, just the truth, please.'

Lila sighed. 'I do, truly, Delphine. It's just I feel...that we don't know each well enough yet, and I'm still only twenty-six. I haven't had time to do my own thing yet, you know?'

Delphine nodded and sipped her wine. 'Darling, I do know. I made the mistake of marrying before I did my own thing – the first time. Thankfully, Richard Sr. was a completely different man to my first husband; we spend as much time apart as we do together, without recrimination and in perfect trust. I get the best of both worlds with him.'

Lila chewed over her words. 'I'm not sure Rich would be up for that. And to be honest...it's the trust part I have a problem with for now.'

She really didn't want to tell Delphine about Camilla, but she realized, now, that it was a big part of her hesitation. 'I've always had trust issues with men,' she confided, trying to deflect attention from Richard, 'so, it's my problem rather than Rich's and something I'm working on.'

'There's no reason you have to get married soon...take your time, make my son wait.' Delphine grinned wickedly. 'I'm sure every bride goes through this. But sometimes, marriage doesn't have to be a prison, sometimes it's the open door. Do you know how many more opportunities you'll have as Richard's wife?'

Lila paled. 'Delphine, I do not want his or your money, I've always made that clear. I'm not a gold-digger.'

'Oh, bless you child I know that. Do you think we'd be so welcoming if you were? That damned Camilla was, ugh. Loathsome creature. You are worth a million of her. But let's be practical; once you're married, you will be rich too. It just goes with the territory. And don't immediately assume that's a bad thing; look what you could do with it. Build better children's homes, work for charities, or pay for further education in your chosen field.'

Lila's eyebrows shot up. 'I had never thought of it that way.'

'Well, do. Money isn't evil, people who spend it selfishly are. And you are not one of those people.'

Lila had to admit she felt better after talking to Delphine, but when she went home that night, she found Richard in a foul mood.

'What's the matter, baby?'

Richard, his tie pulled down and a heavy glass of scotch in his hand, threw a copy of the National Enquirer at her. 'Want to tell me about this?'

She picked it up, seeing her own face staring back at her. She frowned then paled as she saw the headline. *Beauty hits the jackpot with Billionaire #2.*

Oh, fuck...

20

NOW…UPPER EAST SIDE, MANHATTAN

'How do you feel?'

Cora and Delphine exchanged worried glances as Lila looked around the apartment as if she couldn't remember being here. She'd lived here with Richard for the last year, out of convenience for school more than anything, but she had never felt at home here. Her home was the little house they were building out of the city. It was the one place she really felt she belonged with him because she had put in as much work and as much money as she could afford into it.

She smiled at the other women. 'I'm fine. A little overwhelmed is all. I guess I'll just take my case into the bedroom for a minute.'

Cora darted forward before she could grab her bag. 'Don't you dare,' she chided Lila, 'You need to take it easy.'

Lila sighed but smiled at her. 'Sorry. Of course.' She wondered what Cora would think if she knew about the extra-athletic fuck she'd had a few days ago. Lila bit back a grin. *Noah Applebaum…I wish I could stop thinking about you.*

She loved them both but wanted to be alone – *ha, alone.* That was a thing of the past; Delphine had arranged twenty-four-hour security for her. No-one could get close.

Delphine fussed around her, making her tea, plumping pillows until Lila begged her to sit down. 'You're making me dizzy.'

Delphine sat down as Cora reappeared. 'I've unpacked everything so you don't need to,' the young redhead smiled shyly at her.

'You didn't need to do that,' Lila held out her hand to her, 'but thank you.'

For a few minutes, Lila sipped her tea while the others waited. She grinned at their expectant faces.

'Guys, relax, please. I'm good.'

Delphine shared another glance with Cora. 'Sweetheart...do you know what you want to do next?'

Lila nodded. 'Absolutely. I want to see Richard.'

21

THEN...UPPER EAST SIDE, MANHATTAN

C arnegie's new fiancée, twenty-five year old Lila Tierney, is an up
and coming artist studying at the Big Apple's School of Visual
Arts. The couple's engagement announcement hit the society
pages just as it's been revealed that Carnegie is not the first billionaire to
have crossed paths with the raven-haired beauty. Six years ago, billionaire
art dealer Carter Delano was rumored to have dated the young artist for a
few weeks before breaking things off. Tierney was said to be devastated, but
six years later, she's finally got her rich young man...

'I HONESTLY DON'T KNOW whether to laugh or lose my shit,' Lila said,
tossing the rag aside. 'That's so far away from the truth I can't even
tell you.'

Richard was still glowering. 'But you didn't ever mention it.'

Lila shrugged. 'Why would I? Have we ever discussed our exes?'
Except for Camilla, she wanted to add but didn't want to be spiteful.
'And I don't even count Carter as an ex. I was doing a friend a favor by
double dating with him and his brother. Carter and I got along as
friends but we never even slept together. It was nothing.' She looked

at his angry face. 'What are you really angry about, Rich? Because I can't believe it's over this shit.'

Richard's body slumped. 'It's not...I'm sorry, I'm sorry, baby, forgive me.' He dropped into a chair. Lila pulled up a chair and sat next to him.

She took his hand. 'What is it?'

Rich sighed. 'Judith. She was the one who planted the story about you.'

Lila rolled her eyes. 'So what? At least she's staying away from Cora. I can take anything Judith throws at me, I have no skeletons.'

Rich smiled sadly. 'I'm sorry she's doing this to you, darling. And I'm sorry I jumped to conclusions. I guess I...'

He stopped and shook his head. Lila touched his face. 'What?'

'I guess I almost wanted it to be true, that you had some secrets so I could feel some sort of parity. God, I don't know, I just can't get past my...indiscretion.'

Lila sat back and sighed. 'God, Rich...I thought this was done with months ago. Look, it happened, you apologized, I accepted that apology. Let it go.'

She got up, clearly annoyed. Why did he have to keep bringing this up? It was almost like he wanted to feel bad, feel sorry for himself. She went to the kitchen and grabbed a couple of beers from the refrigerator. Closing the door, she looked at the calendar. The wedding was fifteen months away.

Fifteen months. Lila closed her eyes. *What's the matter with you, woman? Why does the thought of being married scare the crap out of you? You love him, don't you?*

I DON'T KNOW. Oh god...I don't know...

22

NOW...RIKER'S ISLAND, NEW YORK CITY

Her heart was thumping hard against her ribs as she walked through to the visitors' room. As she sat down in front of the glass partition, she felt vomit rise in the back of her throat and tried not to gag.

'Breathe through your mouth, honey, it gets easier to bear,' said a kind faced woman to her right. Lila smiled weakly then, as the door to the prisoner's side opened, her stomach dropped.

Rich had aged in the months he'd been incarcerated, his face covered with a thick beard. He sat down and looked at her, placing his hand flat against the glass for moment. Lila tried to smile, put her hand against the glass to mirror him. It was a shock to see him so broken.

He picked up the phone. As she put the receiver to her ear, she heard his shaky breathing.

'Lila...oh god, Lila...' He started to sob and her heart fractured. She wanted to put her arms around him and tell him it was okay.

'I didn't do this, Lila...I swear on everything I am, that I did not do this.'

'I know, Rich, I know...don't you think I know that?'

'I would never, ever hurt you, my love, never...'

He hadn't heard her, she realized. 'Richard. Richard, look at me.'

His sobs became gasps and he looked up, eyes streaming. 'God, I had forgotten how beautiful you are.'

She ignored the compliment. 'Richard, listen. I know you didn't do this. I know with every fiber of my being that you would never hurt me, let alone stab me.'

Rich flinched. 'God...they showed me pictures, Lila, of you, of your injuries, of how they found you...baby, I'm so sorry.'

Lila shook her head. 'Don't think about that. We need to concentrate on getting you out of here.' She stopped, looked away for a second. 'Rich...I know you were...with someone else. It's okay, it really is so don't keep anything from me. I need to know everything so I can help you.'

Richard's face crumpled again and he began to sob and Lila let him cry himself out. 'Rich,' she said softly, 'It's okay. We both have our...mistakes.' She felt strangely disloyal to Noah saying that. 'Please, take a deep breath and tell me everything.'

So he did. To her great relief, it wasn't Camilla he had strayed with this time, but his new assistant, Molly. The affair had only begun three months before Lila's stabbing but she could tell that Molly had been more than a fling. She felt strangely relieved.

After he'd finished, they stared at each other. 'I love you, you know?' he said and she nodded.

'I know. I love you too but Rich, we're not *in love* anymore, are we?'

He shook his head sadly. 'No, I don't think we are. And I hate saying that. I thought we'd be together forever. I hope you find someone who truly deserves you, Lila, I do. And please, whatever happens to me, to us, please don't abandon my family. They love you as one of their own.'

It was Lila's turn to cry now, tears dripping down her cheeks. 'I would never do that, I love them too.'

He put his hand against the glass again. 'Lila...will you come visit me again?'

'Of course. Every day. Every day, Rich, as long as you're in here.'

.   .   .

SHE WAS STILL THINKING about him on the ride home. As the town car sped through the city, she felt a peace settle inside her. Her cell phone rang. Charlie.

'Hey little one, how did it go?'

Lila sighed. 'Good. Really good. Charlie, I need your help...we have to start trying to free Rich – '

'Are you serious?'

Lila pulled the phone away from her ear for a moment. When she spoke again, her voice was strained with anger. 'Charlie, enough. I know Richard didn't try and kill me. I know it.'

'Because of your years of detective training? Or a hunch?'

'You weren't in that dressing room, Charlie, you didn't have a knife stuck repeatedly in your belly, and you didn't hear him, feel him, *and smell him.* Don't you think I would have recognized my own fucking fiancé?' She was mad now, mad at Charlie for his antagonism, his negativity.

There was a silence on the other end of the phone then... 'You're right. I'm sorry, boo. I'm just frustrated that we haven't found whoever did it. I'm scared I'll lose you...but, forgive me, the guy cheated on you if nothing else.'

Lila sighed. 'That's not anything you have to worry about now. We agreed to break our engagement. But that will not stop me from fighting for his freedom.'

Another silence then a soft laugh. 'Sweetheart...I hope that guy knows what he's lost. I'll come by after work and we'll talk.'

'I'd like that.'

WHEN SHE GOT HOME, she showered and then got into bed for a nap. The day had exhausted her; her body ached, her mind fatigued and sad. Her head pounded and she felt nauseous.

She awoke to the sound of someone pounding on the door. She staggered out of bed in her shorts and t-shirt to see her security guard coming in the door.

'I'm sorry to disturb you, Miss Tierney, but there's a police officer here to see you, says it's urgent.'

Lila sighed. 'It's just Charlie, let him in.'

Charlie was grim-faced when he came in but Lila rolled her eyes at him. 'What's with the drama? I was sleeping.'

'Lila...'

Something in his tone made her stop. 'What is it, Boo?'

'Lila...sweetheart, I have something to tell you and it's not going to be easy.' Charlie took her hands, his expression grim but his eyes were sad. He led her to the couch and made her sit down.

Lila looked at him, ice flowing through her veins. 'What?'

Charlie cleared his throat and when he spoke his voice was soft. 'Lila, there was an incident at the prison. In the exercise yard. Some guys were whaling on a new guy and Richard tried to stop it. Lila, he got stabbed, in the back. They called the emergency services straight away and he was rushed here, to the emergency room a little over an hour ago.'

Lila was shaking her head from side-to-side. She wanted to scream, wanted to hit Charlie for what he was about to tell her. 'No...no...'

'Darling...he died forty minutes ago.'

She stared at him in horror. *No...no, this isn't happening...*

RICHARD WAS DEAD.

LEAN INTO ME: SHATTERED BILLIONAIRE PART 2

23

NOW...UPPER EAST SIDE, MANHATTAN

*Reeling from Richard's murder, Lila and the Carnegie family close ranks
and grieve in private. Soon, though, Lila discovers something which could
shatter the Carnegie's faith in her and so she disappears. Her oldest friend,
New York detective Charlie Sherman is devastated by her disappearance
and works with the Carnegie's and their vast resources to find her. At the
same time he and his partner Riley investigate Richard's murder and find
out more about the dead man than they expected. Richard's brother Harry
returns to New York and when he meets Charlie's ex-girlfriend Tinsley,
sparks fly. In Seattle, Noah Applebaum can't get Lila out of his mind and
when he learns of Richard's death, he resolves to track her down. With more
than one person seeking her, will Lila be able to stay hidden and safe, with
the biggest secret of her life...*

U*pper East Side, Manhattan*

THERE WAS a quiet sadness in the apartment as Lila dressed for the
funeral. She still couldn't believe it; Richard was dead. Her love for so

long, the man she thought she would spend the rest of her life with until that terrible day all those months ago. The day she was brutally stabbed and left for dead. Somehow, even though she had loved Richard, she knew that day marked the end of one life and the beginning of another.

She looked around the apartment. It rang with loneliness. *This was never my home,* she thought now. *I may have spent every night here, with Rich, but it was never really my home.* It was too opulent for her simple tastes, too designed, too neat. She preferred her space to be cluttered and cozy.

She had already told Delphine, Richard's mother, that she wanted to move, that being in the penthouse apartment was too painful. Delphine had understood. 'You can go anywhere you want now,' she had told Lila, 'everything Richard had is now yours, with our blessing.'

God. Lila Tierney, the girl from the children's home, the girl who from sixteen to eighteen had lived in an old car, was a millionaire. She would give every penny away to have Richard back in their lives, even though before he'd died, they'd agreed to break up. She still wanted her friend, for herself, for his family.

'I miss you, Boo,' she said aloud to the empty apartment. A knock on the door made her start, chuckle softly to herself. *If this was a movie,* she thought as she went to get the door, *then Richard would be standing on the other side, a big grin on his face.*

Instead, her oldest, most trusted friend, Charlie, half-smiled at her. 'Hey, you. Ready?'

She tried to smile back but just nodded. 'Ready.'

He offered her his arm as they walked to the elevator, his big warm hand covering hers. It wasn't until they were settled in the town car, that it hit Lila. Richard's funeral. Richard was gone. That funny, erudite, adventurous live-wire of a man was dead. How could that be? Her breath hitched and caught in her chest and she felt her composure slip.

Charlie took one look at her and wrapped his arms around her and let her sob out her heartbreak.

24

WESTCHESTER

Harrison 'Harry' Carnegie felt utterly out of place in the home he had grown up in. Having lived in Australia for the last fifteen years, he'd forgotten how organized and structured Westchester gatherings could be. More than that, he hated to see his parents, his sister Cora, so utterly devastated.

Delphine had introduced him to Lila at dinner last night and he'd chatted to the petite brunette, seeing exactly what his brother had in her. What she'd been through this last year...poor girl. And the devastation on the faces of his family was echoed in her lovely, heart-broken eyes. He'd liked her very much.

Now though, circulating through the gathered mourners, Harry felt discombobulated, as if the person they were burying hadn't been his own brother. He and Richard had been close growing up but as their lives moved in different directions, the inevitable distance grew.

And he just couldn't get his head around the fact that not only was Rich murdered, but was in prison at the time. In prison! Harry shook his head – what the hell had happened to his family? His sister Cora was a wreck and, according to his mother, only thirty days sober. He looked across at her now, fragile and sparrow-like in her black dress, and his heart pounded with sadness.

'Hey kiddo,' he said moving to her side and wrapping a big arm around her. 'This is a shitstorm, isn't it?'

Cora smiled up at him through bloodshot eyes. 'This last year, really, Harry.'

'Sorry I wasn't around for it, punkin.'

She wrapped her tiny arms around his waist. 'Don't apologize. I'm glad you were spared at least some of it.' She sighed. 'Lila looks so sick, don't you think?'

Harry glanced over at his brother's ex-fiancée. 'I don't know her well enough to say but yeah, she looks tired. I don't know who half these people are, Cora. Richard's friends? And who's that dude over there that looks like he might go postal at any minute?'

Cora chuckled. 'That's Charlie; he always looks like that but he's a big softy, really. To me, at least, he's been very kind.'

'Little crush, sis?'

Cora giggled through her blushes. 'Noooo....He's Lila's oldest friend, and a cop.' She broke off suddenly. 'His partner, Riley, is lovely too.'

'He's gay?'

Cora laughed. 'No, his police partner, idiot. Hey, come meet some people.'

Harry balked and made an excuse – he really didn't want to meet 'people'. Cora, shaking her head, stuck her tongue out at him and smiled.

'Hermit.'

'Twig.'

'Old man.'

'Wise-ass.'

Harry smiled after his sister....*oh lord,* talking of sisters; Judith was bearing down on him. Out of all the Carnegie children, Harry was the only one she liked – adored, actually. The feeling was definitely not mutual.

Not even pretending to be subtle about it, Harry made his escape to the bar his parents had set up in the reception room.

'Dewer's on the rocks, please.'

The barman nodded and went to get his drink. Harry leaned against the bar and rubbed his eyes. God, let this be over soon, please...

'I heard an accent,' said a voice....an Australian voice. 'Might you be the sibling who escaped all this grandeur to go to the greatest country on Earth?'

Harry grinned and looked up to see a stunningly pretty blonde girl grinning at him. 'I might be. Well spotted.'

She laughed. 'Wasn't hard. I have Oz-dar.'

'The hell is Oz-dar.'

'Like gay-dar, except I can spot an Aussie accent a mile away – even an ex-pat who's caught the lingo. Where did you end up?'

'Melbourne.'

She clinked her drinks glass against his. 'Born and bred.'

Harry smiled. God, she was gorgeous, blonde hair pulled back in a low pony tail, blue eyes sparkling with humor, pink, rosebud lips parted in a wide smile. He stuck out his hand. 'Harry Carnegie.'

'Tinsley Chang.'

Harry raised his eyebrows. 'Chang?'

She grinned, obviously expecting the question. 'My stepdad is Chinese. And lot nicer than my real dad was so when my mum remarried, I took his name.'

'That's cool. I know the weight of having a 'name'.' He motioned around the place, then added hurriedly, 'Not that I don't love my family, because I do.' Sadness enveloped him and Tinsley stepped toward him, placing her hand on his arm.

'I'm sorry, Harry, about Richard, about all this. I got to know him quite well over the last few years; Lila and I used to work at the same bar and Charlie and I used to double-date with them.'

A spike of disappointment went through him. 'Oh, so you and the bulldog?'

She laughed. 'Not anymore, no, but thankfully, we've stayed friends.'

Harry nodded, his mind racing. She was utterly beguiling but a complication he really didn't need at the moment. Unless he was desperately needed, he wanted to get back to Australia and his life there. His shipping business was huge now, built from a small export and import company he'd started with some capital from his father and it had made him a billionaire in less than two years. He knew his father, to whom he was closest, was proud of him but within himself, there was a building dissatisfaction with his life. He wanted to create something, something tangible, with his own hands. He wanted to build boats, beautiful bespoke, hand-crafted sailboats for passionate sailors like himself. He just didn't know how his family would react if the CEO of the world's most successful shipping company was to give it all up to apprentice as a shipwright.

So...Tinsley Chang, no matter how enchanting, was a no-go. *Really. Seriously. You can't go there, man. And guess what, you definitely can't ask a woman out at your brother's funeral, dumbass...*

He sighed. 'Look, I have to get going but it was great to meet you.'

Tinsley nodded, not showing any disappointment or insult. 'You too, Harry. Hey, if you get the chance before you go back to Melbs, drop by the bar and I'll buy you a farewell drink.' She handed him a business card, and smiling, he took it.

'I will, thanks.'

Tinsley disappeared back into the gathering and he watched her go, feeling regretful and yet suddenly more optimistic. This trip home could be different than he'd planned. It could be the moment he finally broke free from his family's expectations, and told them what he really wanted for his life.

25

NEW YORK CITY

A week after the funeral, and Lila was just about finished packing up the apartment. The Carnegie's had insisted that she do whatever she wanted with the place; it was hers. So she decided to sell, find a small place in the city, put the money in a bond somewhere to gather interest. Not that she ever had to worry about money again, of course; Richard had left her his fortune, his properties, his cars, his personal effects. Only his trust fund and his seat on the board of Carnegie's industries went back to his family, the trust fund split between Cora and Harry.

Lila had begged Delphine to come and choose anything of Rich's that she wanted before Lila put it all in storage. 'There's no way I'm more entitled to anything than you,' she told her and Delphine reluctantly acquiesced.

Now the place rang with emptiness, with sadness, with the hole Richard had left. God, they had been so in love in the beginning, so sure that they belonged together. A part of Lila wished they hadn't decided to end things that last time, that Richard had died with the certainty he was loved by her. Which he was, of course; they did love each other – but it hadn't been enough.

And then there was Noah...

Lila sat down on the floor amidst the boxes, her entire body aching. She had pushed herself too far; it was still only a few months since her stabbing. Although she had made a remarkably quick recovery (thanks, in part, to Noah), tonight, her body was hurting – a lot. She lay down on the floor, staring up at the ceiling. She had rented a one-bedroom apartment in the village, and tomorrow she would make the final move and start over.

Except...she didn't want to be here, in New York, anymore. She wanted mountains, and orca, and the Space Needle. She wanted to go home and start her life over there...

And then there was Noah...

'You, again,' she whispered and closed her eyes, recalling his tall, broad frame, those sea-green eyes that twinkled with mischief. She remembered the feel of his skin on hers. At first, only in a professional capacity. The first time they'd met, he'd examined her, fingertips light on her spine, then pressing down, doing a routine exam of her abdomen, her injuries. The look in his eyes when he'd seen the extent of the stab wounds – not pity – not anger, compassion, empathy.

Only now could Lila admit that she'd been hooked from that first day. As they'd progressed through her rehabilitation, she got more and more excited when she knew she was going to see him.

When he started to visit with her after hours, she knew she wasn't the only one feeling it. They would sit and talk about their lives, about everything. She knew he was thirty-nine, from money (he'd rolled his eyes when he'd told her that) and that he loved what he did. They would laugh and joke about the same things, and every night his chair would get closer to her bed.

That last day, she had woken up, knowing that she would see him, professionally, for the last time and Lila knew, with every fiber of her being, that she would have to do...something. She hadn't counted on the passionate love-making on the floor of the rehab room; his gentle but firm touch, the way he caressed her body, the way he looked at her. She could recall every second that his huge, diamond-hard cock thrust into her, that she'd never wanted it to end, coming over and over. His kiss, his mouth on hers.god...

Lila rolled onto her side and moaned softly. Noah...Seattle...so much temptation. Stop it. Get up, go grab some food, and get some sleep. 'Okay,' she said out loud and rolled up, scrambling to her feet.

A searing, tearing pain ripped through her belly then and she gasped, doubling over. Overwhelming nausea and then she was running, just making it to the bathroom in time before she threw up. She vomited until her stomach was empty, and then sat down on the edge of the tub to recover, breathing deeply, trying to quell the nausea. Jesus...she had pushed it too far.

She swiveled around and ran the hot water. A soak would be perfect, then maybe she'd order some Chinese food and...*uh-oh...big mistake.* She bent over the toilet and dry-heaved for a few painful moments. As the bathtub filled, she brushed her teeth, gagging gently, trying to breathe through her nose. Soon, she was sinking gratefully into the tub, letting the warm water sooth her tired body and she felt herself begin to drift. She reached out to grab a bath towel, rolling it up and resting her head against it. So tired, so warm...

She awoke with a start. The water was freezing cold but it wasn't that which woke her. It was the fact that she felt something, even maybe heard something.

Someone was in the apartment with her.

BIG MISTAKE, my darling, sending the security team home for the night. I heard you telling them, in that sweet but firm voice of yours, that you didn't need their protection anymore.

But you were wrong.

That glorious body of yours stretched out in the bathtub, your golden skin, your dark hair piled on top of your head, those dark circles under your eyes. The way those thick, black eyelashes rest on your cheek. Your breasts... I want to reach out and touch them but no...I hold back. I watch the soft rise and fall of your belly as you breathe; admire the scars my knife left on you that day. I imagine going back to your kitchen, finding a knife and returning to plunge it again into your center, watch the shock on your face as you bleed out into the tub. Letting them find you dead and gone.

But not tonight, my love. Tonight, I allow you to live. Tonight, you may dream of days to come, weeks, months, years, in which you will make plans, plans which may never come to pass.

Because, my lovely Lila, I will come back for you...and when I do, you will beg for death before I finish with you. The horrors I will visit on that perfect body of yours before I take your life...

...they will be the stuff of legend.

26

SEATTLE

Noah Applebaum was having a bad day. A *really* bad day. First, a most beloved patient had died unexpectedly on his table, then later, a colleague, a good friend, had quit, telling everybody that he wanted to spend more time at home with his family.

'Bullcrap, Billy,' Noah had said to him, enraged, 'They've forced you out.'

Bill Nordstrom sighed sadly. 'Noah, when you get to my age, you realize – older people are written off. They're worried about their liability. If I make one mistake and a patient dies...'

'That comes with the territory of being a doctor,' Noah shook his head. 'They're fucking cowards, is all.'

Bill, his seventieth birthday just passed, smiled at Noah, his wise old eyes crinkling at the edges. 'Kiddo, I've seen it and done it all. It's time.'

Fuck the Board. Noah had fumed about it all day, his usual good humor missing. *That's not the only thing missing. Lila.* God, he missed her like he was missing a limb. He wanted to see her, touch her, hold her, make sure she was okay, was safe. He had been shocked by Richard Carnegie's murder, had wanted to reach out to her but he didn't know if she would want that, whether it would be appropriate given what had passed between Lila and himself.

That day was imprinted on his memory, the feel of her soft skin, her lips, and the velvety warmth of her cunt...her violet eyes shining up at him. What they did...so unprofessional, so wrong given her situation and her health...felt so right. The moment his cock had slid into her, he knew that he was lost. She was his for such a brief moment in time but his heart was forever hers now.

Missing her was another reason why Noah drove home in a foul mood. When he saw Lauren, his ex-girlfriend of five year ago, parked in her convertible outside his condo, he was about ready to explode.

'What are you doing here?' Short, brusque, hoping she'd take the hint.

She didn't. 'I was just driving past some of our old favorite haunts and I got nostalgic,' she said with what she must have thought was a sensual smile. Noah wasn't impressed.

'Lauren, this isn't a good time.'

He stalked to his front door – and she followed. 'Come on, NoNo; invite me in for a drink.'

Ugh. He'd forgotten about that damned nickname – who calls a six-five forty-year-old man 'NoNo'?

Man, you really are in a dark place...calm down. Noah sighed. 'One drink then. I'm really tired, Lauren.' Please god, don't let her call herself 'LoLo' – there was no way he was up for being 'NoNo and LoLo' tonight. Suddenly he found his humor again. As he walked into the house, he found himself wanting to talk with Lila, tell her about the horrifyingly twee names Lauren would give them. Lila would find it hilarious.

Lauren saw his smile and got encouraged. 'It's been too long, Noah.'

Noah poured the both a drink. 'Tequila is all I have. No lime, sorry.'

'Doesn't matter. How have you been?'

Noah drew in a deep breath. 'Good, look, I don't want to be rude but – '

'Why am I here?'

He nodded, and then relented. 'Not that it's not good to see you.'

Lauren sat back and smiled. 'I really was just passing some of the places we used to hang out, where we had good times. Remember we used to walk your dog at the Gasworks? Sunday afternoons. We'd make huge bowls of pasta when we got home and loll about in front of the TV. for the rest of the day. I miss that.'

Noah sat down opposite her. 'Yes, those were the good days. But, Lauren, they were quickly outnumbered by the bad.'

Lauren's smile faded. 'And I know I was to blame for that, Noah. I was young and greedy and stupid, and I apologize. I was too dumb to see beyond your family, and their wealth.' She leaned forward, her pretty face earnest. 'But, Noah...I've grown up so much you probably wouldn't recognize me. I've made my own money, become fully independent and I want you to know...I'd like to try again.'

Noah opened his mouth to protest but she cut him off, her voice shaking. 'Please, just hear me out.'

Noah gave her a brief, short nod and she smiled gratefully. 'Noah, these last five years apart have been lonely. Yes, I've seen other people but no-one I connected with as much as you. Please, Noah, won't you at least think about it?'

Noah sighed. 'Lauren...it's not that easy.'

She studied him. 'Is there someone else?'

Yes, yes, god, yes. 'It's complicated.'

Lauren's hands were trembling. 'I see. Well...I'm sorry to have bothered you.'

Noah felt sorry for her. 'Lauren, look, if it weren't for – '

'Please don't say whatever it is you're about to,' Lauren cut him off and stood up. 'I don't want your pity, Noah. I came to say my piece and I have. I'm sorry to have bothered you.'

He walked her to the door and as he opened it, she touched his arm. 'I hope she knows how lucky she is.'

Noah felt sadness settle over him. 'It's me who should feel like that. I'm sorry, Lauren, for all of this but I just can't think past her at the moment.'

Lauren nodded then suddenly kissed him full on the mouth. 'Goodbye, Noah. I'll never forget you.'

NOAH SHUT the door behind her, blowing out his cheeks, releasing the tension. If Lauren's visit had done anything, it had just solidified in Noah's mind that he couldn't move on. He wanted Lila so much it physically hurt him to think about her. Screw it, he thought, just get to New York, find her and see what could be.

In an hour, he was on the plane to the Big Apple.

27

MANHATTAN

Harry Carnegie, not known for being nervous, now felt it keenly. He sat with his father, Richard Carnegie Sr., waiting for the older man's reaction to what he had just told him. Richard Sr. stared out of the window. Harry noticed how much his pa had aged in the last year, how quiet and subdued he'd become. They talked every other day on Skype when Harry was back in Australia and although Richard Sr. had never been an exuberant man, he enjoyed joking with his son as they talked. Now, though, his eyes were flat, his posture one of defeat.

'Dad?' The waiting was killing Harry. Richard Sr. blinked as if finally remembering his son was in his office.

'Harrison...you have to do what you love in this life. Do I wish what you loved was running the business you built? Of course, but realistically, who loves that? It's your decision, son. It's not as if you have to get rid of the business, just get some good managers in.'

'That's just it, Dad. I don't want the business; I don't want to be burdened by it. We could sell it for...well...billions. I just want to start over, build boats, and be freer in my everyday life.'

Richard Sr. rubbed his chin. 'Harry, I mean it. It's your decision – you're a young man with every opportunity open to you. Do it, try it out. As long as you're happy, I'm happy.' He suddenly gave his son a wry smile. 'I'd be even happier if you decided to make boats here.'

Harry shifted uncomfortably. 'Dad...'

Richard held up his hands. 'Oh I know, I know. You're an Australian now. We just miss you, is all.'

HARRY LEFT his father's office and decided to stroll around the city. Melbourne had half the population of New York City; here there were too many people in too small a place. Harry always felt like he couldn't breathe when he was here.

He shoved his hands into his pants pockets and felt something slit the top of his finger. 'Son of a...' He pulled the offending object out. A business card. The card Tinsley Chang had given him. Harry sucked his finger to get rid of the blood, and stared at the card. The bar was only a few blocks from here...

Decision made, he turned on his heel and headed into the Village.

'TINS, HELP ME OUT HERE,' Riley Kinsayle grinned at the blonde bar woman. 'Charlie wants me to believe that the reason you two broke up was because of his huge...commitment to work.'

Charlie, sitting next to his partner, grinned at his ex-girlfriend. 'Ignore him; he has the mentality of a four-year-old.'

Tinsley laughed, drying glasses and stacking them neatly behind the bar. 'Riley, I'll tell you the truth....it was just that his cock was too damn big for me.' She winked at Charlie who raised a glass.

'That's my girl.'

Riley cackled with laughter then sighed. 'At least you got some action; I can't even remember the last time I got laid.'

'Probably because you're always talking about it and not doing anything about it,' Charlie muttered, rolling his eyes.

Tinsley chuckled then her smile faded. 'You guys any closer to finding out who tried to kill Lila? Because if it wasn't Richard then...'

Riley shook his head soberly and Charlie looked morose. 'No and it's driving me crazy. She's driving me crazy too; she doesn't want to believe it was Richard Carnegie but at the same time, now she doesn't want extra protection. She let Carnegie's security go, you know?'

'And you're frightened that someone will get to her?'

Charlie sighed. 'Look, truth. I still think it was Carnegie. I think he knew their relationship was rocky, that his family adored Lila, that the only way out that he didn't look like the bad guy was if she were murdered by some stalker. He may not have wielded that knife but I'll bet my life that he knew who did.'

'And you have proof of that, detective?'

All three of them started at the voice behind them. Harrison Carnegie stared at them with unfriendly eyes. 'My brother is dead. His fiancée does not believe in any way he could do that to her and she's right. Richard wasn't capable of the kind of violence it takes to stab an innocent woman fourteen times in the belly. He wasn't capable of violence, period.'

Harry's eyes met Tinsley's for the briefest second then he turned and stalked out. The three of them were frozen for a second then Tinsley darted out from behind the bar and after Harry.

OUTSIDE, she glanced around quickly and found him walking quickly down the block.

'Harry! Wait!'

He didn't stop and she found herself running down the block after him. He reached the corner just as she grabbed his arm. 'Harry, please, wait, we didn't mean anything. We're just worried about Lila, is all.'

Harry stopped and she took her hand from his arm. He looked down at her, his eyes full of conflict. 'He was my brother, you know?'

Tinsley nodded. 'I do know, and for what it's worth, I'm with Lila. I hung out with Richard long enough to know that he was a good guy. If he wanted to break up with her, he would have. This was some other crazy.' She half-smiled. 'Lila does have a tendency to attract them. It's that face and body of hers, it drives men wild.'

Harry smiled softly. 'She's a beauty, alright, but then so are you.'

'Sweet talker.'

Harry gave a loud, genuine laugh then. 'It's true. Look, I'm sorry I got the wrong impression; I just thought you guys were dumping on my brother.'

Tinsley felt a little uncomfortable then decided the truth was the best way to go with this guy. 'In all honesty...I think Charlie always had a problem with Richard. Charlie and Lila grew up together, they protect each other like siblings, and they fight each other like siblings. They were street kids, you know? So Charlie isn't impressed with wealth. I believe he was of the opinion that Richard thought he could buy Lila.'

'Again, Rich – '

'Oh I know. Richard proved himself over and over but, hey, you know...Lila's Charlie's responsibility – at least that's what he thinks.'

Harry nodded. 'Got it.' He sighed, looked around at the busy streets. 'Look, I don't particularly want to go back to that bar but what say I meet you for drinks tonight somewhere else?'

Tinsley smiled. 'That sounds great; I was hoping you'd stop by. I guess this means you're going back to Melbourne soon?'

HARRY GAZED DOWN AT HER, her bright, blue eyes so kind and warm, a faint flush of pink on her cheeks, her hair all mussed up from working. Something shifted inside him and he found himself smiling back at her. Tentatively, he stroked her cheek – just a tiny movement but their gazes locked – and held.

'Soon but not just yet. I'd like to see you...what say Mona's at eight?'

Tinsley grinned widely and Harry felt his cock twitch, aroused by her loveliness. He could imagine taking her in his arms, her lithe body curving around his, her small breasts against his chest...

'I'll be there…look, I have to get back or Riley will have drunk the profits. See you tonight.'

With a wave, she was gone, darting quickly away from him and disappearing into the crowds.

Don't get too involved, Harry told himself, *it's a nightmare waiting to happen.*

But he walked back to his hotel with the biggest smile on his face.

LILA SAT on the edge of the bathtub in her new apartment and closed her eyes. She counted three minutes out in seconds, carefully not thinking about anything else but the seconds ticking by. Definitely not thinking about what she thought was happening to her; the days and days of sickness and pain. Definitely not thinking about what she would do. And most of all, definitely not thinking about what it could mean to every single relationship in her life.

One-hundred-and-eighty-seconds. Done. She opened her eyes and looked down at the small plastic stick on her bathroom cabinet.

Oh shit. Oh *shit*.

NOAH HAD BEEN in New York for two days and hadn't found her. If he was being honest, he didn't even know where to begin looking for her. Well, that wasn't exactly true; there was one way but he'd exhaust every other option before he got in contact with Charlie Sherman. Although he'd had very little contact with the man, his fierce big brother stance made Noah wary of going to him. What would he say? *Oh, hey man, just checking in on my old patient…*Sherman would see through that immediately and his guard would go up. No, there must be some other way.

Noah had a few friends here, some connected with his family. Maybe one of them had an 'in' with the Carnegies? Now you're thinking, he told himself, 'let's do this.'

. . .

NOW THAT LILA lived only a couple of blocks from the bar, Tinsley could go there after work and see her friend. She handed over to Mikey now and snagged her bag from the backroom.

'Going to see Lila,' she hollered as she left.

'Give her my love,' Mikey shouted back and Tinsley grinned. They were her little family away from home. When Lila had been stabbed, Tinsley had been heartbroken, scared, and she visited Lila almost as much as the Carnegie family. They were such a sweet family that she felt immediately at ease with them. And now there was Harry Carnegie...

Just friends, she told herself firmly. *Just two Aussies going out to bond over their homeland.* Yeah, Harry wasn't really an Aussie but fifteen years in the country – she reckoned that counted. And it truly, truly had nothing to do with his warm brown eyes, his broad shouldered body, and those big, gentle hands. *Nope, nothing.*

When she got to Lila's building, she rode the elevator up to the third floor and made her way to Lila's apartment. She carried a bottle of tequila Mikey had given her, and she wore a huge smile as Lila opened the door, which faded when she saw Lila in tears.

'Hey, hey, honey, what's the matter?'

Lila burst into fresh sobs and Tinsley couldn't make out a word she was saying. She wrapped her arms around Lila, kicking the door shut behind her. She steered Lila towards the couch and let her cry herself out.

'Ssh, ssh, just tell me, what's wrong?'

Lila, her face awash with salty tears, looked at her with desperate, hopeless eyes. 'Oh god, Tinsley...I have fucked up. I have fucked up royally and I don't know what to do...'

As she cried, Tinsley hugged her tightly, her own heart thumping. Whatever it was, it had scared the crap out of Lila and Tinsley wondered if it was something she could come back from, or if her friend really was in trouble...

'DR. APPLEBAUM?'

Noah turned to see the tiny redhead looking up at him. Cora Carnegie. He smiled. 'Hello, again, Cora, how lovely to see you.'

His face remained smooth but inside, his heart began to thump expectantly. What if Lila were here too? He'd felt bad, finagling a last minute invitation to brunch as the guest of some of his parent's oldest friends but they had warmly welcomed him, showered him with questions about the older Applebaum's, and the food was incredible, piles upon piles of fresh baked pastries, fresh fruit, scrambled eggs with truffles scattered liberally on top of them. Noah had started to enjoy the gathering almost separately from his plan but now; Cora Carnegie was standing in front of him.' She was even thinner than he remembered, the skin of her face pulled taut, her eyes almost sunken. Noah's heart went out to the young woman. 'I was so sorry to hear about your brother,' he said in a soft tone, 'I can't begin to imagine what it's been like. How are your mother – and Lila?'

He hoped his question didn't sound desperate but Cora didn't pick up on his eagerness. 'Mom's okay, getting through it. She's here, somewhere, I know she'd love to see you. What are you doing in New York?'

Where's Lila? Where's Lila? 'Just here for a few days seeing old friends,' He nodded to the hosts, 'my parent's best friends, really. Have you eaten?' He stopped himself from telling her she should but she nodded.

'Like a horse,' she smiled suddenly, 'I know you doctors – but don't worry, this,' she gestured to her slender body, 'is just from stress. It always happens when something awful happens; I just can't keep weight on. But I promise you, I do eat.'

Noah smiled ruefully. 'Sorry, it's none of my business. Talking of doctoring,' - Ugh, dude, really? That's the best segue you can come up with? – 'How's my actual patient? Lila?'

Cora's smile faded. 'We don't know.'

Noah frowned. 'What do you mean?' Cora looked as if she were about to cry and Noah gently steered her into an outer room. 'Sit down, sweetheart. Here' some water.' He found a pitcher and poured her a glass. She sipped it, smiling at him gratefully.

'I'm sorry, Dr. Applebaum.'

'I'm not on duty, Cora, call me Noah.'

'Noah,' she said shyly and sighed. 'It happened about a week ago. Her friend, Tinsley...did you meet her?' Noah shook his head, his heart thumping with rising panic. 'Well, Tinsley went to her apartment and Lila was crying and rambling about how she had 'fucked something up' and that it was really bad and she didn't know what to do. Tinsley tried to talk to her, find out what was going on but Lila wouldn't say, just kept saying she had screwed things up so bad.'

Noah's heart was beating out of his chest. 'So what happened next?'

Cora leaned forward, hugging her arms around herself as if her stomach hurt. 'Tinsley said that all of a sudden, Lila just got calm – I mean, way too calm for how upset she'd been. Told Tinsley she loved her but she needed to be alone now. So Tinsley left – oh, and went on a date with my brother but that's another story – and the next day, Mom and I went to see Lila – and the apartment was empty. I mean empty, empty. She'd asked the super to let us in if we wanted and we found a note.'

This was not good. 'What did it say?'

Cora hesitated and then reached for her clutch. 'Read it. I can't stop looking at it.' She handed him a letter. It was written on a heavy cream, obviously expensive paper, and Noah couldn't help be thrilled at Lila's scrawling handwriting.

DEAR...EVERYONE,

I AM SO *sorry about this but I can't think of anything else to do but go away. From New York, from all of you. Know that I love you all, so, so much and I will forever be grateful for your love and your generosity.*

I did something I can't undo. Please don't worry, it's not illegal or life-threatening but I have to do it alone. Maybe one day, I'll be brave enough to tell you.

．　．　．

PLEASE, *don't try to find me.*

I LOVE YOU ALL,

Lila

NOAH REREAD the letter three times. 'There was a separate letter for Charlie but it was in a sealed envelope. He hasn't told us what it said.'

Of course not. Not for the first time, Noah felt irritated with Charlie Sherman. At the same time...Charlie had known Lila for much, much longer than he had – and how well did he, Noah, know Lila anyway? *One fuck does not make you soulmates.* But the way he felt about her....

'Noah? You look upset?'

Shit. He smiled at Cora. 'I'm just concerned. It's only a few months since she was stabbed; she shouldn't be on her own. If there are complications...' He trailed off, realizing he wasn't helping Cora's anxiety. 'Look, she's an adult, I'm sure she's fine. Sometimes people just need space. Let's hope that's all it is.'

Cora nodded, again tears were threatening. 'Dr.....Noah, would you stay in touch? I feel better talking to you; the rest of us are way too close to her.'

If only you knew. Noah nodded. 'Of course.'

LATER, Noah drove around to where Cora said Lila's old apartment was and parked outside, looking up at the darkened windows. *Where are you?* He felt like a stalker, flying across a continent for a woman he'd slept with once. *What the fuck am I doing?* He started the car and drove back to his hotel. *Forget her. You don't want this drama.*

Except when, later, he lay in bed staring up at the ceiling, all he could think about was Lila. That day, in his rehab studio, when she'd made it clear she wanted him; there had not been a doubt in his mind that making love to her was all he wanted. And the feel of her skin under his fingertips, the softness of her thighs around his waist as he moved inside her...

'For the love of God!' He rolled onto his side and gazed out of the window at the night. 'Where are you?'

Don't try to find me. Well, Lila, you didn't write that note to me so, beautiful, I can ignore your wishes.

I will find you...

'Okay. Let's try this again...third time lucky.' Harry grinned at Tinsley as they sat in the small cocktail bar. Tinsley laughed, shaking her head ruefully. Their first date – sort of date – was a washout. After she'd been with a distraught Lila, Tinsley had been distracted and subdued. At the end of the date, he'd driven her home and she'd apologized profusely.

A couple of days later, unable to get her out of his head, he called again and now, smiling at her, he tapped her glass with his.

'I promise, this time, no annoying cop friends andno freaking out over Lila,' she said.

'Still not heard from her?'

Tinsley shook her head. 'She doesn't want to be found and I respect that. I miss her, of course, we all do, but she's doing what she needs to do.'

Harry took a slug of his beer. 'Can I be honest? I'm a little pissed at her. I don't think she realizes what her taking off has done to my family, especially Cora. My sister is fragile and she loves Lila like a sister.'

Tinsley nodded. 'I know. Lila's not perfect, by any stretch but because, most of the time, she's so level she gets tarred with that brush. Don't judge her too harshly; she's been through hell.'

Harry sighed. 'In that case...why don't we change the subject? I want to know about you, Tinsley.'

Tinsley grinned. 'What do you want to know?'

'Everything. Family?'

'Mum, dad, two older brothers called Tyler and Joseph. Both are a pain in my ass but I begrudgingly love them.' Her smile said it was more than begrudging love. 'They're typical surfer types; really, if you described a stereotypical surfer dude, that's Ty and Joe.'

'What about you?'

'Went to college near home, came here to start art school. Dropped out when I got interested in managing a bar instead. Mikey sold me half the business last year. I love it.'

Harry nodded. 'That's great, finding your dream.'

Tinsley nodded. 'I know it's not everyone's dream but I love the life. I'm a night owl, and a people person, I love meeting new people. Hell, I even enjoy a good bar brawl.'

Harry grinned. 'Suddenly I'm having flashbacks to the wild west.'

Tinsley chuckled. '*Red Dead Redemption,* actually.'

'You game?'

She nodded. 'You?'

Harry looked embarrassed. 'The whole thing passed me by, if I'm honest.'

'So what's your dream?'

He smiled. 'Building boats and by that, I mean catamarans, sail boats, that type. Getting my hands covered in varnish, and jammed full of splinters from good wood.'

Tinsley's eyes were wide. 'That, I wasn't expecting.'

Harry grinned. 'What were you expecting?'

'Well, just, you know, your brother was more about the bling – not over the top and crass, but as much as he tried to hide it, Rich liked his cars, and his penthouse and his Saville Row suits. You seem to be the plaid wearing step-child,' she added with a wicked grin.

Harry laughed. 'Is that the hipster version of the redheaded-stepchild?'

'It is, except you're not a hipster.'

'Thank god. Well, I guess, me and Rich had a lot of differences. He was more spontaneous. I like the slow burn.'

It wasn't intended, but at his words, their eyes met and held. Tinsley's cheeks colored a little but she raised her chin and her sapphire eyes twinkled. 'You do, huh?'

God, she's delicious. 'Yes, ma'am.'

She smiled as she sipped her drink. 'I like that.'

He reached out and stroked her cheek with the back of his hand and she leaned into his touch. 'Tinsley...I had all sorts of reservations about getting involved with someone. I still have those reservations. I can't promise anything...I want to go back to Australia; it pulls me back, constantly, something deep in me. But I like you. A lot.'

She nodded. 'I understand, I really do. I've never done long-term, not even with Charlie. I'm not sure I'm able to do commitment. But I can do fun.'

Harry smiled. 'We're on the same page.'

A small smile played around her lips. 'Almost. I'm a contradiction. I don't sleep with anyone on the first date.'

Harry chuckled. 'This is our *third* date.'

'The first two were disasters, they don't count,' she waved her hand dismissively and he laughed loudly.

Tinsley leaned forward, and with a finger, traced a line down his inner thigh, slowly, lightly, until she placed her palm over his groin. Harry felt his cock respond but he smiled lazily at her as she cupped him through his jeans.

'I'm looking forward to seeing more of you,' she said, 'but forgive me if I want to explore that slow burn.' She removed her hand, and threw back the rest of her drink. 'Pick me up tomorrow, my place. We'll see if that slow burn is more of a flash burn.'

She winked at an astonished Harry and walked away. He watched the sway of her hips as she sauntered out of the bar, the way she looked back at him and grinned. Confident. Sexy.

He was looking forward to the next night. Flash burn indeed...

28

SAN JUAN ISLAND, WASHINGTON STATE

Was it stupid, coming back here? Was it too obvious, would they come looking? Lila had avoided – painfully – going back to Seattle so she picked a place up on San Juan Island, somewhere where she could walk around without being recognized but was still close enough to civilization. She wanted to be alone, not isolated.

Alone. Did she really want that or was she in Washington State because at least this way, she could be near to Noah. You'll drive yourself crazy, she remonstrated with herself. Stop thinking about him. Noah Applebaum was not an option. Not now.

She sat on the porch of the little cottage she'd rented, that looked out over the Haro Straight. There was a decent bit of land with the property which she loved – privacy. Every morning since she had come here, she had taken her breakfast out on the porch, sitting at the small wrought iron table with her cereal and her tea. It was so quiet, so serene. She would periodically see orca in the water, marveling at their graceful movement despite their size.

It was almost heavenly. She sighed now, placing her hand over her belly, still not quite believing that a tiny being was inside there. Noah's baby. The day she had found out, she had flipped, lost it. It couldn't be, not now, not with all this going on – what the hell would she tell the Carnegie's? *Oh hi, yeah, we've just buried your son and my fiancé but guess what? I'm having my doctor's baby! Surprise!*

'Jeez,' she said to herself, cringing. Tinsley had happened upon her when she was in the middle of her meltdown but Lila didn't tell her about the baby. She just shut down on her and Tinsley, obviously hurt, had tried to be a friend. When the realization hit that the only way to handle this was to leave, Lila's mind had calmed, had stilled and she'd calmly and politely asked Tinsley to go. Lila felt a pang now; Tinsley was a good friend and she deserved better than the brush off she got.

Lila absentmindedly stroked her non-existent bump and wondered if she could risk emailing Tinsley to apologize. Get a temporary email address then delete it after she'd sent the mail. She couldn't risk discovery, not by Tinsley, not by the Carnegies and not by Charlie.

And definitely not by the stranger who'd broken into her house that night. Every time she thought about it, she was surer someone had been in her apartment while she was asleep in the bath. When she'd gotten out of the freezing cold bath, wrapping a towel around her nakedness, she'd grabbed a full shampoo bottle to use as a weapon and marched with purpose around the whole apartment. Nothing. No-one.

But her things were moved. Her laptop, which she was certain had been shut off, was on, the browser open. She'd looked closer then recoiled with a gasp. Horrific images of murdered women, all of them stabbed.

Then she got mad. She stalked around the apartment again, this time armed with her own knife, checking every possible place a person could be. When she was satisfied, she let out a scream of rage.

She remembered that scream now; it had been a howl of anger, fear, and utter exhaustion. Whoever stabbed her still wanted her dead, that was clear.

So getting away was a no-brainer. Lila breathed in a lungful of cold, fresh, clean air and wondered what to do next. For once, she was glad of Rich's money, that it gave her breathing space to work out what to do next. She wanted to completely remodel this house, get it ready for the baby. The baby's room was the one room she would not spend Rich's money; she just couldn't do it. Not for another man's baby.

So she would need a job. Minimum wage, stacking groceries until she was too big – she could do that. She would do that.

'You and me now, beanpod,' she said softly then went inside to change.

NOAH PRESSED his lips against her throat, his big hands sliding around her back and stroking the soft skin. God I missed you...

The way she whispered his name as he stroked her thighs, pulling them around his waist and slipping his hand between her legs to stroke her sex, feeling the warmth, the dampness as she gasped at his touch. Lila...

Her violet eyes shone with love for him as his cock, so huge, so heavy, drilled deep into her ready cunt, her sharp intake of breath as he filled her, the friction between them driving them both wild as he moved in and out of her, their lips hungry against the others. Noah braced his hands either side of her head and slammed his hips against hers until she was moaning and coming and she looked so, so beautiful that he came over and over and over...

NOAH STARED up at the ceiling of his bedroom. Every night he lay here awake, unable to sleep, remonstrating with himself. *You slept with the woman once. That's it. Stop obsessing.*

But it was the fact that she was missing that bothered him. Cora had told him that it wasn't anything sinister but he couldn't help but worry. Someone had tried to kill her before now; who's to say he – or she – wouldn't find her again and they would never know, never be able to protect Lila from her killer.

Damn it, Lila, why'd you make my life so damn complicated? Noah shook his head. He'd never taken advantage of his family's wealth and connections much before, but earlier today, he'd called the private investigators his father used and set them on a countrywide search for Lila. Invasion of privacy? Maybe, but if they found her, he'd instructed them not to make themselves known to her, to keep a distance. Then he would make his decision as to how to approach her. Jeez, what a mess.

He couldn't get an image of Lila's murdered, mutilated body out of his mind. *Please, god let me find her before he does...*

With that thought screaming through his mind, Noah flicked the lamp off and tried to go to sleep.

29

MANHATTAN

Harry was early. Tinsley grinned at him as she opened the door, her hair still wet from the shower, the zipper on the back of her dress still undone. Harry raised his eyebrows at her.

'Sorry, I got home from work late, could you zip me up, please?'

Harry laughed. 'Sure thing...' He let his fingertips drift up her spine before he pulled the zipper up and she shivered with pleasure. She turned around and slid her arms around his waist.

'Thank you.'

He smoothed the damp hair away from her face and pressed his lips to hers. 'My pleasure,' he murmured, breathing in her clean, soapy scent. 'Although I'd rather be taking it off entirely.'

Tinsley chuckled quietly. 'Anticipation is the name of the game tonight, Mr Carnegie. Lots of kissing first...kissing and food, because I am starving.'

They both laughed. 'What are you in the mood for?'

'Hamburgers,' she said immediately, 'all flame-grilled and juicy.' She made the words sound so filthy he gave a little growl and she laughed. She slid her hand over his demin-clad cock. 'Patience. It'll be worth it, I promise.' She grabbed his hand and put it under her dress. His cool fingers found hot bare skin. No underwear. Harry groaned and buried his face in her neck.

'Tinsley Chang, I swear you'll be the death of me.'

She grinned. 'Harry...I swear, tonight will be the best of your life. Are you up for adventure? Whatever it is?'

Harry nodded. 'Whatever it is.'

THEY ATE at a local burger place, family-run, huge sandwiches, thin but incredibly tasty patties smothered in mustard, mayo, pickle and lettuce. The sauces dripped down their fingers and made a mess but they didn't care. There was something so carnal, so sensual about the way they ate them, licking their fingers so suggestively that they both ended up laughing. Afterward, they went to a low key bar and drank mojitos.

'I feel like I wanted to ask you more about your life, but tonight doesn't feel like the right time.'

She nodded. 'Tonight is all about the physical, Mr Carnegie.'

Really, he'd never met a woman so unaffected, so confident in her sexiness. It drove him wild.

'So what do you like? Are you a straight up missionary girl....wait, I think I know the answer to that.'

Tinsley sipped her drink. 'Harry, I don't believe in limitations or labels. I don't believe in holding back. If I want someone, and they want me, why pretend to follow social norms that say a woman should be coquettish or pretend to a reservation she doesn't feel. That just gets in the way of a good fuck.'

Harry raised his glass to her. 'I'll drink to that.'

She grinned. 'I bet you do. Harry...where's the wildest place you've had sex?'

He considered. 'Probably under the bleachers of my college football field.'

'Is that it? Was it during a game?'

Harry grinned sheepishly. 'Nope, sorry. How about you?'

Tinsley took a long moment before she answered. 'There's a club

I go to sometimes.'

Harry caught her tone and grinned. 'Oh, '*a club*'.'

She laughed. 'Yes, and it's exactly what you think it is, but it's a safe space to...try new things.'

'Like?'

'Bondage.' She studied his eyes for his reaction but he returned her gaze steadily. 'It depends what you're into, of course.'

'And you've tried out everything the club has to offer?'

Suddenly her smile widened into a face-splitting grin. 'Nope, not once but I thought I'd try and freak you out.'

They both laughed then, Harry shaking his head. 'Woman, I tell you, when we get out of here, I'll make you pay for that.'

'Sounds promising.' Her eyes dropped deliberately to his crotch then back to to his eyes. Harry growled.

'Damn, when you look at me like that...'

Tinsley got up suddenly and held out her hand to him. 'Come with me.'

Ten minutes later they were on the top of her building, looking out over the lights of New York City. Harry caught his breath. So beautiful...the city glittered below them and now, as he turned to face her, those lights were reflected in Tinsley's blue eyes.

'God, but you're beautiful,' he murmured and gathered her to him. As they kissed, his hands roamed over her body; her own fingers went to the button of his jeans.

As she freed his engorged and throbbing cock from his jeans, he slid his hands under her dress and pushed her up, lifting her in one easy movement. He pressed her back against a concrete wall and thrust into her damp and ready cunt. He gave a shivery moan as he heard her gasp. 'I'm going to fuck you long and hard, pretty girl,' he growled into her ear and heard her shaky, almost breathless laugh. He thrust deep and long, right to the core of her, again and again and again, his cock wanting more and more of this feeling, his senses exploding. Tinsley wrapped her arms around his neck, keeping eye contact with him, forging a connection. Her lips were rough against his, her fingers twisting in his hair, her nails dragging along his scalp with a feral intensity.

'God...Harry...more...' His hips increased their pace, his cock thickening inside her, stretching the tight muscles of her vagina as he pounded into her. They both came too quickly, Harry groaning as his thick, white semen pumped deep into her belly; Tinsley gasping and moaning as he used his hand to tease her clit, her entire body vibrating with pleasure.

They stayed connected as they caught their breath. 'Wow, oh, wow,' Tinsley managed to gasp as she grinned at him. 'That was incredible.'

Harry chuckled, kissing her deeply, his cock already stiffening again inside her. 'I could do this all night...and guess what? That's exactly what we're going to do.'

Tinsley threw her head back and laughed. 'I'm in.'

Harry grinned wickedly. 'Actually,' and he began to move in and out of her again, '*I'm* the one who's in.'

'God, you're delicious,' she whispered, kissing him then as her excitement grew again, she closed her eyes. 'Yes...just like that, *yes....yes...*'

THEY ENDED up back at her place, fucking on the floor, the bed, in the shower. At four am., finally sated and exhausted, they made their way to the diner at the corner of her street and had pancakes and syrup. Harry, his free hand covering hers, smiled at her. 'You working tomorrow?'

She shook her head. 'Day off. Why?'

'No reason. Just wanted to see if you felt like fucking for a full twenty-four hours?'

She giggled at his cheeky expression. 'Who wouldn't with you?'

Harry thanked her. 'You're incredible. I gotta say...never had it so good.'

'Right back atcha – but don't tell Charlie that,' she rolled her eyes and chuckled.

Harry scooped a forkful of pancakes into his mouth. 'Why did you and he break up?'

Tinsley's smile faded a little. 'Charlie is a great guy, heart of gold, very protective. Too protective for my liking. I'm a free-wheeler, Harry, it's in my blood. I don't do commitment, I don't do being asked where I am all day.' She sighed. 'I understand why Charlie was extra-protective given what happened to Lila, but it brought us into conflict. In the end I had to sit him down and explain my...ethos, I suppose you would call it. I live, I love but I am my own person.'

Harry was nodding with understanding. 'I think that's fair. So you decided...?'

'We'd be friends and I'm so grateful that we are still friends. I know your brother and Charlie didn't always get on, but I swear....I wish I could find a way to set him up with someone who deserves him.'

'Momma Bear.'

Tinsley grinned. 'Definitely not a mama. Kids aren't in my plan.' She looked at him as if expecting him to protest but he nodded.

'That's fair enough. Not entirely sure I want them myself. Not got to that point in life yet. What?' He asked when she chuckled...

'No, nothing, except it's just woman are expected, almost as soon as we hit puberty, to address the question: do you want children? And the reason is always given – because the clock is ticking. Men never have to worry about the ticking clock or the expectations that a woman will *always* – even secretly – want a child. When we say we don't, there's always a counter-argument – *Oh, you'll want one eventually*. Well, not me. I don't hate kids; I just don't want one of my own.' She looked at his face and grinned. 'Sorry, bug bear of mine.'

'Completely valid. I get it too...I'm not one for commitment or the saccharin stuff. Tinsley, you're beautiful and sexy and I love spending time with you. I love fucking you. No strings.'

'Word, brother,' she tapped her coffee mug against his. 'Now, if you've finished eating, I think you'd better take me back to bed.'

. . .

HE WATCHED them as they left the diner. He'd started following the blonde woman, knowing she was Lila's best friend, wondering whether she knew where Lila was. He'd been prepared to get the information out of her with violence, if necessary. And now he discovered she was banging Richard Carnegie's brother. 'All getting a little incestuous,' he murmured. Still, she would be alone at some point then he would get to her.

He was absolutely sure his knife would make her tell him everything, and then when she did, he would silence her forever.

30

SAN JUAN ISLAND, WASHINGTON STATE

Lila sat happily at the register of the bookstore. She had been expecting to score a job at the farmer's market or the grocery store but when she'd come into the bookstore three months ago, trying to find something new to read, she'd seen the 'Assistant wanted' notice and eagerly applied.

Now she was settled here. The bookshop was owned by Ronnie and Flynn, partners in business and love, who were built like loggers and yet possessed the sweetest natures of anyone she'd ever met. They'd just adopted twin daughters and Lila watched the two men dote on the girls. They'd hired her to run the bookshop, impressed by her literary knowledge, and she found they stepped back from the business more and more. She didn't care; she loved it here, talking with customers about books, making recommendations. She even loved cleaning and tidying the place. It was a haven. The whole island was, and she'd found herself relaxing here, her mind finally peaceful after the months of turmoil. The island had a terrific medical center with warm and efficient staff and she liked her obstetrician, Dr. Low, very much. The young Chinese woman had told her what she could expect during her pregnancy, and had advised her on any extra precautions she should take because of the damage to her belly due to the stabbing.

'You'll probably find your scars itch a lot so plenty of cream. Internally, well, we'll have to see. You're still tender, your muscles still weakened. But I'll keep a close eye on you. I take it the pregnancy wasn't planned?'

Lila had shaken her head but now, as she thought back, she found herself wondering. She had not even for a second, considered an abortion. She was absolutely pro-choice, but when it came to this baby...would she have felt the same if it had been anyone else's child but Noah Applebaum's? Even Richard's?

She asked herself over and over why she couldn't get Noah out of her head. She reasoned with herself but there it was – unfinished business. She wrestled whether to tell him about the baby and found herself confiding in Ronnie and Flynn, asking them what she should do.

'We can't tell you that, honey, but the man deserves a shot at whether or not to be involved.'

Lila chewed her lip. 'It was a one-time thing though.'

Flynn rolled his eyes. 'But you're crazy about him, anyone can see that. Just go be with him.'

Lila sighed. 'It's not that easy. Firstly; I have no idea if he feels the same way or if I was just a one-time thing. Second – my fiancé was just murdered. It's bad enough I'm having another man's baby....god, what a fucking mess.'

She thought about that conversation now, grateful to Ronnie and Flynn for their honesty but it was still unresolved in her mind. Now she was nearly five months along, her belly softly curved outwards, small but still noticeable. She was surprised the baby was so small; with Noah's height she figured it would be a monster but no, her little bean was just that. Little. She stroked a hand down her belly. Now; whatever happened, she was already attached to the little critter. No turning back now, she smiled to herself.

The bookshop was quiet today. The weather had turned rainy and cool, and the sky was black with storm clouds. Lila was checking a new delivery, scanning the books into the shop's computer system and pricing them. So absorbed was she, she barely heard the shop door open, the small bell chiming.

'Hi.'

She froze and her breathe caught in her throat. No, not like this. She grabbed hold of the counter in front of her, shifting slightly so the box of books was a wall in front of her. Protection. Deflection. She took a breath in and looked up.

Noah Applebaum stood in front of her, impossibly handsome in his sweater and jeans, a smile that reached his green eyes. His dark hair was a little longer than she remembered, and he was taller too, wasn't he? Yep, that's the stuff to focus on now, you idiot. She stared back at him.

'Noah...what are you doing here?'

His smile didn't fade. 'Why do you think? I tried to get in contact with you in New York after Richard died but Cora told me you'd done a vanishing act. Then, the other day, a patient of mine was telling me how she'd seen this very beautiful young woman in the bookshop where she lived, and that she seemed familiar. She'd remembered about the bridal store stabbing in New York, remembered your face from the photos.'

Lila's eyes narrowed. 'What else did she tell you?'

Noah looked confused. 'Huh? Nothing, just that.'

'You're lying.'

That shook him. He obviously had expected a warmer welcome than the one she was giving him. 'What? No, I...'

'If the woman exists, she would have told you something else about me. Something big. Noah...how did you find me?'

He opened his mouth to protest, then had the grace to look ashamed. 'I'm sorry; I didn't want to freak you. I thought if I played it like it was a coincidence, a passing remark, it would sound better than I hired a detective to find you. Several in fact.'

Lila closed her eyes. 'Oh, god...'

'Lila, I'm sorry, I was just so concerned. Whoever stabbed you is still out there, I wanted to know you were safe. And I wanted to see you. Of course, I wanted to see you.'

Lila felt like crying. One side of her wanted to run into his arms but the other, the rational side, was irritated and frightened and god...so many emotions. She clutched the box of books in front of her. 'I think you should go,' she whispered. 'I can't do this.'

She hated the hurt in his eyes. 'Noah...things have changed. I'm not engaged but I'm not free either. As much as I...' she trailed off and just looked at him. He was everything she wanted, desperately wanted. The time they had spent together when she was in hospital had been incredible. The connection they had forged, nothing like she had experienced before. She adored everything about this man; his intellect, his goofy sense of humor, the pattern of moles on his right cheek which looked like the Big Dipper. She had felt most safe when her skin was next to his and yet now, standing less than a few feet away from him, she had never been more terrified.

You have to do this; you have to tell him why. It's only fair.

'Noah, I...' her voice cracked and he stepped forward to comfort her. She shook her head and he stopped. 'Noah,' she began again, string this time, 'there's something I need to tell you. A big thing.'

He gave her a crooked smile. 'The big thing my imaginary patient would have noticed?'

She didn't return his smile. 'Know that I...didn't want to burden you.'

He was confused now. 'Whatever it is, Lila, please, just tell me.'

Lila hesitated for a long moment, and then with a big intake of breath, she stepped around the counter and finally faced him, her hand on the small bump in her abdomen.

Noah stared back at her in disbelief.

31

MANHATTAN

Riley Kinsayle didn't have his usual smile on his face as Tinsley greeted him that evening. "Sup, dude?'

She pushed a beer towards him but he waved it away. 'Charlie's in the hospital.'

Tinsley was shocked. 'What? How?'

'He took a beat down by some junkies on a bust that went FUBAR. Doc's say he'll be okay but, god, Tins...'

Riley looked so shaken that she rounded the bar and hugged him. 'God, that's horrible. Which hospital is he in? I'll go see him.'

Riley told her. 'But leave it until tomorrow; they're only letting police in at the moment.'

Tinsley sighed and rubbed her eyes. 'God, I thought all this violence was over and done with. Was it a bust gone bad?' She indicated the hot coffee pot and Riley nodded gratefully.

As she passed him the drink, he took a long sip, obviously not caring if the hot liquid burnt his mouth. 'Nope, Charlie was following a lead on Lila's attacker. He must have gotten too close.'

Tinsley's eyes widened. 'Wow. Oh wow.'

Riley studied her, his dark eyes searching her face as he drank some more coffee. He put the cup down. 'Tinsley...he was asking for Lila.'

'What?' Tinsley felt like she might cry. Riley sighed.

'Tins, if you know anything about where she is...tell me. Please. She'll want to know about Charlie and he needs her now, like never before. *Please*.'

Tinsley sighed. 'Riley, I honestly don't know where Lila is. I did get one email from her, telling me she was sorry for disappearing but it was for the best. When I tried to reply, the message bounced back.'

Riley chewed over this information. 'Do you still have her email?'

Tinsley nodded. 'Good,' Riley said, 'then maybe we could trace where it came from. Huh. Ironically, the Carnegie software would probably do it for us and – '

'Riley, *no*. She doesn't deserve to have her privacy violated like that, it's not right.'

'Her best friend has just been attacked, Tinsley.' Riley's voice had an uncharacteristic tone – angry, full of blame and she whirled around, irritated herself.

'I know that but it's not Lila's fault, is it?'

Riley dug in his pockets for some cash for the coffee, shaking his head, obviously pissed. 'Tins, I want you to know that you could be charged with impeding an investigation.'

'The hell I am – Lila didn't beat up Charlie, did she?'

Riley slammed the money on the bar and walked out.

32

SAN JUAN ISLAND, WASHINGTON STATE

Noah stared at Lila's belly for the longest time then slowly he met her gaze, his eyes cold. 'Is it mine?'

Lila's hands were sweating and her heart thudded heavily against her ribs. 'Of course it is,' she whispered. 'There's been no-one else since that time.'

'That *one* time,' he said. Almost in disbelief.

'Are you angry?'

He shook his head. 'Not that you're pregnant, Lila, no, I'm not angry about that.' He stepped towards her, his eyes full of hurt. 'But I am angry that you kept it from me. That's my child too.'

'We had one day together, Noah. I didn't want to dump this in your lap, especially not after everything, and it's not like we were in a relationship to begin with. And I had to consider the Carnegie's in this too. How do you think they would have felt? Me pregnant with another man's baby when their son, my fiancé, has just been killed?'

Noah stared at her, shaking his head. 'The only person who matters here is our child, Lila. You're keeping it?'

'Of course.' Her voice broke then and tears dropped down her cheeks. He raised his arms to hold her but she backed off. 'No, please, don't touch me. Noah, I am sorry but as far as I'm concerned, there's nothing to be talked about.'

Noah lost it then. 'You cannot do this, Lila, that's my child! Don't you think I want to be involved with his or her life? Help to raise them. I want...'

'What? What do you want, Noah?'

He stopped mid-rant. 'I want you, Lila. I want you and our baby.'

Lila closed her eyes. She had dreamed of hearing these exact words – just not like this. 'Noah, I can't. I just can't. I'm scared that if we try – and fail – losing you would break me. And, even though I feel something real and tangible for you, we still don't know each other that well.'

'Bullshit,' he said fiercely, 'I do know you. I know you love with your whole heart. I know that when you sleep, you favor your left side, sleep with one hand under your face. I know you like orange Jello and also the lime. I know that I would walk through fire to see you happy and safe...'

Lila gave a sob, and in a flash, Noah had locked the door to the shop and pulled down the shade, coming to take her in his arms. She didn't resist.

'Lila, sweetheart, I can't get you out of my head. I had to find you, tell you how much you mean to me. Try to see if we could make a go of it together. It wasn't a one night stand for me, Lila; it was the beginning of something else. And now I know that's true. Look, I'll transfer to the medical center here, rent somewhere, so that if you need me, I'll be here. Always. I won't ask you to make a commitment to me, just let me be around, involved.'

She looked up at him through tear filled eyes, searching his clear green eyes for clues to how he really felt. All she saw was hurt – and love.

'Noah...'

His lips crushed against hers, hunger, pain in his kiss and his arms wound tightly around her body. Her hands slid onto his face as she responded to his kiss, fingers knotting in his hair.

Noah's hands slid under her dress, caressed her swollen belly, then his hand slipped between her legs, stroking and touching through her underwear. 'I want you so badly,' he murmured against her mouth and she moaned softly as his fingers snagged in her panties and slid them down her legs.

Somewhere in her hazy, lust-delirious mind, it registered that making love to this man here at her workplace, in the middle of the day, was insane. But she couldn't stop. God, the sweet taste of his mouth on hers, his eyes sweeping all over her, making her sex tremble and dampen, his big hands on her skin.

He lowered her to the floor and covered her body with his own, kissing, nibbling at her earlobes, pulling the straps of her dress down so he could take her nipples into his mouth, sucking on them, teasing them into a frenzy. His mouth moved down to her belly, his hands gentle, his lips against it, tender as he stroked it.

'I want you inside me,' she managed to gasp, smiling, Noah kicked his jeans off, his cock rising, hard and huge against his stomach. The sight of it made her cunt pulse with desire and when, at last, for only the second time, he entered her, she sighed with happiness and content.

I'm being fucked by this beautiful man, whose baby I'm carrying inside me. In this moment, I have everything I've ever wanted...

As they made love, Noah, tender to the last, kissed her softly, passionately, gazing into her eyes. His cock drove her onto almost unbearable pleasure, her rounded belly hard against his, her nipples brushing against his hard chest.

She gazed up at him and thought, *oh how I love you, you beautiful man* and for one blissful moment, she imagined what it might be like to imagine a life together, here on this island, anonymous and peaceful.

Her orgasm dashed any thought of anything from her mind and as she came down from the high, she heard Noah groan and his seed spilled out of him into her belly.

'Lila, Lila, Lila...'

His plaintiff whisper made her want to cry but instead she fixed her mouth on his. Noah stroked her face as they embraced, then as they broke for air, he gazed down at her.

'Lila...please, can't we at least try? To be a family? You, me and the little one? Let's at least, try.'

Hope sprang in her for the first time and she nodded, her eyes filled with tears, seeing the joy started to flood into his eyes. 'Yes,' she said simply. *Yes.*

33

MANHATTAN

Tinsley was shaking. Never, *never,* had she seen Riley so worked up. Yeah, okay, his partner had been shot, but to attack her for protecting Lila's privacy. Something was going on with Riley, something other than Charlie getting shot.

Tinsley sighed, trying to calm herself. The Riley she knew and loved – he was nowhere to be seen in the angry man who had just left. 'Jeez,' she said to herself.

LATER, when Mikey had come in for his shift, Tinsley took off, and, still pissed at Riley, had ignored his entreaty to stay away from the hospital. She was in luck; the cops there let her in with no argument.

Charlie was sitting up in bed, staring at a ballgame on the TV. His left shoulder was heavily bandaged, his arm in a sling. There were patterns of cuts and bruises all over his handsome face. He looked tired but his eyes lit up when he saw her.

'Hey cutie pie, what are you doing here?'

She rolled her eyes, kissing his cheek. His stubble tickled her lips and she felt a pang of nostalgia when she would wake up to him kissing her awake. *Water under the bridge, kiddo.*

'Riley came to see me, told me you'd gotten yourself beaten up. I heard by an eighty-pound elderly nun. With a limp.'

'More like sixty four-hundred-pound sumo wrestlers. With actual hammers like in the cartoons.'

Tinsley laughed, glad that Charlie retained his sense of humor. She touched his injured arm lightly. 'How bad is it?'

He shrugged – then winced at the pain. 'Couple of chipped bones, hairline fractures. Should be fine in couple of months.'

Tinsley nodded. 'Good thing it's not your jerking off hand.'

Charlie gave a bark of gruff laughter. 'Yes, it is. Although, you know you can always help me out with that.'

As he laughed again, she swiped at him, blushing. 'Filthy boy.'

'Talking of which, how goes it with Harry? Those Carnegie boys do like to mess with my women,' he grinned to show he was joking.

'Just fine and dandy,' Tinsley felt weird discussing her relationship – if she could call it that – with her ex-boyfriend but Charlie to her now was a good friend – her best friend, if she was being honest. She grinned wickedly at him. 'Anyway, a little birdy told me that you had your own fan in that family – a certain little redhead?'

Charlie had the grace to look sheepish. 'It's just a crush; she'll get over it. Cora just needs some looking after, is all. I'm old enough to be her dad.'

Tinsley smirked. 'That's true, granddad. Hey, listen...Riley came to see me, to tell me about you and I'm afraid we got into a bit of an argument and I wanted to come explain myself to you.'

Charlie held up his good hand. 'Hey, I'm staying out of any arguments between the two of you. That's a lose-lose for me.'

Tinsley frowned. 'But it does kind of involve you – well, Lila, at least.'

'How so?'

'He asked me if I knew where Lila was, that if I knew, I should tell you because you needed her, you asked for her when you were hurt.'

Charlie stared at her. 'Tins, I did no such thing. Lila is where she needs to be right now; I would never intrude on that for a few cuts or bruises. You sure he said that?'

'Well, seeing as it was the crux of our argument, I'm pretty sure. I told him I didn't know where she was and he kinda freaked out on me. Big time.'

Charlie looked astonished. 'Riley? Riley freaked out?'

Tinsley nodded. 'Yup, that was pretty much my reaction. Listen, you sure you didn't ask for her when you were brought in, maybe you were out of it?'

He shook his head. 'Nope, absolutely positive.'

She looked at the bruising on his head and wondered if he had concussion. 'How can you be so sure?'

Charlie sighed. 'Because, Tins...I already know where Lila is.'

34

SAN JUAN ISLAND

He drove them across the island in his Mercedes, back to the home she had found for herself. Shyly, Lila took Noah's hand and he looked over and smiled at her. 'Hey, beauty.'

Lila shook her head, smiling. Something had to give. Something would go wrong. If she's learned anything from the past year, it was that no-one got everything they'd ever dreamed off just like that. There had to be catch, a pay-off, a twist in the tale.

But right now, for once, she let herself believe. After making love in the shop, they'd dressed, tidied the place up, and re-opened but the rain kept the shop empty and so instead, they talked.

'Why did you keep the baby?' He asked gently. 'You could have just had it...dealt with, and no-one would have known.'

'Because it was yours,' she whispered softly, earning herself a passionate kiss.

They'd talked practicalities. 'I could just resign,' he said easily, 'but I have patients that I want to see through their treatments. So, for now, I'll commute. I'll get a place near you so I don't crowd you.'

She shook her head. 'No, don't. Just stay with me, don't make this more complicated than it is. And sometimes, if you'll have me, I'll come into the city.'

Noah was clearly delighted. 'We're going to do this, Lila, all the way. We're going to make it, I swear.'

She wanted to tell him she loved him in that moment but she funked it. It was too soon; she thought to herself, it was just lust. Well, she thought with a half-smile, lust – and a baby on the way. But if she was honest, she didn't want to say it yet. She wanted to say it in a moment where it wasn't being swayed by sexual arousal, or panic, of fear, or anything. She would know when the moment was right.

Her home came into view and Noah whistled. 'That's nice,' as he pulled up to it and she was surprised.

'It's just a cottage, pretty scrappy too,' she smiled as he helped her out of the car. She opened her mouth to continue but then saw he was gazing down at her, his eyes intense. 'What is it?'

'Pregnancy suits you,' he said softly, 'you're even more beautiful than I remember.'

Lila flushed with pleasure and embarrassment. 'I'll remember you said that when you're holding my hair back because I'm throwing up everywhere.'

'You've had sickness?'

Lila grinned at him switching automatically to doctor mode. 'I have a great OBGYN, relax. You can just be the Daddy.' She flushed again and her eyes filled with tears and it was Noah's turn to ask what was wrong.

'Nothing, these are happy tears. I never thought this – us – would happen.'

Noah wrapped his arm around her. 'Well, then, show me to your castle.'

35

MANHATTAN

Tinsley had to wait to find out how Charlie knew where Lila was because no sooner had he dropped that bomb on her than the doctor had arrived to check him. She hovered impatiently outside his room until the doctor, shooting her an amused glance, left the room, then when she went in, she saw Charlie was up and getting dressed.

'Doc says I can go home,' he said cheerfully. Tinsley gaped at him.

'You're not going anywhere until you tell me how you know where Lila is,' she said, gently pushing him back on the bed. Charlie sighed.

'She wrote me, remember, when she left? She asked me not to tell anyone where she was but, of course, she was going to tell me, wasn't she? So, that's how I know and no, I'm not going to tell anyone, not you, not the Carnegies, and certainly not damn Riley.'

'What is his problem, then? Why does he want to know where Lila is so badly?'

Charlie's face set in its grim expression. 'I don't know, but I'm going to find the hell out.'

Harry Carnegie read through his emails hurriedly, not really taking much notice of them until he reached the last one. Then he cursed loudly and grabbed his phone.

'Yeah, what?' Brent, his associate back in Melbourne, mumbled into the phone and too late, Harry realized the time difference. It was four am. in the Australian city.

'Brent, look, man, I'm sorry to wake you but I just got the email about the Landecker deal. To renew the contract, they want a price cut of seventy per cent....are they kidding with this?'

He pictured Brent sitting up, rubbing his bearded face and by the grunting noises he heard, he was doing just that. 'Look, mate, things have been screwy here ever since you left. I can't do it all on my own. Yeah, we dropped the ball on that contract and they snuck in with a last minute renegotiation. We need you back, man.'

Harry sighed. 'Yeah, I know. Look, I didn't mean to stay here so long...listen, I'll get my stuff in order here and I'll come back early next week. Can you hold on signing anything until then?'

'I'll try.'

Harry said goodbye and ended the call. 'Damn.' He had known that postponing and postponing his return to Melbourne would come back to bite him in the ass eventually, but he was having such a good time here. And yeah, that was entirely down to Tinsley. They had stuck to their agreement – fun, no commitment, easy come, and easy go. But, despite himself, he'd grown attached. His spirit lifted every time she smiled at him; his entire body worshipped hers when they made love. She *fit* him.

Not only that but during the time home, he'd reconnected with his family – each of them: Delphine, Richard and Cora – and felt a closeness to them he'd never felt before. Yet Australia was calling him home. It was his home. All of his friends were there now, the friends of his youth in Westchester all scattered and gone.

His sister, still reeling from Rich's murder and Lila's disappearance, had been leaning on him and he had to admit, she was a really good kid with a lot of potential – if she could keep it together. Tinsley had equally taken the young woman under her wing.

Tinsley Chang...darn it if she hadn't gone and gotten under his skin. Harry shook his head. This was exactly what he'd tried to avoid his whole entire life.

Falling in love.

Tinsley's cell phone buzzed just as she was climbing the stairs to her apartment. She had insisted on getting a cab with Charlie to his apartment and cooking for him. He had rolled his eyes but she knew he was grateful. Despite his protestations, his injuries had made him ache and she fussed over him, feeding him pasta and making him promise to take aspirin and go to bed.

Before she went, he'd called her back. 'Tins...don't mention our conversation to Riley. Let me look into it a little.'

She smiled ruefully. 'I don't think me and Riley will be talking about anything much for a while so I think I can promise. Look, I have to go into work for a couple of hours...sure you don't want me to come back and check on you later?'

Charlie chuckled. 'No, Mom, I'm good. I'll call you tomorrow.'

Now, she took out her phone and checked the caller i.d. and smiled. 'Harrison Carnegie, you won't believe the day I've had.'

'Bad or good, sweetheart?'

She balanced the phone between her ear and neck and she dug in her bag for her keys. 'Um, I'd say, a bizarre day. You okay?'

'Oh yeah, yeah...listen, can you meet me for drinks?'

'When?'

'Um, kind of now? I'm outside.'

She laughed, letting her front door close again and turning back to the stairs. 'You doofus, why didn't you just catch up with me?'

'Didn't want to intrude.' There was a chuckle in his voice. Tinsley jogged down the stairs and out onto the street.

'You mad man,' she said into the phone as she saw him. He was leaning against a very nice Porsche.

'A loaner from my dad,' he grinned as he held the door open for her. He took her to a quiet bar on one of the side streets.

'The amount of time I spend in bars, I should just put a bed in the corner of mine and have done with it,' Tinsley said as they found a quiet booth. The waitress came over and took their orders.

'You know, Melbourne had a wealth of bars just crying out for a manager like you,' Harry smiled but she could see wariness in his eyes.

'I love New York,' she said, gently. 'Melbourne will always be home for me, but my heart is here now. What's up, Carnegie? You look squirrely.'

He grinned wryly. 'You know me too well. I have to go back to Melbourne. Next week. I've been neglecting the business and I've exhausted my partner's patience.' Tinsley found she couldn't speak for a moment but then she nodded. 'We knew this wasn't a forever thing, Harry. We said it wouldn't be.'

He nodded, somberly. 'We did.'

They sat in silence for a few minutes, the atmosphere between them awkward. Harry sighed and took her hand. 'Look, truth time. I didn't want to get involved. But something happened when I met you – '

'Don't say it, please,' Tinsley begged him suddenly, 'don't make this harder than it has to be. We're both adults, and this is the real world. A long distance relationship isn't what either of us want or need. Let's just...god, Harry don't look at me like that...' She broke off and looked away.

'I'm sorry. But I'll miss you more than you know,' his voice was gruff.

Tinsley half-smiled at him. 'I never said I wouldn't miss you like crazy. You'd better stay in touch.'

'I will.'

'When do you leave?'

'Monday.'

'God, so soon.' Another silence.

'Tinsley, would you spend the weekend with me? I mean, I have a family thing on Sunday, and I'd like you to come with me to that too if you would like, but the rest of the weekend...'

'Me, you, my bed and food delivery,' she said firmly and grinned. Harry laughed softly.

'Well, that sounds about perfect.'

Tinsley gazed at him. 'For what it's worth, these past few months with you? Best of my life.'

Harry leaned forward and brushed her lips with his. 'Ditto.'

Much later, they walked hand-in-hand to her apartment, stopping every few minutes to kiss. As she slid her key into the door, she stopped and frowned, pushed on the door without turning the key. It opened. 'Shit.'

Harry stepped in front of her, shielding her as they entered the apartment. He quickly stepped into each room.

'No-one here. Anything missing.'

Tinsley, on edge, glanced around the kitchen then went into the living room. 'Fuck,' she said and with a resigned sigh, she pulled her cellphone from her pocket. Harry looked confused and she raised a hand, signaling she would explain in a minute.

'Charlie? My apartment's been broken into and guess what's missing? Yep, that's right. Okay. Okay, see you in a few.'

She ended the call and looked at Harry. 'It's a long story, but Charlie's on his way over and I'll explain them.'

Harry shook his head. 'What's going on? What was taken?'

She sighed. 'My laptop, Harry. My laptop with possibly a way to trace where Lila went. Jesus.' She sat down heavily on her couch.

'What's the big deal about that?' He sat down beside her, putting his arm around her shoulders.

She put her head in her hands. 'Harry...whoever took my laptop broke in to take it. That person does not have good intentions for Lila. That person could be the one who wants to kill her.'

I know where you are now, my darling Lila. Soon, so soon, we will be together and I will show you how much I love you – again. My knife will sink into your flesh once again and you will smile and thank me for the gift I am giving you. I will watch as you fight the loss of control as your rich ruby blood covers us both, as all the breath leaves your lungs and the light in your lovely eyes starts to dim and flicker.

. . .

BUT FIRST, *Lila, first I need to make another pay for their treachery, for keeping you from me. Someone you love will pay the ultimate price, my love.*

Watch. Despair. It will be your turn soon...

36

SAN JUAN ISLAND, WASHINGTON STATE

Lila stretched her body like a cat, and turned to face her sleeping partner. Noah Applebaum is in my bed, she said to herself a little smugly. She gently touched her fingertips to his cheek, felt the beginnings of stubble. She loved the feel of his sculpted cheekbones, the short, thick dark hair at his temples, the way his ears were slightly too big. Thank god for them, she grinned to herself, or you would be too perfect, Doctor.

On cue, Noah opened those clear green eyes of his and smiled. 'Wasn't a dream, then?'

'Wasn't a dream.'

He cupped her face with his big hand. 'Just checking you're real.'

She chuckled. 'I have the very real morning breath to prove it.'

'I don't care.'

She giggled as he tickled her. 'You will, I was too, um, occupied last night to brush my teeth.'

'In that case, I apologize for not brushing mine either but I don't apologize for distracting you.'

Lila stretched again and he ran a leisurely hand down her body, settling on the small bump. He traced the still pink scars that crisscrossed her navel, made more vivid by the pressure of the pregnancy. 'Do you know the sex yet?'

She shook her head. 'No, I'm old-fashioned like that, I wanted to wait but do you want to know? Because we can go find out.'

Noah considered, his hand gently stroking the bump in which his first child slept. 'I'm not sure...can I think about it?'

'Of course, I want you to feel you are making as many decisions as me. God, this is difficult for me to get a handle on.' She pulled herself into a sitting position, grinning as Noah eyed her breasts lasciviously. 'Yesterday I was alone. Now the man I've been dreaming of for months is in my bed and we're talking about our child.' She shook her head. 'Crazy.'

'You've been dreaming about me?'

She touched his face. 'I thought about you every day, every minute. I know it's crazy, but I spent three years with Richard and yet in those few weeks when we spent time talking when I was in hospital, I learned more and shared more with you than with anyone. Even Charlie. It was just...right.'

Noah sat up and took her in his arms. 'Screw the morning breath,' he said, 'that deserves a kiss.'

Eventually they made it out of bed and into the shower. They tried to make love, giggling and splashing, but Lila's bump kept getting in the way.

'The acrobatics will just have to wait until the little one is born.'

THEY MADE BREAKFAST TOGETHER, Lila scrambling eggs, Noah grinning as she whipped them. 'Your sweet little ass jiggles when you do that.'

She grinned and exaggerated the movement then pointed at the pan he was holding, 'Your pancakes are burning.'

'You better bet they are,' he muttered, but he turned back to the stove.

They sat out in her favorite place on the deck, eating breakfast.

'It's so peaceful here,' Noah said, 'I kept waking up last night because of the quiet. How'd you find this place?'

'Realtor,' Lila suddenly looked downcast. 'It's small but its location made it perfect for a hermit like me. Rich...left me some money and I hated to do it but I had to use some of it to buy this place.'

'Hey, you had to do what you had to do.'

Lila sighed. 'The thing is, Noah, Richard and I had ended our engagement a few days before he was murdered. We both knew it hadn't been working, even before I was stabbed, but because we were such good friends, and the family was excited, I think we made a silent agreement to go through with the wedding. One of the many reasons I know it wasn't Richard who tried to kill me is that there wasn't a sly or vindictive bone in his body. If he had really wanted out, he would have talked to me.'

'You miss him?'

'Of course, but I miss him as my friend, not my lover.' She looked a little nervous as she answered his question but he smiled.

'Lila, he was your fiancé for three years. Do you think I wouldn't expect you to talk about him?'

Lila half-smiled. 'Thank you. The reason I took the job in town was that even though I used Rich's money to buy this house, I refuse to use his money to pay for the baby.'

Noah nodded. 'That's fair but you don't need to worry about that anymore.'

Lila looked uncomfortable. 'I really get a reputation as a gold-digger.'

Noah laughed. 'You will not but, hey, does this make me your third rich man?'

She groaned as he laughed. 'Oh, that sounds terrible!'

Noah leaned over and kissed her. 'Listen, I have an idea...'

Lila was still shaking her head. 'God, what now?'

He laughed again. 'In honor of your spectacularly successful gold-digging career – '

'Stop it!' but she was laughing hysterically now, and his eyes were twinkling with merriment.

'I think we should call our first born...*Kanye.*'

Crying with laughter, Lila flicked a piece of pancake at him. 'That's it; you're not naming our child.'

'And your name from now on will be 'GD',' he ducked to avoid a whole pancake.

'Stop, I can't breathe,' she said, gasping. She put her hand on her chest, breathing hard. Noah sat back, grinning.'

'Well, it's ridiculous; anyone who spent even a minute with you would know you're no parasite. Believe me, I know those types of people, men and women. I've dated a few.'

'*Men* and women?' She was joking now but Noah, his grin widening, nodded.

'Yes. Does that bother you?'

Lila was taken aback. 'You're bisexual?'

'No, I was messing with you. But that's my point. You don't know until you know someone what they are like, what they do. If people want to paint you as something, they will until they know you. And anyway....fuck 'em.'

She was looking at him, her eyes both wondering and curious. 'Noah Applebaum, I really have never met anyone like you.'

'Right back atcha, shorty.'

'I'm tall.'

'I'm a doctor and five-five isn't tall.'

'That's heightism and just when I was being so understanding about your taste for cock,' she stuck her nose in the air for a moment. 'Seriously though, it wouldn't have bothered me if you were bisexual.'

Noah shrugged. 'Wouldn't bother me either. But I only have eyes for one person.'

She blew him a kiss then checked her watch. 'I have to be at the bookstore by ten.'

'And I,' he said regretfully, 'have to go back to the city, at least for today. I'd like to come back tonight, if that's okay?'

She smiled. 'Bring a big, full suitcase of your stuff. Make yourself at home.'

Noah leaned over and kissed her, then leaned his forehead against hers. 'You and me and Kanye make three.'

She giggled. '*Not* Kanye. You insist on that, I'm calling you 'Applebum'.'

'Like I haven't heard that before.'

They drove into town together then, kissing her goodbye, Noah stroked her face. 'Until tonight, then.'

She got out of his car. 'Hurry back to me.'

'I will. You and little K look after yourselves.'

'Hahaha, get lost, Applebum.'

She watched as he drove down to the harbor where the ferries connected to the mainland. Again, she marveled at the change in her life within one day. She smiled to herself. A new day, a new life.

She unlocked the bookstore and went to work.

37

MANHATTAN

Charlie Sherman walked into the precinct on Monday morning and went straight to his captain. The man listened as Charlie outlined his concerns about Riley Kinsayle but Charlie could see he wasn't taking him seriously.

'Charlie, what happened between you two? It's been months that you've had this distance and now you come to me with this idea that Riley Kinsayle – that goofy man-child - could be obsessed enough with Lila Tierney to want to kill her? Even though he's shown no sign of psychopathy...ever?'

'I know it sounds crazy but listen...why else would he be so desperate to find her? They're not that close.'

'Maybe he thought he was doing something nice for you?'

'I wouldn't risk exposing Lila because I got beat up a little. Riley knows that.'

The captain shook his head. 'No, I'm sorry, Charlie. You got beef with Riley, you two work on it – outside this precinct. I mean it. Any trouble, I'll suspend both of you.'

Charlie was fuming by the time he went back to his desk, even snapping at his friend Joe Deacon, who came to give him a message. Joe held his hands up and backed off immediately.

. . .

RILEY NEVER SHOWED up to work. At half past five, Charlie called his cell phone for the twentieth time. The captain, who had been keeping an eye on the desk-bound Charlie, came to the door of his office. 'Still nothing?'

Charlie shook his head. The captain sighed. 'Okay, well, why don't we send a unit over to his apartment, check it out?'

'I want to go.'

The captain rolled his eyes, knowing it wasn't worth arguing. 'Okay, take a patrol, but you stay behind them, Sherman, agreed?'

'Agreed.'

HE RODE in the back of the cruiser as they weaved their way towards Riley's apartment in Queen's. As they parked outside, Charlie looked up at the building. There were no lights in Riley's window.

'Guys, stay vigilant. If he is in trouble, we don't want to make it worse.'

The two patrolmen, whose names he didn't know, went in first. They knocked at Riley's second floor apartment door but there was no answer. Charlie nodded at the door. 'He's a cop and he might be hurt or...'

'Understood.'

The burlier of the two kicked the door in. 'Riley? Riley Kinsayle? It's Charlie, dude, yell if you're hurt.'

No answer. Charlie flicked the overhead light on. Riley's apartment was clean, tidy, no sign of any disturbance. On the table, a laptop was open and switched on.

Charlie sighed. 'Jesus, Riley.' It was Tinsley's laptop. Charlie shook his head, and then looked up sharply. 'You guys hear that?'

The other men shook their heads and Charlie nodded towards a closed door, flicking the catch of his holster and drawing his pistol. The other men followed suit and led the way. As the first cop entered the room, he yelled that it was clear, and switched a light on.

'*Holy motherfuck,*' Charlie heard him hiss, 'Sherman, come take a look at this.'

Charlie followed the other cop into what he saw was Riley's bedroom. The bed was made, and it wasn't until he was fully in that he saw what the cop had seen. He sucked in a deep breath as if the shock was palpable. Riley's bedroom wall was covered in photographs. Every one of them a different scene, a different day. They only had one thing in common.

Every single of one of them was of Lila...

BREATHE ME: SHATTERED BILLIONAIRE
PART 3

Building a new life in Washington State, Lila doesn't stay hidden for long when a lovesick Noah tracks her down. Stunned by the news that she is carrying his child, Noah tells her he wants to try to be a family with her and their baby. Lila is swept away by this handsome man and they begin to build a life together. In New York, Charlie Sherman becomes increasingly suspicious if his partner Riley's behaviour and when Riley goes missing, Charlie makes a shocking discovery which could put Lila's life at risk once again...

38

MANHATTAN

'Oh my god.' The words were hissed from between Charlie Sherman's lips as he stood in Riley's apartment. Endless images of Lila assaulted his vision, photographs obviously taken without her knowledge over what looked to be the last few years, since she'd been in New York. Richard was in some of them, and as Charlie looked closer, he saw hazy images taken of the couple through windows. Intruding on private moments.

'Sherman, take a look at this.' One of the cops accompanying Charlie motioned at the wall and Charlie shifted to see what he indicating.

'Fuck.' Angry now. Photos of Lila in the hospital bed, barely alive, tubes in her arms, down her throat, spots of blood on her skin. Charlie shook his head.

'How did I not see this?'

'Kinsayle's long gone,' the other cop was rifling through Riley's closet. 'Looks like he packed in a hurry.'

'Dammit, Riley,' Charlie turned and stalked from the room, calling back to the other, 'don't touch anything else, get C.S.I. down here.'

Charlie went straight back to his captain and told him what had happened. This time, the other man took him seriously.

'Okay. Do we know where Lila Tierney is?'

Charlie gave a quick nod. 'But I don't want her scared. Let me go to her, explain what's happening.'

'Fine, I'll clear it. Charlie, if you find Riley...take him alive, if you can. No matter what he's done, if he's done anything, he's still a cop. Due process etc.'

Charlie nodded. 'Duly noted.'

CHARLIE DROVE straight to the airport and caught the next flight to Seattle. On the plane, he rubbed his face trying to figure out the story. Lila moves to New York, Charlie with her. He gets Riley as a partner and because he is always around Lila, Riley and Lila spend a lot of time in each other's company and innocent, joking flirtation occurs. But maybe it wasn't a joke to Riley....maybe he became infatuated, believed himself in love and when she had met Richard, jealousy reared its hideous and destructive head and Riley's obsession began.

Charlie narrowed his eyes, deep in thought. Riley had played the waiting game, waiting for Lila to see the rich fuck for who he really was, waiting for them to break up but a few days before the wedding was actually going to take place, Riley snapped. Followed Lila to that wedding boutique and stabbed her viciously. *If I can't have you, no-one can...*

Charlie snorted, shaking his head. Oldest play in the book. Crime of passion. And now they were looking for mild-mannered, jovial Riley Kinsayle.

Charlie closed his eyes, exhausted. The sooner he got to Lila, the sooner he would be there for her, being the best friend she always leaned on. He couldn't wait.

39

WASHINGTON STATE

L ila smoothed her cotton blouse over the ever-growing bump and grinned. 'I'm sure I just felt her kick.'

Noah, propped up on his elbow beside her, smiled. 'Her?'

'I just have a feeling.'

Noah chuckled and slid his big hand over her belly, and waited. Nothing. 'I think you imagined it.'

'Maybe but won't it be exciting when we know for sure?'

'It will.' Noah glanced at his watch and groaned. 'God, I have to get to work.'

IT WAS STILL DARK OUTSIDE. Noah's attending position at one of Seattle's most prominent hospitals meant a long commute every day to the city and now, as Lila saw the dark shadows under his eyes, she frowned. 'Baby...you know, I could always move to the city again, save you having to travel every day.'

'You'd be more exposed in the city,' he said, kissing her softly on the lips. 'I don't mind travelling. Besides, I love this place, it's a haven.'

She stroked the hair at his temples. 'We could keep this place for the weekends. I hate that you're exhausting yourself for my benefit.'

'For your safety,' he corrected, smiling. 'And for your peace of mind.'

Lila lay back on the bed, thinking. What was she so frightened of? It wasn't even her attacker finding her – it was the Carnegies. If they should find out about the baby before she had a chance to explain... god. She looked at Noah now.

'Noah, I think I need to reach out to Richard's family and let them know that...we're together at least. If they know I'm in a new relationship, maybe I can fudge the dates of my pregnancy. God that sounds bad – I just don't want them to get hurt, is all.'

Noah nodded. 'I get it, Lila, I really do. And this is all so new, you, me, us and the little bean. Tallulah.'

Lila laughed. 'No way, Jose. Anyway, I'm going to do that, get in contact, start rebuilding bridges. Then, how about we stay at your place in the week, come back here for weekends?'

Noah considered then smiled. 'Does sound tempting,' he admitted, stroking her face, 'and think of all that time on travelling I could save...what could we do to fill that time?'

She grinned back at him, then moving, she straddled him, taking his already-stiffening cock in her hands. 'I wonder.'

Noah's hand roamed all over her body, cupping her breasts and stroking her rounded belly. 'Have I told you how beautiful you are, lately?'

She chuckled. 'Way too often. I'm getting a big head.'

Noah looked down at her hands working on his cock. 'So am I, by the looks of it.' He groaned softly as she moved the tip of his cock up and down her wet sex.

'Do you like that?' She whispered, her gaze intense on his. He nodded, his hands on her breasts, his thumbs stroking a rhythm over her nipples. Lila cupped his balls in one hand and gently massaged them. 'And that?'

'God, yes...' Her gentle hands worked his cock until it stood rigid, engorged. She traced a pattern with her fingernail gently on the sensitive tip.

'That?'

Noah's answering moan made her smile. She guided him inside of her and began to move, gazing down at this wonderful, gorgeous man. His hands were on her hips then, fingers massaging the soft flesh as she rode him. His cock, so big, so hard, plunged deep into her and she moaned as Noah began to stroke her clit, increasing the pressure as she quickened her pace. God, it had never been this good with Richard, or anyone else. Her body seemed to fit Noah's perfectly despite the disparity in height between them, his cock fit inside her, stretching her, hitting all the nerve endings in her cunt.

Their movements became frenzied, fucking each other harder and harder until they both shuddered and moaned their orgasms, Noah's cock pumping thick, hot semen deep inside her. They caught their breaths, laying side-by-side, staring at each other.

Finally, Noah brushed his lips against hers. 'Lila Tierney…I am crazy in love with you.'

Lila smiled delightedly. 'You are?'

'Hell yes.'

She kissed him. 'Good. Because I've been wanting to tell you that for ages. I love you, Doc.'

He gathered her to him, and then slid a hand down to her belly. 'Family,' he said simply and she nodded, tears in her eyes.

'Yes,' she said softly, 'family.'

I SEE YOU. I see you with him, laughing, loving, fucking.

YOU WHORE. You filthy fucking whore.

WHOSE BABY IS THAT? His? I'll cut that thing out of you, Lila, after I've killed you, and send it to him. Here's your kid, bastard, oh and by the way,

Lila is dead, my knife buried deep inside her. This time, you won't be able to save her, you fuck.

THIS TIME *my knife will gut the life right out of her.*

SOON, *Lila, soon.*

LILA FELT ALMOST GIDDY, like a schoolgirl getting a date with the best looking boy on the football squad. *Noah Applebaum is in love with me,* she thought to herself, as she flitted around the bookshop, tidying, repricing books on sale, unpacking new deliveries. It had been a busy morning, a beautiful Washington day outside had brought waves of tourists over on the ferries from the mainland and it seemed that every single one of them had come to the shop. A few locals had said as much, some of them squinting at the newcomers as if they were rabid interlopers. Lila grinned to herself; she loved this little book-shop with its large windows and light wood bookshelves, the airiness of the space, the calm, and the peace. At one end, there was a selection of large, battered couches which patrons could sit and read all day if they wished.

Yeah, if she did move to the city during the week, she would miss this place. Maybe she could work out a new arrangement and she could commute for a couple of days, at least until the baby came. She would be loath to give up on this place entirely.

So deeply engrossed in her thoughts, she didn't see him standing at the door watching her, a small smile on his face.

'Hey, Boo.'

Lila looked up startled. Her immediate reaction was joy when she saw her oldest and closest friend standing at the door; then the next minute, she blanched. 'Charlie...what are you doing here?'

He stood aside to let some patrons out then came to the counter.

'Got all sorts of answers for that, but the most important one was... god, I missed you.'

Lila froze for a moment then suddenly darted around the counter and threw herself at him. 'Oh, Charlie, I missed you so much.'

He swept her up and spun her in his arms. 'Hated every minute without you.' He put her down and only then seemed to notice her swollen belly. His eyebrows went up.

'Food baby?

She grinned, flushing furiously. 'Actual baby. Long, long story.'

Charlie looked stunned. 'Is this happening or is this a fever dream?'

Her color deepened. 'Charlie, there's so much I have to tell you but first...why are you here? Apart from missing me.'

His smile faded and he glanced around at the other patrons – most of who were eavesdropping on the scene. 'Is there somewhere we can talk privately?'

Lila glanced at the clock. 'I'm off in an hour...look, there's a coffee-house across the road, can you wait?'

Charlie nodded. 'Okay, in an hour then.' He looked her up and down. 'You look radiant, Lila. Oh hey,' he said suddenly, 'who's the father?'

She grinned at his expression. 'I'll tell you everything in an hour, I promise.'

An hour and fifteen minutes later, Charlie sat back in his seat, running his hand through his dark hair. 'The good doctor, hey?'

Lila nodded. 'I'm crazy about him, Chuckles. He is the person I was meant to be with...you'll like him, I know it for sure.'

'Hey, the few times I met him, he seemed like a stand-up guy,' Charlie agreed, 'and he helped you recover so I'm always going to owe him one. So when...' He gestured to her burgeoning belly and Lila flushed again.

'A few days before Richard died. At our last physiotherapy session.'

Charlie threw back his head and laughed. 'Wow, Lila...'

She tried to smile. 'I know, so unlike me and just...I don't want to call it wrong but it was probably not the appropriate time. But, god, Charlie, I'd just come back from the dead and I wanted him.'

Charlie leaned forward, taking her hand. 'Hey, hey, I'm not judging you. I say good for you. After all those years with that – '

'Charlie, no. Richard's dead, let's not...' She choked up, tears in her eyes. 'The reason I left New York was the baby. I knew it had to be Noah's and that fact alone made me want this baby so much. I had fallen in love with him almost as soon as I met him – not that I told him that.' She grinned shyly. 'In fact, when I came here, I told no-one, not even Noah. I didn't want him to think he was trapped. Lucky for me, he tracked me down.'

'And now you're making a go of it?'

'We're making our family. That you're here makes it even more of a family. How did you find me, by the way?'

Charlie frowned. 'Your letter, remember? You told me you were going back to the place where we met. You probably meant Seattle but I remember I first met you here. The children's home had brought us here on an outing – you came along later that day with Susanna...remember?

She shook her head. 'No...god, I don't.' She gave a small laugh. 'Well-remembered, though.'

Charlie grinned. 'The rest was easy, just asked around at the grocery store, the local medical center. Strange how a cop's badge will get you the information you need.'

Lila rolled her eyes, laughing. 'Yes, it's a mystery. Guess my well-laid plans fell through if it was that easy to find me.'

Charlie's smile faded. 'For a cop, yes, and that's another reason I came. Lila, I have some bad news, shocking news really.' He took a deep breath. 'Boo, I think we know who it was who stabbed you.'

Lila began to tremble, her hands shaking and she put her tea cup down. 'Who?' Her voice was low, almost a whisper.'

'Riley.' He watched her expression go from shock to horror to fear.

'Oh my god...' Lila closed her eyes. 'Oh god, please no.'

Charlie frowned. 'Lila, is there something you haven't told me about you and Riley, something you've kept from me?'

She shook her head but didn't look at him. 'No. God, how do you know?'

He told her about the incident with Tinsley and then what they'd found in Riley's apartment. 'As soon as I saw that wall of photographs of you, I knew. He's obsessed, Lila. Dangerously so, we think.'

'Then why haven't you arrested him?'

Charlie looked at with soft, dark eyes. 'Sweetheart, because we can't find him. Riley's missing.'

LILA STILL FELT sick as they drove back to her cottage. Riley...She couldn't believe it and yet when she thought back to that awful day in the bridal boutique, when she'd opened the curtain and her attacker had driven that knife into her belly over and over...it made a strange kind of sense. Her stabber had been the right size for Riley, certainly, tall and well-built but that didn't mean anything. Richard, Noah and Charlie were all of a similar height and build as Riley.

But there was another reason it made sense...one that she always looked back on with shame...

...she had cheated on Richard with Riley.

40

MANHATTAN

T *hen*

IT WAS AFTER PARIS, after they'd travelled around the world back-packing and when Richard had finally gotten his way and treated her to the most luxurious Parisian dream vacation. After that.

They'd gotten back to New York and returned to their everyday lives; Richard running his billion-dollar corporation and Lila back at school and at the bar. Now that school was coming to an end, her schedule was light and she had more time to think and hang out alone.

Which was proving to be a big mistake. She had been triggered by a photograph in a society magazine of Delphine's.

CAMILLA VAN DER HAAS, 27, leaving Butter with her new flame, Eric John Markham, 39. Miss Van Der Hass is the daughter of billionaire property

magnate, Regis Van Der Haas and Lavinia Fortuna. Mr Markham is the
head of MarkoPharm, the pharmaceutical giant.

THERE WAS a photograph of Camilla in a stunning, red silk slip dress,
her long tawny hair tumbling down her back, her wide smile open and
knowing. Her escort was blandly handsome in a forgettable way but it
was Camilla Lila couldn't take her eyes off. *That knowing look. I could have*
any man I wanted and I know it, it seemed to say. *Especially* your *man,*
Lila...who do you think you are, you jumped up gold-digger from nowhere?

Lila had made a face at the photograph and threw the magazine
down. Fucking bitch. And why had Lila let Richard off so easily? He
fucking *cheated* on me, she told herself.

She was in the bar, cleaning up. It was late and the bar was almost
empty of patrons. Saturday night...late.

'I've been watching you clean the same spot for the last ten
minutes, with a face that says '*Imma gonna cut ya bitch*'.'

Lila looked up and smiled. 'Hey, you, I didn't even see you. When
did you get here?'

Riley Kinsayle smiled at her. 'Like I said, ten minutes.'

Lila chuckled. 'Man, I'm sorry, what can I get you?'

Riley looked around the otherwise empty bar. 'You sure? I mean it
looks like you're ready to shut up shop for the night.'

Lila hesitated then went to the door, closing it and sliding the bolt
across. 'Lock-in for two?'

Riley grinned delightedly. 'Hey, I'm always up for that.'

Lila grabbed a couple of beers and they snagged a table in the
middle of the room. Tapping the neck of his bottle to Lila's, Riley took
a swig. 'So, why the face?'

Lila shrugged. 'Nothing. Not much...god...it's just one of Richard's
exes.'

'Been bothering you?'

Lila gazed at him for a long moment. 'Riley, if I tell you something...will you promise to keep it to yourself, not even tell Charlie?'

He put his hand over his heart. 'My word is my bond, Lila.' He studied her closely. 'What is it, sweetheart?'

She sighed. 'Richard cheated on me with one of his exes. Camilla. She's an Upper East-sider, all designer labels and perfect hair.'

Riley cussed. 'Are you kidding me? Is he an idiot?'

Lila tried to smile. 'Oh, yes. But I give him credit for telling me straight away, the same day.'

'You do? I don't,' Riley was clearly pissed now. 'What fucking idiot cheats on *you*?'

Lila flushed, waving off the compliment. 'No, I mean, he's an idiot for sure, but I don't think it was intentional.'

'So he tripped and his dick fell into her snatch by mistake?'

The image Riley conjured was so comical that Lila burst out laughing and he grinned. After a moment, Lila stopped laughing. 'Riley, you always manage to cheer me up.'

'Maybe cos I'm awesome,' He waggled his eyebrows at her making her grin, but then he fixed her with a stare. 'Please tell me you've kicked him to the curb.'

Lila shrugged and Riley sighed. 'Lila...don't you know that he's lucky to have you? That any guy would kill for a woman like you?' He looked down at his hands briefly. 'I would.'

Lila got up and went to him, hugging him tightly. 'Thank you, Riley...'

He got up from his chair and wrapped his arms around her. 'Anytime, beautiful, anytime.'

They stayed like that for a beat too long then Lila pulled away – but looked up at him. For a heartbeat, they stared at each other then Riley dipped his head and kissed her. It was a sweet but firm kiss and Lila responded, her lips against his, her hands flat on his chest. When his fingers slid under her t-shirt, for a second, she thought about stopping him.

But she didn't...he was here and Richard wasn't...and she needed to be held and loved by someone good and pure, who would never hurt her...

It seemed only a beat before Riley was pulling her t-shirt from her, his eyes fixed on her full breasts, her stomach. 'Wow. Oh wow,' he said softly, 'you don't know how long...'

'Ssh,' she smiled up at him, 'No words.'

Riley smiled and then they were pulling at their clothes and tumbling to the floor naked, and Riley was hitching her legs around his hips and thrusting into her.

'Oh god, Lila...Lila...'

The way he said her name made her feel so special, like Richard had in the beginning, so full of love, and wonder. Riley was a skilled lover, all his attention riveted on her and her pleasure and he made her come, a long, drawn out sigh of an orgasm shuddering through her body. Afterward, they held each other and talked and laughed – easy, casual, and friendly.

Lila tucked her t-shirt into her jeans and then grabbed his hand. 'Hey, Riley...listen, I had a really good time tonight and I...'

Riley stopped her with a kiss. 'Just between you and me,' he said, '*this* night belongs to us even if there are no more nights like it.'

Lila smiled at him fondly and touched his face. 'You are such a good friend, Riley.'

There was something in his eyes that made her chest hurt, a sadness, a disappointment but he smiled at her. 'Always, Lila. Always.'

AND THERE HADN'T BEEN another night like that. To Lila's great relief, Riley's manner towards her hadn't changed – he was still the warm, goofy friend to her, still flirted outrageously as if they had never been intimate. When Charlie was there, the three of them acted as they always had, Lila and Riley teasing Charlie about his grumpy manner.

IT HAD BEEN a week before Lila and Richard's wedding when it happened. Lila was celebrating her last night at the bar and all of her friends were there. Champagne was flowing easily but Lila had notice Riley sticking to soda water all night. Eventually she got him on his own.

'Why aren't you drinking, Smiley Riley?' Lila had been drinking and was a little light-headed. She swayed and he steadied her, smiling.

'Because I'm a lousy drunk,' he said softly, 'and tonight of all nights, I didn't want to be that guy. The guy that tells you he's crazy about you and has been for years. The drunk guy you look at sadly and shake your head at and wonder why you invited him. The one who gets drunk and begs you not to marry the rich guy because he, the drunk guy, is in love with you. And look, I went and said all that stuff anyways.'

Lila stared at him and Riley looked away from her gaze, giving a little laugh.

'Oh, Riley...' Lila felt awful, putting her hands on his face. 'I'm so sorry.'

He shook his head. 'Don't be, it's not anything you have to be sorry for. I misjudged my ability to stay...distant.'

Lila stood on her tiptoes and kissed him. 'You know I love you too, right? Just I'm not...'

'*In* love with me. That's okay, shorty, as long as we're still friends.'

'Always,' she said fiercely, 'always.'

He'd held her for a long minute then gently pushed her away. 'Go. Go be happy ever after, Lila, go enjoy the rest of your life.'

Four days later, a man with a knife – possibly Riley - tried to end her life and very nearly succeeded.

41

SAN JUAN ISLAND, WASHINGTON STATE

Noah frowned as he opened the front door to the cottage. Normally, Lila would be waiting on the front porch for him, would throw herself into his arms. Today, nothing.

'Anyone home?' He called, his heartbeat quickening before he heard her voice.

'In here, baby.'

The living room. He dumped his bag and coat and went in – and stopped. Charlie Sherman stood and held out his hand. 'Hey, doc.'

Noah blinked. 'Hey yourself.' He shook Charlie's hand and bent to kiss Lila's cheek. She smiled at him, and he saw strain in her expression.

'Has something happened?'

He sat down next to her and put his arm around her. Charlie watched them and when Lila just nodded, Charlie picked up the story for her. Noah whistled.

'So this Riley...he's missing?'

Charlie nodded. 'Which is why I'm here. I know Lila wanted space and I was happy to leave her be...but things have changed, escalated. And now I know that you two are together, and that there's a little one on the way...I felt like it was my duty.'

He trailed off but smiled. Noah felt irked. 'You know, we have got security in place. You may not see it, but it's very discreet. We have this.'

Lila squeezed his hand. 'Honey, Charlie came to warn us about Riley, not to tell us what to do about it, right Charlie?'

Charlie held up his hands. 'Sure, sure, sorry if I caused offense. I'm just used to being Lila's protector. Forgive me.'

Noah nodded tightly, his eyes narrowing and Lila sighed. 'Okay then,' she pulled herself up, 'if you guys are done pissing around me, then I'll go make us something to eat.'

Noah got up, his expression apologetic. 'No, you won't. We'll get take out. That okay with you, Charlie?'

'Of course.'

LATER, when they'd eaten and Charlie had gone back into the city to his hotel, Lila and Noah lay in the bathtub together, Lila leaning back against his chest and Noah's fingers stroking her belly bump. He drew a six on it and she giggled. 'I know can you believe it? Only three months to go.'

'Should we discuss names? Have you any ideas?'

Lila smiled around at him. 'A few...but I'm scared you'll hate them.'

'Hmm,' he considered, 'well, how's about you tell me yours and I'll tell you mine and we'll see where we're at.'

'Okay.'

'Good. If it's a boy...William.'

She grinned. 'I like that. William Noah...or Noah William. Noah Applebaum II.'

'Oh no,' he protested, 'I find dudes who name their kids after them so very, very conceited. What was your boy's name anyway?'

'Noah,' she sulked as he laughed, 'but I do have some spares. How about Gyjoo – Gee-shooo?'

'What the hell kind of name is Gee-shooo.'

She grinned wickedly. 'It's spelled G. I. J. O. E.'

It took Noah a second then he splashed her. 'G. I. Joe, very funny.'

'Sorry but I really only had Noah for my boy choices, but I really do love William.'

Noah cheered. 'So I get my choice? Victory!'

Lila rubbed her belly smugly. 'Only if it's a boy, mister, and as I'm baking this thing, I know for a fact it's a girl.'

'Oh you do, huh? Hit me with your choices then.'

'Okay I'm doing this, top three in reverse order, okay?'

Noah sighed dramatically. 'Just get on with it, woman.'

Lila chuckled. 'Okay, in third place...Olivia.'

Noah thought about it. 'Yep, nice, continue.'

'Second place... Emeliana.'

'Hmm, not sure, it's nice but with Applebaum? That's a mouthful.'

Lila pouted. 'Then you're probably not going to like my first choice.'

'Go for it.'

'Matilda.'

'Hmm. Matilda Applebaum. Matty Applebaum. You have a deal.'

She turned and faced him, the surprise obvious on her face. 'No way, you agreed that easily?'

'It's a gorgeous name for our gorgeous girl, Lila Belle. And by the way, what say we talk about making this all official?'

She stopped and looked at him, her face paling. 'What?'

Noah grinned. 'Don't panic, I'm not proposing...*yet*. I mean, if we're having a baby, I'd quite like him or her, Matty or Willy,' - he grinned at her pained expression – 'to meet my family so that means I'd like you, my darling one, to meet my family. I warn you – they are crazy.'

'Good crazy or bad crazy?'

'It's a fine line.'

Lila nodded slowly. 'Okay then, I'm all for crazy. Wow, I get to meet the Applebaum clan.' She kissed him, her lips curling up in a smile against his mouth. 'Any family that bred you can't be all bad.'

Noah chuckled. 'Thank you, I think. And sorry about earlier with

Chuckles. I was oversensitive, the guy just wants you safe same as me.'

Lila sighed happily, resting her head in the crook of his neck. 'Oh and by the way....there's no way in hell we're calling our son 'Willy'.'

They both laughed and then Noah tickled her until she was screeching with laughter then kissed her until the water got very, very cold.

42

SEATTLE

'I could have come back to the island,' Charlie said the next morning as they sat in the coffee house, 'You didn't need to haul your cookies here, Boo.'

Lila smiled at him. 'It's no problem...in fact; I got extra time with Noah coming into the city, so it all worked out. Also, I'm going to stay at his condo here more often now that I'm not 'in-hiding' as such.'

Charlie stirred his coffee. 'Are you sure that's wise? We still don't know where Riley is.'

'I won't take any unnecessary risks,' she said, rolling her eyes. 'No more wedding fitting rooms for me.'

Charlie winced. 'Don't joke about that, Lila. Was the worst day of my life.'

'Mine too,' she said, half smiling. 'Charlie, I want to know what you've been doing, or rather who? Any chance you and Tinsley could hook up again?'

She looked so hopeful that he grinned. 'The honest answer is I don't know. She was dating Harry for a while.'

Lila's mouth dropped open. 'Harry...Carnegie?'

'The very one. Nice guy, actually, better than – '

'Charlie.' Lila glared at him over her coffee mug.

'Sorry, old habits,' but he smiled. 'Yep, they were hot and heavy for a while but then he went back to Australia.'

'Tinsley upset?'

'I honestly couldn't tell you. She and I were kind of distracted with this Riley thing. I haven't spoken to her since I got here.'

'I should call her.'

'Yes, I know she misses you. Lila?'

She was staring out of the window and when she turned to face him, there were tears in her eyes. 'Charlie, I want to talk to the Carnegies, I do, but I have no earthly idea of what to say to them, especially now.'

She looked down at her swollen belly, placing her hand protectively over it. 'I could wait until after the baby is born but I don't want it hanging over me. Noah says to rip off the Band-Aid.'

'Noah's a smart guy. Look, there's no easy way to tell them what you gotta tell them, Lila. Just do it.'

Lila suddenly chuckled. 'Jeez, Charlie, tell me how it is, won't ya?'

'That's the way we do it, Tierney.'

The waitress brought their breakfasts and Charlie fell on his pancakes as if half-starved. Lila looked at him fondly. 'Dude, you need to get back with Tinsley. Be truthful; did you ever really get over her?'

Charlie shrugged. 'I'm not someone who gets over things, Lila, you know that. I just go with the flow.'

'Hmm,' Lila squinted at him. 'Is it wrong I want you to be as happy as I am now?'

'No, kiddo, it's not wrong, it's not wrong at all. Just sometimes it doesn't happen for people and I'm okay with it. As long as I got my girl,' he tapped his fingertip against her cheek and she bit it, giggling.

'Of course. Hey, listen, Noah's asked me to go with him and meet his family.'

'Scared?'

'More excited. I can't wait.'

. . .

DR. APPLEBAUM?'

Noah turned to the woman behind him. Joanne Hammond smiled at him and Noah smiled. They had met a few times when he had been dating Lauren Shannon; they were co-workers and Joanne had none of Lauren's pretensions. Joanne was the trusted second-in-command of Derek Shannon - Lauren's father – and the life blood of his PR company. He adored Joanne because she ran the place like clockwork – and put up with Lauren. Noah had met her at a company barbecue and was instantly drawn to her wit, sarcasm and cynicism. It had always irritated Lauren that Noah and Joanne were friends – which made it even more enjoyable.

'Joanne! It's good to see you...I *think*. You okay?' He hugged her.

'I am – but Mackie's in for his diabetes again.' Joanne, a small, athletic woman with dark skin and silver eyes smiled but she looked tired. Her husband, Mackie, was a war veteran who'd gotten depressed after he'd left the military and gained enough weight to trigger type two diabetes later in life. A good man, Mackie had been hospitalized a couple of times and Joanne, almost in her seventies now, was exhausted.

'Come have a coffee with me while the doctor's in with Mackie,' Noah said now, seeing his colleague talking to Mackie, 'then you can catch me up.'

EVEN THE STOIC Charlie was impressed when Lila showed him into Noah's condo. 'Okay, should have gone to medical school.'

Lila chuckled. 'I know, right? To think he trusts us, two street kids, here alone? Shall we case the joint?'

Charlie, laughing, shook his head. 'You know, we were never really street kids, well, not until we were old enough to be thrown out on our own.'

'We managed.'

'We did.'

Lila made them both drinks. 'Let's go out on the balcony because we're fancy.'

'Always a good reason.'

Noah's balcony had astonishing views over Elliott Bay and they put their feet up as they settled back into the uber-comfortable deck furniture. The day was bright and cold and the Olympic Mountains soared high on the horizon.

Lila looked over at Charlie. 'Chuckles, can I ask you something?'

'Anything.'

'Do you think I get involved with too many rich men? I never intend it that way.'

Charlie laughed. 'Lila, have you looked in the mirror? You attract every type of man. And it's only really been Richard and Noah – two entirely different situations. Everyone else you've dated has been pretty low rent.'

'Don't say that, they were all great guys – one of them especially,' she grinned at him. 'You'll always be my first love, Chuckles.'

'Right back at ya, Saddlebags.'

Lila almost snorted her juice out of her nose. 'That's so cruel, but hilarious. I'm going to be huge soon at this rate.'

'You could be the size of Madison Square Garden and still be the most beautiful girl in the world.'

'Honey tongue!' She giggled as he doffed a pretend cap. 'Stop flirting with me, Chuckles, I'm gestating.'

'Fair point,' Charlie sighed. 'Look at that view. God, I miss this city.'

Lila swigged a gulp of orange juice. 'You could always move back here.'

Charlie looked over to her and smiled. 'I can't follow you around my whole life, sweetheart. Besides, if you want me to get with Tinsley again...'

Lila threw her arms in the air. 'Yes!'

'There you go.'

'I want you to get married and have a million kids.'

'Steady on, girl.'

'Then come live here in Seattle.'

Charlie sighed. 'Jeez.'

Lila grinned and then gasped, bending forward and clutching her belly. Immediately Charlie was alert. 'What? What is it, Lila?'

Lila didn't answer for a moment then looked up, her eyes shining. 'She just kicked. That's the first time I've felt it. Oh my god, Charlie, give me your hand.'

She grabbed his arm and placed his hand over her belly. She stared at him, smiling. Charlie started slightly then removed his hand.

'This isn't right, it should be Noah...'

'He's not here, doofus,' she grabbed his hand. 'Noah knows how these things work, you can't have perfect timing, He'll just be glad I had someone I love to share the moment.

NOAH TRIED to smile as he balanced the phone between his neck and shoulder and changed out of his white coat. 'Darling, that's wonderful. I can't wait to get home but my dad's asked me to meet him for dinner after work. Will you be okay for a couple of hours?'

'Of course, I'll order takeout, get Charlie to stay with me. I'm so excited though, Noah, I can't wait for you to feel her.'

Noah chuckled. 'You're convinced it's a girl, aren't you?'

'You betcha. Well...say hi to your dad for me, tell him I'm looking forward to meeting him.'

'Probably better if I tell him *about* you first...then somehow try to work in 'Hey, dad, also, you're going to be a grampy!'.'

Lila laughed. 'Well, good luck with that, buddy. I love you.'

'Love you too, beautiful.'

ON HIS WAY OUT, he stopped by to see Joanne and Mackie. Mackie was asleep and Joanne was sitting by his bed.

Noah – ever the doctor – checked Mackie's charts. He tried to keep the grimace off his face but Joanne knew him too well.

'Yep,' she said, 'Mackie's circling the drain. His words, not mine. But he won't buck up and take responsibility for his health. He eats,

Noah, from the minute he gets up to when he goes to sleep. Maybe not always unhealthy stuff but you know as well as I do, anything in excess...'

Noah nodded, sighing. 'Sure do. Look, has he tried any psychotherapy to deal with his eating disorder?'

'A bunch of them. Nothing sticks. He's resigned to dying, Noah, says he'd rather die happy.'

Noah was irked. 'And what about you?'

Joanne just looked at him and he nodded. 'Yeah, I know. Listen, I have to go meet my dad.'

Her eyes lit up. 'You going to tell him about the baby?'

Noah smiled at her expression. 'Yeah...wish me luck. Hey, listen, don't say anything to Lauren, will you?'

Joanne rolled her eyes. 'As if I would. Good luck with your girl, Noah, you deserve a sweetie.'

'I'll come by tomorrow, see how things are.'

As HE DROVE to the restaurant to meet his father, he thought about spending the next fifty years with Lila, as Joanne had done with Mackie. Would they still be as devoted? He had never been more sure of anything. He and Lila were best friends, They were each other's protector, mind, body and soul.

Noah Applebaum had grown up seeing first-hand what an unhappy marriage could do. His father, Halston, had been a terrible, violent husband to his mother, even when she was dying of cancer. More than once, he, Noah, had stepped between them and taken his father's blows. When his mother had finally died, she'd kissed Noah and told him that she was happy to go and to get away from his father.

But his mother's death had changed his father. A full-on break-down followed and intensive therapy at the most expensive spas in the world and his father was someone else entirely. The first thing he'd done when he returned to Seattle was seek Noah out and apologize. And it wasn't some sappy apology culled from a program; it was a genuine from the heart plea, not for forgiveness but for a second chance. And his dad hadn't held back; he began a foundation to combat domestic abuse, gave interviews where he freely and ashamedly admitted to being an abuser, and was a committed public speaker on the subject. Noah, already in his twenties and cynical hadn't been convinced of the turnaround until he reluctantly attended one of his father's events. After some speeches, his father asked for a volunteer from the audience, for a woman who had been badly abused. There was hesitation and eventually a small bird-like woman had come to the front.

Hal Applebaum had asked her to stand opposite him, and then he met her gaze. 'I am your husband, your brother, your demon, your nightmare. I am standing here stripped of every bit of anger. Say what you always wanted to say, scream your rage at me, tell me everything you wanted to say when you were being abused.'

The woman had been nervous at first, her voice barely audible, but as she began to speak, to vocalize her hurt, her pain, the atmosphere in the room was electric. Noah found himself almost unable to breath as the woman started to yell, scream pull at his dad's shirt, express every ounce of pain her abuser had visited on her and his dad just took it. When the woman's sobs had quieted, Hal took her hands.

'I'm not your husband,' he said softly, 'and you're not my wife. He never apologized to you and my wife never heard me apologize. This won't make up for that but I think it will help both of us. I'm sorry. I'm so sorry that this happened to you, there is no excuse for all the hateful things you heard, for the pain inflicted on you. You are strong and kind and beautiful and any man who treats you less than a goddess is not worthy of you. I'm so, so sorry.'

The look on his dad's face – Noah knew that not only was he talking to the tormented woman in front of him, he was talking to Noah's beloved mom.

Afterward, he'd approached his dad. The two men stared at each other, then Noah held out his hand and his dad broke down. Tears rolling down his face, he pulled his son into a hug.

'I know this doesn't make anything right,' he said, his voice breaking, 'but I'll spend the rest of my life trying.'

IT HADN'T SOLVED their problems overnight but they worked on it. Now Noah enjoyed a warm but separate existence from his father. He had remarried, a lovely woman called Molly, and now his father lived in Portland with her and Molly's teenage son, Kyle. Kyle and Noah bonded quickly and now Noah considered Kyle a brother. The younger man had graduated *summa cum laude* and now worked as a journalist in Kuala Lumpur.

Noah walked into the restaurant and saw his father and Molly waiting for him. They hugged him hello and they chatted easily while they were seated.

Halston smiled at his son. 'I hear great things about your work, son. Saul Harlow says you could be the youngest Chief of Surgery in a generation.'

Noah thanked him. 'But, actually, Dad, Molly, there's something else I have to tell you – something pretty big.'

And he told them about Lila and the baby. Both Hal and Molly were surprised, shocked and then delighted. 'Well, this is extraordinary news,' Hal clapped his son on the back, 'Congratulations, Noah, that's wonderful.'

'So exciting,' Molly squeezed Noah's hand, her soft face lit up. Noah grinned at them.

'So, I want you to meet Lila – you will love her.' His smile faded a little. 'I should tell you...she used to be engaged to Richard Carnegie.'

'Wait,' his dad frowned, 'She's the young woman who was attacked, right?'

'She was stabbed, yes,' Noah's mind went back to when he'd first met Lila, 'They still haven't found the person who did it so we've had to up security.'

'Awful,' Molly looked upset. Noah smiled at her.

'Lila's much better now; I mean, there's still some way to go with her range of motion but we're waiting until after the baby is born to complete her rehab.'

'When is she due?'

Noah cleared his throat. 'About three months.'

His dad's eyebrows shot up. 'And you're just now telling us?'

'It's a long story.'

43

SEATTLE

Charlie Sherman left Lila at the condo and went to meet his compatriots at the Seattle police department. The detective he met with, a middle-aged tired looking man named Cabot Marin, greeted him with a resigned sigh. 'If I earned a dollar for every nut-bag stalking a woman...'

Charlie filled him in on Lila's case. 'No, I have to be fair, apart from Riley's disappearance and what we found at his apartment, we have no other evidence to suggest Riley is the man who stabbed Lila, or that he has ever committed any crime. But he is our only lead and the fact he went missing on the day we linked him to the attack...'

'Yup. Sometimes we have to go where the investigation points, even if it is somewhere that's uncomfortable. Well, look, we already know that Dr. Applebaum had employed extra-security – they applied for concealed weapons licenses, which they were granted. Miss Tierney appears to be well-protected, both out on the island and at the doctor's condominium. Is she the type to follow instructions to keep herself safe?'

Charlie half-smiled. 'Not in the least, which is what worries me. Lila is street-smart but headstrong – she rubs against any restrictions.

She says she won't take unnecessary risks but if I were Riley, I'd wait for the necessary risks and strike then.'

Cabot Marin nodded. 'Yup. Well, all we can do right now is be vigilant.'

Charlie shook his hand. 'I appreciate it.'

HE LEFT the police building and walked back to his hotel. He had told Lila he would meet Noah and Lila for breakfast the next day and then fly back to New York. He pulled out his phone and dialed a number, smiling when he heard Tinsley's Australian accent. 'Hey, you,' he said warmly, 'you got any plans for tomorrow night?'

44

SEATTLE

Noah crept quietly into the bedroom, pulling his clothes off and hanging them over the chair, as quiet as he could be. Lila was asleep, lying on her side, one hand under her cheek, the other reaching out towards his side of the bed. Noah slipped in beside her and she stirred, opening her eyes and smiling at him.

'Hey gorgeous.'

Noah brushed his lips against hers, tasting her minty toothpaste on her breath. 'Hey yourself, baby.' He nuzzled her nose with his, then slid his arms around her and pulled her close. She smelt of sleepy warmth and fresh linen, and her skin was so soft, he couldn't help but run his hands over her bare skin.

'Your hands are cold,' she grumbled but giggled when he tickled her.

'I love you when you're all sleepy like this,' he ran his fingers through her hair; 'you're so funny.'

She grumbled something unintelligible.

'What was that?'

Lila rubbed her eyes. 'Sorry, I said, how was your dinner with the parental units?'

Noah smiled. 'Good...they can't wait to meet you but they had to go back to Portland tonight, so Dad suggests we go down there for the weekend. What do you think?'

'I'm in. Hey, the baby's kicking again.'

Noah slid his hand onto her belly and she guided it to where the baby was kicking her. Noah's eyes widened. 'Wow...that feels so weird.'

'Doesn't it? God, she's a little bruiser too, I swear, she's been kicking up a storm all day. Go to sleep, Matty Apple.'

Noah grinned. 'Matty Apple?' Lila smiled and kissed him.

'I maybe know a way to, um, rock her to sleep.' She pulled herself up and straddled him, reaching for his cock.

Noah lay back, and relaxed as she stroked him gently between her hands then traced the tip up and down her sex.

'Do you want me?' Lila asked softly and he nodded, unable to tear his eyes from her body, lit by the moonlight flooding into the room, her dark hair tumbling down in messy waves.

They made love slowly, each movement sensual and languid, drinking each other in. When they had finished, Noah wrapped her in his big arms and they fell asleep.

The phone woke them both a little before three am. Lila groaned as Noah reached for it. 'Yup? Okay. Okay. I'll be right in.'

Lila protested as he slid out of bed. 'What is it?'

'A patient took a fall...Mackie; he's sort of a friend. He wasn't even supposed to be out of bed...damn it.'

'Did he hit his head? Is that why they called you in?'

'Yes...god, I'm sorry, baby.' He was frantically pulling his clothes on, now.

'Don't worry, I hope he's okay.'

He leaned over to kiss her. 'Will you be okay?'

'Of course, go, go.'

'Lock the door behind me.'

She followed him sleepily to the front door and kissed him again. 'Go save a life, superman.'

She closed and locked the door behind him and went to bed, not seeing the alarm pad blinking. She curled up beneath the covers and was asleep in minutes.

She didn't hear the doors to the balcony being slid open and a figure entering her home. The intruder made their way to the bedroom and stood at the side of Lila's bed, watching her sleep...

NOAH WENT to look for Joanne just after six am. The woman was staring out of the window of the relatives room at the dawn creeping over the horizon. She saw his reflection and turned and by the expression on her face, she was already prepared for his news.

'I'm so sorry, Joanne.'

She nodded once. 'I know. I felt him go...not just tonight but years ago. It wasn't a life, Noah, he's at peace now.'

'What about you? Will you be okay?'

She smiled at him and patted the seat beside her. Noah sat down and took her hands in his. She smiled at him. 'I will be,' she said, 'and probably sooner than I ought to be. What was it in the end, the fall?'

Noah nodded. 'The hell of it is that if he had been healthier, he might have made it but because of the smoking, he was already depriving his brain of oxygen. His cause of death will be hypoxic brain injury due to fall and life style choices.'

'Well,' Joanne was stoic, 'that's just it. They were *his* choices.' She sighed and got up. 'Guess I'll just go home then. Will they take care of Mackie until I can get things arranged?'

'Of course,' Noah stood and hugged her. 'I'm so sorry, Joanne, again, if there's anything I can do.'

'You've done plenty,' she said, 'if Mackie'd had any chance after that fall, it would have been you that handed it to him. Some people can't be saved.'

AFTER SHE'D GONE, Noah slumped down into a chair and buried his head in his hands. Jeez, how quickly lives can change. He thought of

Joanne going home to an empty bed for the first time in fifty years. *God...*

An image of Lila in that fitting room all those months ago...okay, so he hadn't been there but he'd seen enough stabbing victims – and now he pictured her, curled up in a fetal position, her blood pooling around her, her hand pressed hard against her belly as she tried to stem the blood....*stop it. That's in the past.*

He got up and strode to the doctor's changing room, stripping off his scrubs and dumping them in a laundry bin.

He didn't know if it was the combination of losing Mackie, the lateness of the hour or the visions of Lila bleeding that haunted him, but he knew that right now, there was only one thing he wanted to do.

Get home. *Now.*

BARELY BREATHING, she kept her eyes closed but her senses were on the edge as she listened to the intruder walk around the condo. She'd woken – but thankfully not opened her eyes – when she heard the floorboards creak and immediately felt the presence next to the bed. She waited for the knife or the bullet or hands on her body but none came.

She risked opening her eyes a crack. She saw the figure through the doorway in the living area, and mentally ran a scan of anything in the bedroom she could use as a weapon. Her eyes lit upon a small marble lion's head sculpture on Noah's nightstand.

She smiled grimly to herself and shifted slowly across the bed to grab it. She sat up and slid out of bed and to the door, peaking around it to see where the intruder was. The kitchen area. Good.

Lila slipped into the living area silently, her bare feet making no noise on the carpet. As she reached the intruder, they turned and Lila raised the sculpture. The intruder batted her arm away but Lila let go and the marble lion's head smashed down on the intruder's shoulder. A high-pitched yell – feminine – made Lila lose concentration for a moment then the assailant was on her, hands around her neck, choking, pushing her down to the floor. Lila rammed her fingers into the attacker's eyes and there was a scream – this time, Lila was sure. It was a woman.

'Get off me, you fucking bitch,' she kicked the attacker in the groin and she rolled off of her. Every single emotion that Lila used to feel defending herself on the streets came back to her, and she darted around the prone attacker, yanked open a drawer and pulled out the biggest knife she could find and held it in front of her.

'Come at me, bro,' she growled, fury raging through her, daring the attacker to try again.

Instead, the attacker gave a sob and crumpled to the floor. Lila stared at the figure in black in disbelief, then reached over, flipped on the lights and yanked the mask from the attacker's very blonde head. The young woman didn't look at her.

'I'm sorry, okay-y-y-y,' her voice wobbled as she sobbed, 'I just wanted to see you.'

Lila dropped her arm but not the knife. 'Who are you?'

The woman looked up finally, and Lila saw she was young, about Lila's age, and very pretty – when she wasn't covered in snot and tears.

'Are you Lauren?'

Noah had told her about his ex-girlfriend months ago, when Lila was still going through rehab. The girl nodded.

'I'm sorry,' she said again and scrambled to her feet. Lila took a step back and raised the blade in front of her. Lauren held up her hands.

'I promise, I never intended to hurt you...I'm sorry about before but you did just hit me in the shoulder.'

'You broke into my home.'

Lauren nodded, looking at her curiously. 'Who are you?'

Lila took a deep breath in. 'Lila Tierney. I'm...with Noah now.' Almost unconsciously, her hand moved to her belly, protectively and Lauren's eyes followed.

'Oh.'

'Yes.'

Lauren's eyes filled with tears again. 'Noah's?'

Lila nodded. 'Look, Lauren, could you just...go? Or tell me what you want? If you leave now, I won't tell Noah – or the police – this happened.'

Lauren nodded but dipped her head shyly. 'Just a couple of questions before I go and I won't bother you anymore.'

Lila sighed. 'What do you want to know?'

Lauren studied her. 'Where did you meet Noah?'

Lila hesitated. 'At work. His work.'

'You're a doctor?'

'No.'

'A patient?'

Lila hesitated. 'Not any more. Look, Lauren, I'm sorry but you really have to go now.'

'I will, I will, just...do you love him?'

Lila's expression softened. 'Very much.'

'And he loves you?'

'That's what he tells me.'

Lauren smiled sadly. 'He never once told he loved me.'

'I'm sorry,' Lila said evenly. Lauren nodded and walked to the front door.

'I am, too. Sorry if I hurt you, I didn't see you were pregnant. Good luck with it all.'

'Goodbye Lauren.'

LILA CLOSED the door after the woman and leaned back against it, shaking her head. 'The world is full of fruit loops, little Matty,' she said to her bump. She was getting used to that name – if it was a boy, he might have to be called Matthew, she pondered now as she locked the door and this time remembered to set the alarm. She locked the balcony windows – how the hell did Lauren climb up this high? Crazy.

She padded back to bed but couldn't sleep, instead staring at the ceiling. All the adrenaline had left her body now, and the shock of the assault began to sink in.

'Jesus,' she whispered to herself. *Will I ever be safe again?* Every time she felt settled, something happened to rock her equilibrium. Eventually she fell into an uneasy sleep, full of nightmares and dreams of being stalked by an unknown menace.

LILA FLIPPED the pancakes onto a plate, covering a yawn as she listened to Noah and Charlie talk. Noah had come home a couple of hours after Lauren had left and one look at his face told her that Mackie didn't make it. She held out her arms and he had gone into them, holding her tightly. They held each other until they both fell back to sleep and when Charlie had rung their door bell, they both groaned.

Charlie grinned at them both, their hurriedly tugged on clothes and bed-head hair. 'Should I give you an hour? I can come back.'

Noah and Lila waved away his suggestion. 'You're family,' Noah said and Lila shot him a grateful smile. Her two favorite men in the world were getting along and that made her unbelievably happy.

But now, of course, they had to go and spoil it by talking about Riley. She wondered if she should tell them that she'd slept with Riley that night so long ago. *God, am I a slut?* She shook her head. Both of the men in this room, Riley, Richard, a couple of guys when she was younger. By modern standards she was practically a novice.

'So, best thing to do is take normal precautions, lock doors, set alarms, don't go walking alone at night.'

Lila turned and stared at Charlie and he grinned. 'Thought that would get your attention.'

Lila waved the pancake slice at them both. 'You two know I'm in the room, yes?'

Noah snorted with laughter. 'Lila Belle, it's your safety we're concerned about, is all.'

Lila turned back to the stove, hiding a guilty expression. She'd promised Lauren she wouldn't say anything....ah, screw it, the woman had broken into their home.

'Well, in that case, you might want to tell your ex-girlfriend not to break in in the middle of the night.' She dumped a plate of pancakes on the breakfast bar a little too hard. Noah blinked.

'Excuse me?'

Lila sat down and looked at both men. 'Lauren. She shimmied up the side of our building last night, came in through the balcony. I had to throw down with her.'

Noah bugged at her. 'What the actual fuck? Why didn't you say anything? I'll fucking kill her...' He stood up but Lila grabbed his hand.

'Sit. Down. Now. No biggie,' she stared him down. Noah sat.

'*Whipped,*' muttered Charlie but Lila glared at him. Noah looked between the two of them then rubbed his face trying to wake up enough to think clearly.

'Let me get this straight. Lauren broke into this house last night?'

'Yup.'

'And you, what, wrestled?'

'She was snooping around, I ambushed her, she choked me, and I kicked her in the lady nuts.'

Charlie spat his coffee out, choking on laughter.

'This isn't funny,' Noah snapped at the laughing man. 'Jesus Christ, Lila.'

Her face softened. 'It's fine, babe. We calmed down, talked stuff through. She's a weird one but no harm done. Mostly. I may have fractured her shoulder with your lion's head thing.'

'This just gets better.' Charlie looked at Noah's set face and shut up again.

'You have to tell me stuff like this. Where the hell was security?'

'To be fair, they weren't expecting Spider Woman.'

Noah sighed. 'We're moving. If someone can get in that easily...'

'No way, I love this place.'

Noah shook his head. 'We'll talk about this later.'

Charlie cleared his throat. 'That's my cue.' He stood and Lila hugged him, pouting.

'You really have to go?'

''Fraid so, munchkin.' He hugged her back tightly. 'I'll see you both soon.'

'Sure we can't take you to the airport?' Noah shook Charlie's hand.

'Thanks but no, cab's easier.'

'He hates goodbyes,' Lila rolled her eyes, 'He cries. You should see it, it's like *Love Actually*.'

'Yeah, yeah, yeah,' Charlie waved her teasing away. 'Take care of each other.'

WHEN CHARLIE HAD GONE, Lila knew Noah would want to return to the subject of Lauren so she pre-empted him. 'So, you should have maybe told Lauren about the bambino.'

Noah sighed. 'I don't see that it's any of her concern; we were over months ago.'

'Still, your really quite recent ex has a baby on the way. That's gotta sting.'

'Do you care?'

Lila considered. 'I suppose not. I felt sorry for her.'

'Don't. She's a viper, don't trust the innocent little girl act.'

'Oh, I don't. Look, can we not talk about her anymore?'

Noah smiled and wrapped his arms around her. 'Good idea. Thank god it's the weekend. What shall we do?'

She laughed at his suggestive grin. 'Well, apart from that, we could see if your dad and step-mom want to come out to the cottage with us?'

Her voice shook at the end, nervous, but Noah grinned widely. 'Really? You ready?'

Lila kissed him and nodded, her eyes excited. 'I'm ready.'

45

MANHATTAN

Tinsley Chang cheered as Charlie made his way into the bar that night. 'At damn last,' she said, going to hug him, 'Man, I want all the gossip.'

Charlie chuckled, but lowering his tone, he glanced around the busy bar. 'Any sign of Riley?'

She shook her head, her smile fading. 'No, dude, I'm sorry.' She looked over at Mikey who was behind the bar. 'Dude, I'm taking off, you all set?'

Mikey waved her away. 'Go on and leave me, you thankless wench.'

Tinsley laughed then dragged Charlie out onto the street. 'We're going to my place. I bought some micro beers and we can order pizza and we are going to talk, Sherman.'

'Pregnant.'

'Yes.'

'Lila is *pregnant*.'

'Like I said.'

'*Six months* pregnant.'

Charlie sighed. They'd been over this again and again but Tinsley was still looking at him as if he'd gone mad. 'I don't know what else to tell you, Tins.'

'With the hot doctor's baby?'

'You think he's hot?'

'Is the sky blue?'

Charlie was a little irked and didn't hide it well. Tinsley prodded him. 'You're still my favorite, Chuckles. So, she's happy?'

'Getting there, I think. She's freaking out about what to tell the Carnegies. Talking of whom...how's your man, Harry?'

'Half a world away,' Tinsley said matter-of-factly. 'We've talked a few times. Mostly about how great Melbourne is.' She smiled to herself. 'Makes me kinda homesick.'

'For Australia or Carnegie?'

Tinsley considered. 'Harry and I had a great time but I think we weren't meant to be long term. I don't do long term.'

Charlie huffed out a laugh. 'I know that.'

She sighed and pulled her legs up under her. 'You were my longest...thing.'

Charlie grinned. 'Why, thank you.'

'Don't be gross.' But she giggled. 'But seriously, I'm just doing my own thing lately. This Riley thing is really getting to me though. Woods came to see me.'

Charlie looked up sharply. 'He did?' Woods was Riley's brother; the two had an antagonistic relationship and Charlie had never warmed to the guy. Pretentious, arrogant – the opposite of easy going, affable Riley.

'Wanted to know if I'd seen Riley. I thought you'd talked to the family?'

'Not yet, not until we known for sure that Riley's a suspect. God,' Charlie ran a hand through his hair. 'It's driving me crazy, not knowing and – '

He stopped as his cell phone buzzed. 'Gimme a sec. Yeah?'

Tinsley watched his face as he listened. It changed from annoyance to concern.

'Yeah, yeah of course, I'll be straight there.'

He shut off his phone and turned to her. 'It's Cora Carnegie. She got caught in the middle of a drugs bust.'

'Oh, no, poor kid.'

Charlie sighed and stood. 'I'm sorry, Tins, I have to go.'

'Of course.' She walked him to the door but as he stepped out, she stopped him. 'Listen, if Cora...doesn't want to go home tonight, bring her here. It'll give her some space, to think, to rest without...you know.'

Charlie smiled down at her. 'You're a peach.' He hesitated then kissed her, full on the mouth, brief, quick, then jogged down the hallway to the stairs.

Tinsley closed her door slowly, her emotions in turmoil. She didn't want to get involved with anyone so soon after Harry and especially if it would risk the friendship she and Charlie had built but...*that kiss. Damn...*

Tinsley shook her head. She was still reeling from the news about Lila and the baby. Tinsley grinned to herself and wished there was some way she could get in contact with Lila, talk to her. Charlie had said Lila wanted to get in touch but she needed to talk to the Carnegies first, explain. Tinsley didn't envy her friend that conversation.

She didn't envy that conversation at all.

46

SEATTLE

Lauren gave a squeak of shocked surprise as Noah gripped her upper arm and steered her into the nearest coffeehouse.

'Sit down and shut up,' he snapped at her as he summoned the waitress and ordered black coffee.

'I don't drink coffee,' Lauren tried to hide her nervousness. Noah looked about as angry as she'd ever seen him and it didn't take a genius to figure out why. Unconsciously, she touched her shoulder, still badly bruised from where Lila had struck her a few nights ago.

'It's not for you,' Noah retorted then relented and ordered a chamomile tea for her.

Lauren tried a winsome smile. 'You remembered.'

Noah's expression was thunderous. 'You're lucky you're not sitting in a police cell. What the fuck did you think you were doing breaking into our home in the middle of the night?'

Lauren dropped the pretense. 'Fucking bitch, I knew she would rat me out.'

'You don't say a word about Lila, do you understand?' Noah's tone was low, dangerous and Lauren looked away from the fury in his eyes.

'I just...wanted to see who replaced me. And, goddammit, Noah, you should have told me she was pregnant.' Tears welled in her eyes and she made a show of brushing them away.

The waitress came with their drinks, her eyes flicking between the two of them, obviously curiously about the tension. Noah gave her a wintry smile and thanked her, and the waitress, disappointed moved away.

'I don't owe you a damn thing, Lauren. You and I were over months ago, before I even met Lila.'

'Exactly,' she hissed. 'And yet she's already pregnant? You bastard, you know how much I wanted a baby.'

Noah sighed. 'But I didn't want children with you, Lauren. Hell, I didn't want them with anybody until I met Lila. I'm sorry if that sounds cruel but you and I were not destined to have a happy ever after. We want different things.'

Lauren was quiet for a long moment and when she met his gaze, her expression had turned to one full of spite. 'I could always tell her you were still banging me after you met her.'

Noah wasn't troubled. 'She would know that wasn't true.'

'Psychic, is she?'

Noah gave her a humorless smile. 'And when would you say this so-called 'banging' occurred?'

Lauren smiled. 'In between you first banging her and when she got pregnant.'

Noah grinned then. 'Here in Seattle, was it? Did I swing by your apartment after seeing her?'

Lauren's bluster faltered. 'Noah...'

'Thing is, Lauren,' Noah was enjoying himself now, 'unless you invented time-travel in a very fast jet plane, that would be physically impossible. Not only was I in *New York*, but there was no time between the first time Lila and I were first intimate and the time she got pregnant.'

Lauren's eyes grew wide and her smile turned nasty. 'Wow, that's fast work. I've got to give it to her, that's fast gold-digging work.'

Noah's eyes were dark. 'Lila has no need to desire for my money; don't judge her by *your* standards, Lauren.'

Lauren flushed red but lifted her chin. 'I don't need to; getting knocked up on the first date speaks for itself.'

'I was already in love with her,' Noah said softly, quietly and with such feeling that Lauren couldn't help the gasp of distress.

Noah sighed, reached into his pocket for some bills to pay for the coffee. 'I've said what I came to say, Lauren. Stay away from Lila, stay away from me.'

Lauren narrowed her eyes. 'And what if I don't?'

Noah smiled coldly. 'Then Daddy Dearest will find out what a psycho his darling daughter is and bang goes your trust fund. Believe me; it wouldn't take much to convince him.'

'You wouldn't,' she hissed at him, eyes blazing.

'If you ever come near me and Lila again, I have his number on speed dial. Remember that.'

And he was gone. Lauren was suddenly aware that other people in the coffeehouse were staring at her. She lifted her chin, stood, threw some money for her tea on the table– she was damned if she would let Noah pay for her – and stalked out.

Fucking, fucking, fucking bitch. She should have known Lila Tierney would tell Noah about the break-in. Well, she would pay for that little indiscretion...because Lauren knew who Lila Tierney was and soon, so would the rest of the world.

47

MANHATTAN

Charlie came by the nest morning. 'How is she?'

Tinsley beckoned him into the kitchen. 'Still asleep,' she said, 'and I don't think she's at all happy about being here.'

Charlie looked confused. 'But she said she didn't want to go home.'

Tinsley rolled her eyes and smiled at him. 'You are clueless, Charles.' She stuck her head around the door to check Cora wasn't around then turned back to him. 'She wanted to go home with *you*, Charlie.'

Realization dawned and he groaned. 'Oh, god.'

'Exactly. Being shacked up with your ex-girlfriend is not what she planned. Still, she went straight to bed, not very chatty either. Will she be charged?'

Charlie shook his head. 'She was just at the wrong place at the wrong time, she hadn't even been using, thank god.'

Tinsley felt a pang of jealousy at the fondness in Charlie's voice but turned away to hide it.

'I can't tell you how grateful I am you offered to let her stay here,'

Charlie said softly, and he touched her back, stroking down it. 'Her coming home with me would not have been a good idea.'

Tinsley looked up at him and he smiled. 'Cora's not the one I'm interested in,' he whispered and bent his head to kiss her. Tinsley closed her eyes and sank into the kiss, winding her arms around his neck. God, she had missed this man, his machismo, his strength. Harry had been a wonderful diversion and one she would never forget but...Charlie Sherman....damn...

She regretfully broke away from him. 'We can't do this now, Charlie, not with – ' She jerked her head towards the bedroom door where Cora slept just as they both heard the front door slam.

'Shit.'

Tinsley went to the bedroom and it was empty. 'She saw us.'

Charlie sighed. 'Looks like it. God dammit.' He went to the window. 'Getting in a cab.'

'She really isn't your responsibility, Charlie. And we don't need to be ashamed of wanting to be together.'

Charlie looked at her, his mind obviously on overdrive. Tinsley sighed.

'Look...go to work, check she got home safely. That's all we can do right now.'

'will you be at work later?'

'Only until eight.'

'I'll come pick you up and we'll grab some dinner. Cool?'

She smiled and went to him. 'Very cool.' They kissed again, briefly and then Charlie was gone.

CHARLIE CALLED her about five pm. 'Hey, Tins, look I'm sorry, I have a lead on Riley in Queens – I have to follow it. Can you get home safe?'

Disappointed, Tinsley told him she could and when her shift at the bar was over, she grabbed her bag and went out into the night. She walked briskly, the cool night air refreshing after the sweaty atmosphere of the bar. At her apartment, she took the stairs one at a time then skittered to a stop. Woods Kinsayle was standing outside her apartment. Tinsley considered turning around but then Woods saw her. He looked exhausted and stressed out.

'Hey, Woods,' she plastered a smile on her face. She'd never liked the man, thought he treated Riley appallingly.

'Tinsley, hey, look, sorry about this. I was passing and it was a whim to stop and come see if you'd heard anything.'

Tinsley felt sorry for him. 'Look, Woods, come in, we'll have a drink and talk. Sound good?'

She saw his shoulders slump with relief. 'Sounds great.'

ONCE THEY WERE SETTLED, with cold beers, on her couch, Tinsley looked at him. 'Woods, I really don't know what else I can tell you except maybe that Riley's absence doesn't look too good for him.'

Woods shook his head. 'I know. But, Tinsley, really – can you imagine Riley hurting anyone, let alone Lila, who he adored?'

Tinsley had thought of little else. 'No, I can't but that doesn't mean that, in a moment of madness, he didn't.'

Woods sighed, frustrated. 'But look, the manner of the attack, the brutality. If Riley had a moment of madness, why wouldn't he have used his gun? Why did he run? Wouldn't a murder/suicide situation have been easier to believe? Riley shoots Lila, realizes what he's done, then kills himself?'

'I'm not a psychologist,' she said gently and Woods nodded.

'I know, I know, I just running through all these scenarios in my head. What does Charlie say?'

Tinsley shifted uncomfortably. 'I think he doesn't want to believe it's Riley; at the same time he's desperate to protect Lila.'

'Which I know is totally fair...god, but he doesn't have to tell our parents that not only is Riley missing but a suspected would-be-killer.'

She put her hand on his shoulder. 'I know. I'm sorry, Woods, really.'

He only stayed a little while longer, then left. Tinsley sighed. God, what a mess this all is.

She toyed with the idea of take-out but then fell asleep on the couch watching TV. before she could decide what to get.

SHE AWOKE with a start and almost screamed. It was dark, the TV. had been shut off and at the side of the couch where she was lying stood a figure in black. She saw the glint of light from the knife he was holding. She reacted immediately, kicking out at the intruder, catching them on the knee, hearing an annoyed grunt. Male.

Riley. And he was here to kill her...

No, no, no. As he lurched forward to grab her, she ducked under his arm and threw herself at the door, twisting the handle before she felt the knife slice into her back.

Not deep. She screamed and lashed out behind her as he came for her again. She opened the door and banged him with it, using every inch of her strength to twist and turn out of his reach, still screaming for help. None came. The knife sank into her side and she jerked away from him and almost fell down the stairs leading out onto the street.

She was half crying with fear, half screaming, cursing the cowards who would not help a woman in distress. The attacker grabbed her arm, wrestling her to the ground. Tinsley fought with every piece of strength she had left, twisting her body as he jabbed at her with the knife.

Suddenly there was a group of young men, yelling and the knifeman disappeared. Tinsley couldn't believe it. She lay bleeding on the sidewalk as a couple of the guys knelt down to take care of her. They helped her to her feet when she said she was okay.

'Looks like he got you a couple times,' a kid, no more than twenty, peeled off his over-shirt and pressed it against the worst of her wounds.

In minutes, paramedics and police were there and in a daze, Tinsley was whisked off to the emergency room. Different voices talked at her for a while but seeing she was in shock, soon left her alone. Her wounds weren't serious but she was sore and covered in blood.

What the hell happened? Her brain was a fog, not helped by the morphine the doctors had given her for the pain.

It was only when she heard Charlie's deep voice, raised and angry and scared, that it hit her.

Someone had tried to kill her.

Breathing became hard and as Charlie came into view, Tinsley finally broke down. Charlie took her into his arms as she sobbed, telling her over and over that it was okay, and she was safe now.

48

SEATTLE

Noah watched fondly as Lila demolished a stack of pancakes and a side of bacon. As she chewed she grinned at him and he laughed. 'How are you not the size of a house?'

Lila swallowed her food. 'Believe it or not, it's just the last couple of days I've felt this hungry.'

He took her hand as they sat in the diner. 'You excited to find out the sex of our bambino?'

It was their final scan and last night, Lila had told him she was sick of waiting to find out whether their little Matty was a girl or a boy. Noah hadn't needed much persuasion to agree.

'I'd like us to start looking at family homes for us,' he said and she nodded.

'That would be good...I'd like to keep the cottage on the island; it such a good little weekend place.'

'I agree but I think we need something more suitable than the condo here.'

'With a garden and a white picket fence?' Lila chuckled and he grinned.

'Hell, yes a white picket fence.'

Lila stirred her hot milk. 'Noah, would you mind very much if it wasn't in one of those gated communities? I know between us we could probably buy an entire community to ourselves, but I want our kids to be best friends with the kids on a normal suburban street, ride their bikes, play pea-knuckle.'

Noah burst out laughing. 'Do you even know what pea-knuckle is?'

Lila grinned. 'No idea but you get the picture.'

Noah nodded mock-seriously. 'Yep, you want our kids to grow up in the 1950's.'

She flicked some milk at him. 'I was thinking more 1980's, E.T. in the basket at the front, Grandpa.'

Noah shook his head smiling. 'I adore you, Miss Tierney. Come on, it's time.'

HAND-IN-HAND, they waited for the OBGYN to start the scan. Lila winced; once as the doctor took a look at her still vivid scars, even more prominent now her belly was swollen, then as the doctor squeezed the cold gel onto her skin.

Lila suddenly felt nervous...she so wanted a girl that she was scared that if it was a boy, she wouldn't love it as much. She looked up at Noah, who smiled down at her, and she felt better. A little boy – a little Noah. Of course she would love him, *god,* she would love him...

'Okay, let's go...' the doctor, gazing at the screen and pressing the sensor into Lila's stomach. She moved it around for a while but didn't say anything. Lila glanced at her face.

'Can you see what sex it is?'

She felt Noah squeeze her hand and when she looked at him, there was something in his eyes that made her feel cold. She looked back at the doctor and suddenly her throat felt full of cotton wool.

'Dr. Stevens?' Noah's voice was flat. 'What is it?'

The doctor put down the sensor and turned to them. She seemed to have trouble getting the words out.

'Noah, Lila, there's no easy way to say this...'

Lila moaned when she realized what the woman was about to say. 'No...no...please, no...'

'I'm so sorry, but I can't find a heartbeat, or any signs of life.'

Noah made a noise, a groan, a heart-wrenching sound as Lila shook her head furiously.

'No, that's not possible, I felt her, I felt her kicking...'

'When did you last feel that?'

Lila's tears were falling unchecked. 'Yesterday, yesterday my baby was kicking me...oh god, oh god...'

Noah wrapped his arms around her, his face creased with pain and sorrow. 'Lila...'

'Check again,' Lila almost screamed, 'check again. Maybe she's asleep.'

'Lila, darling, there's no heartbeat,' Noah said in a broken voice and Lila crumbled.

'I'll give you two a moment,' the doctor – a friend and colleague of Noah's – looked as upset as they did, and she left the room, closing the door behind her.

'How? How can this be?' Lila asked desperately, clutching at Noah, who shook his head.

'I don't know, sweetheart, sometimes it...just...happens.'

They clung to each other then, Lila sobbing, Noah's own face wet with tears. Finally, calming down, Lila closed her eyes. 'I wanted her so much, you know? I was so excited to have your baby, Noah; I know we can have more but...'

'It's okay,' he said wearily, heartbroken, 'it's okay, sweetheart, to mourn our child.'

There was a knock at the door and the doctor came back in. 'I'm so sorry, to both of you, It's rare but late term miscarriages can happen. Have you had any trauma lately?'

Lila gave a hollow laugh. 'Where do I start?'

Noah cursed under his breath, and then apologized to them both. 'Lauren. Jesus H. Christ.'

The other doctor looked confused. Lila, head in hands, told her about Lauren's break-in and their subsequent fight. Dr. Steven's eyes were big and she shook her head.

'You should call the police, report this. Obviously we won't have the full cause of death until the autopsy,' she took Lila's hand, sympathy in her warm brown eyes. 'Lila...I'm sorry to add to your pain but we need to make a decision now. Because of how late it is, we'll need to either give you medicine that will induce birth straight away or wait for your body to naturally go into labor. That takes about two weeks but, Lila, it is risky to leave it and risk infection.'

'I have to give birth.' Lila's voice was flat.

'I'm afraid so. Caesarian is too risky, especially in your case. I'm so sorry. I'll give you and Noah some time to discuss what you want to do.'

IN THE END, they all agreed to get it done, get through the worst part. Lila gave birth to their stillborn daughter at four am. the next morning and afterward, they were left alone with her to say goodbye. Lila couldn't take her eyes from the small perfect features; Matilda Tierney Applebaum was a beautiful baby – with her tiny eyes closed, she looked as if she was asleep.

'I keep looking at her and everything in me is hoping that she'll just take one breath, live here with us, even if it's only for a moment. Just hear our voices one time.' Lila's voice broke, her body wracked with exhausted, heartbroken sobs. Noah's tears joined hers, dripping onto their daughter's tiny forehead.

'We love you, Bean,' Noah kissed his child's cold skin then kissed Lila's temple. They stayed there for hours, the three of them, their family until the doctors came to take Matty away.

49

MANHATTAN

Tinsley woke in Charlie's bed. At the hospital, after being stitched up and refusing to stay overnight, Charlie had overridden her objections and taken her back to his place. There he quizzed her on every detail of the attack until she was dropping from exhaustion. He apologized and put her to bed in his freshly changed bed. She had grabbed his hand as he turned to give her some privacy and just said, 'Stay.'

Now she woke, cradled in the strong cage of arms, breathing his woody scent in, listening to his breathing. *Safe.*

Her wounds were sore now, her muscles aching but god, she was happy, *amazed* that she was still alive. Now all that was left was confusion; who the hell would want to kill *her?*

She realized the magnitude of confusion that Lila must have felt – and with the pain Tinsley had felt, she couldn't comprehend the pain of being stabbed repeatedly, deep in the belly, that Lila had experienced. She felt weirdly closer to her absent friend and, now she felt desperate to see Lila, to talk with her, for that female warmth and understanding.

Tinsley looked at Charlie's face as he slept, deep lines of worry etched on his forehead even at rest. 'Charlie,' she whispered, then pressed her lips against his. Charlie opened his eyes and smiled at her. She wanted to tell him then that she wanted to go to see Lila but as he smiled down at her and kissed her again, nothing else in the world mattered, nothing existed except for them, here, now.

Tinsley pulled him on top of her and wrapped her long legs around his waist. For a second, he looked amazed, then wary. 'Are you sure?'

She nodded. 'I need you, Charlie...' and with a groan he buried his face in her neck and they began to make love, slowly, gently at first. As they lost themselves in each other, Charlie hitched her legs around his waist and drove his cock deep into her. Tinsley gasped, a mix of sweet pleasure and pain, then as she moved with him, their gazes locked and she gave herself over to the feral animal in her and they fucked long and hard, the intensity never letting up until they were both groaning and breathless, shattering climaxes ripping through them. Charlie moaned as his cock pumped thick, creamy cum deep inside her velvety cunt and Tinsley reveled in the feeling of his weight on top of her.

He made her come again with his mouth, again and again until she was exhausted and crying, then he gathered her into his arms and held her so tenderly as she let out all the tension that had built up inside her over the last twenty-four hours.

TINSLEY WAS STARTLED. 'REALLY?' They were sitting in his kitchen and she had just told him of her wish to see Lila. Charlie had shrugged and nodded. 'Okay.'

He grinned at her now. 'Of course, I've been thinking the same thing and I know she misses you. Also I want you far away from your apartment, the bar and anywhere else Riley might look for you so I do have selfish reasons too.'

Tinsley sipped her coffee. 'I need to talk to Mikey first.'

Charlie cleared his throat and grinned, his face reddening slightly. 'Kind of already did. Sorry if that was overstepping.'

Tinsley sighed. 'On this occasion, you're forgiven. How long did you get me?'

Charlie leaned over to brush a lock of blonde hair from her cheek. 'As long as you need. That's Mikey talking as well.'

Tinsley was relieved. 'And Lila? Will she be okay with it?'

Charlie nodded slowly. 'I haven't called her yet, but I think so. Especially now,' he added with a knowing grin and Tinsley chuckled. 'Look,' he said, checking his watch, 'how about this. You go grab a shower and I'll call her then we'll go together to your place to pack, grab a flight this afternoon?'

Tinsley frowned. 'What about your work?'

'Don't worry about that, I got some time owed.'

AFTER SHE'D SHOWERED, checking her wounds in the mirror – a long slice down from her shoulder blade down her back, about three or four inches long; small cuts in a pattern over her left breast; a deeper wound in the soft flesh of her hip. *God, I'm so lucky.* As she dressed, she threw back a couple of aspirin with the rather stale glass of water by the bed.

When she was done, she went back into the kitchen – and stopped. Charlie was staring into the middle distance, an unidentifiable look on his face, his phone on the table in front of him.

For a second, every horrific scenario ran through her head. Had Riley finally got to Lila?

'What is it?'

Charlie shook his head. 'It's Lila. She's lost the baby.'

50

SAN JUAN ISLAND

Noah stroked Lila's soft hair as they lay on the bed together, facing each other, talking softly. She had wanted to come back to the island rather than the condo, the place where they knew now the baby had died. The pathologist had been quick, patient and kind. The placenta had partially detached during the fight with Lauren and the baby stopped getting the nutrients it needed to survive.

Lila reacted with just a tight nod but Noah had walked out for a few seconds, trying to keep his temper in the face of Lila's absolute grief.

They had a small burial service; Lila had wanted a Jewish funeral for Matty and so Noah performed a small service in the non-denominational chapel. It had been a day of unbelievable pain for both of them.

Now, they lay together, trying to assuage some of that pain by just being together. Charlie had spoken to Noah and Noah had gratefully told him and Tinsley to come. Lila too, had said she didn't want to be one of those women who moon about and waste time wishing that things could be different.

'Talking of different,' Noah said now, 'I'm thinking of giving up my practice at the hospital. I've done everything I can achieve in my field...I'd like to go into research, maybe teaching. And that's something we could do anywhere, Lila. What do you want to do?'

Lila sighed. 'I want to go back to school, finish out my Masters, and see where we go from there.'

Noah half-smiled. 'Still want the picket fence?'

A look of pain crossed her face briefly but she nodded. 'I do. With you. Nothing else matters, Noah, not to me, except you now. But I won't be defeatist, or,' – and she smiled for the first time in days – 'be a kept woman. I've decided I don't want to keep Richard's money. I never wanted it in the first place. If the Carnegie's won't take it back then I'll tell them I'm giving it to charity – one of Richard's that he supported or a few of them, I don't know. I'm rambling, I know.'

Noah kissed her gently. 'Ramble away. And I agree with you...why hold onto something that never felt right? It's not as if we can't afford it.'

'I need to pay my own way,' Lila said firmly then her shoulders slumped. 'But I realize I can never compete.'

'It's not a competition and it's just money. I would give away every cent as long as I have you.'

'Romantic but totally impractical, that's why I love you.' She cupped her cheek in her palm.

'When we're married, it'll be legally yours anyway,' he said but didn't say anymore.

'I'm glad Charlie and Tinsley are coming today.'

'Me too, baby.'

WHEN THEIR GUESTS ARRIVED, it gave them both a release. Tinsley and Lila held each other for the longest time, Lila horrified to hear what had happened to her friend. Tinsley and Charlie, Lila noted, were closer than ever. At least one good thing had happened and Lila was glad. 'I've put you in the front bedroom, I hope that's okay,' she said so nonchalantly that the other three looked at her askance and she broke into giggles. God it felt good to laugh.

'Subtle as a sledgehammer as always,' Charlie grumbled as Tinsley laughed. Noah checked Lila's cheek.

'Momma Bear,' then realizing what he'd said, he froze. Lila, despite the jolt of pain, smiled at him.

'Always Momma Bear,' she said softly. 'Now, come, people, let's eat.'

After lunch, Noah's phone buzzed and he grimaced. 'Looks like I have to go to the city for a work thing. Will you be okay?' He left the question hanging, looking at Lila.

She nodded. 'Of course, honey.'

He kissed the top of her head. 'I'll see you later. Charlie, can I grab you a sec?'

Charlie followed him out to his car. Noah took a deep breath and fixed him with a steady look.

'You locked and loaded?'

Charlie smiled grimly. 'You bet I am. Don't worry...nothing's going to touch our girls.'

Noah shook his hand. 'There is back-up should you need it – Lila knows where the panic buttons and alarms are.'

'Don't worry, dude, I got this.'

'I know, I trust you.'

51

SEATTLE

I n the city, instead of driving to the hospital, Noah headed downtown to the business district, pulling into the underground parking garage of one of the high-rise office buildings. Joanne was waiting for him. 'I can get you through security easier,' she said when he asked her what she was doing.

Noah stopped. 'You'll be fired.'

She laughed. 'Hell no I won't, not when he hears what you have to say.' She put a hand on his arm. 'I'm so sorry, Noah, about the baby. I don't have the words.'

'Neither do I, Joanne, but thanks. Is she here?' Joanne was showing her credentials to the security guards.

'And utterly clueless as ever. I'm looking forward to this.' Security waved them through and they stepped into the foyer of the Shannon Media building.

Noah smiled grimly as they got onto the elevator. 'Believe me, so am I.'

DEREK SHANNON HAD BUILT his company over forty years of hard, hard work, to the detriment of two marriages and, he believed, of his fathering skills. Lauren had the talent but none of the application, or hunger that he had, or required in his staff. But he was too kind-hearted to do anything about it, relying more and more on Joanne, who ran the company with such efficiency that Lauren was merely a figurehead. Strangely it had worked out well; Lauren glad-handed the clients, Joanne happy to stay out of the limelight. But lately, Lauren had grown morose, sulky and become that thing Derek had always feared – spoilt.

Derek Shannon could trace the very day it had happened; it was the day Noah Applebaum had decided he'd had his fill of Lauren's princess act and cut her loose. Not that Derek blamed Noah; he had liked the intelligent young man very much and had hoped he would have some influence over Lauren. But once Lauren had discovered that Noah was from old money – forget it. Lauren wanted to be a trophy wife and never have to work. Derek actually admired Noah for saying no to Lauren and ending things but that was also the problem – Lauren was never dumped; she *always* did the dumping. And it rankled.

RIGHT NOW, as he spoke to his board members, he kept glancing over at his daughter, who was staring out of the window, clearly bored. Derek sighed inwardly then looked up as Joanne entered the room with Noah Applebaum. Derek's face lit up.

'Noah! How wonderful to see you,' he strode forward and took his hand, pumping it vigorously. Lauren was halfway out of her seat, looking shocked and alarmed but Joanne, very deliberately stood with her back against the only door to the room, and stared her down. Her gaze, full of disgust, said *Try it, bitch, and I will take you down.* Lauren quelled under the gaze of the much older woman.

Noah too glared at Lauren then turned back to Derek, who was looking mystified. 'Derek, I'm sorry to intrude on your meeting but the reason I came was this. You need to know about what kind of person your daughter is.'

'Noah, please,' Lauren began but Noah raised a hand and she

shut up. 'Derek, a few days ago, your daughter broke into my home in the early hours of the morning and assaulted my girlfriend. My six-months pregnant girlfriend. Lila was defending herself and Lauren attacked her.'

'Lauren, what the – '

'Two days ago, Lila lost the child due to the attack. Our daughter died in utero. Lila had to give birth to a stillborn baby and yesterday, we buried her.'

Lauren's face drained of all its color and there were gasps around the table. Joanne looked sick and Derek, seeming to shrink into himself, stumbled and had to grasp the table. He looked at his daughter.

'Dad – '

'Lauren, is this true? Did you break into Noah's home and attack his girlfriend?'

'She hit me first!'

Noah rounded on her. 'You had broken into our home in the middle of the night! I should tell you, Derek, that my girlfriend is Lila Tierney.'

'That name is familiar,' Derek said weakly and Noah nodded, his face hard.

'She was stabbed last year, brutally and she nearly died. At the time, she was engaged to Richard Carnegie.'

'Oh my god...'

Lauren, seeing the look in her father's eyes, started to plead. 'I just wanted to see her, who she was, why Noah was moving on so fast. She attacked me; she hit me with something, look!' She tugged her blouse down to show them the large bruise on her shoulder.

'You broke into the home of a survivor of attempted murder in the middle of the night just to see her?' Derek's voice was flat now, angry. 'And you wonder why she hit you first? And when you saw she was pregnant?'

'No, no, no, I swear, after I saw she was pregnant I didn't do a thing.'

. . .

NOAH CLOSED HIS EYES. He would never, ever strike a woman but Lauren was making it hard for him to remain calm and focused.

'But you tried to choke her before,' Noah said, his rage a roiling thing inside him. Everyone else seated around the table, Joanne at the door, was riveted on the three people at the center of the drama. Lauren took a deep breath.

'Daddy,' she stepped towards her father but he moved back, staring at her aghast.

'Who have I raised?' His voice was a whisper. 'What kind of person are you, Lauren? You were given everything. Everything. Including more chances than most people would ever dream of. And finally your recklessness has cost a life.'

Lauren started to cry but it was Derek that Noah felt bad for, but then he thought of Lila and Matty and his resolve hardened. Derek put a hand on his arm.

'What do you want me to do, Noah? I will try to make this right, I swear to you.'

Noah sucked in a lungful of air. 'No-one can do that, Derek, not when our child is lying in a grave and not in her mother's arms. But there has to be consequences.'

Derek nodded. 'I understand. Do you want me to go to the police, or handle this in-house?'

'I'll leave that up to you, Derek, I've said what I came to say.' He stepped closer to the man and leaned in to murmur 'Leave Joanne out of this, she was doing the right thing.'

Derek nodded tightly, glancing at his deputy. 'You can trust me on that one, Noah.'

Noah nodded at him, then the others, ignoring Lauren and walked to the door.

'I'll make this right, Noah.'

Noah nodded again and left the room followed by Joanne. In the hallway they hugged, not needing words, then Noah rode the elevator down to the foyer. Before he went to get his car from the parking lot, he walked out into the fresh air, down the side alley of the building and threw up and up until he was dry-heaving.

52

SAN JUAN ISLAND

'It is gorgeous here,' Tinsley said, her arm linked with Lila's as they walked around the state park. Lila was pointing out all the places she used to come walk when she got here, mostly to watch the orca from the shoreline. They found a bench and sat down. Lila looked at her friend.

'How are you? I mean, after the attack. You seem surprisingly well.'

Tinsley sighed. 'I'm angry more than anything. Who the fuck could do that? Break into my apartment like that? And my fucking neighbors...' She gritted her teeth and shook her head and Lila took her hand.

'Tins, you can stay with us as long as you need.'

Tinsley grinned then. 'Lila Tierney, if this is more of your plotting to bring all of your friends to Washington...then I'll admit it's tempting when it's as beautiful as this.'

'All of my friend except one. I just can't believe that Riley is the suspect. Riley...he looks like a giant teddy-bear; he *is* a giant teddy-bear. I can't get my around it but Charlie is convinced.'

Tinsley's smile faded. 'I know. Part of me wants to scream at Charlie, don't be so fucking ridiculous! But until we find Riley...'

Lila looked away from her friend and Tinsley could see tears glistening in her eyes. 'Lila...'

'In my head,' Lila interrupted her, 'we find Riley, he's a bit banged up but okay and he tells us he found who it was but they tried to silence him. Then he and Charlie go catch the bastard and...'

'We all live happily ever after. I'm sorry, kiddo, you know better than most. It ain't gonna happen.'

～

LATER, at home, Lila and Noah were alone. Tinsley and Charlie had gone to collect some takeout from town – were giving the couple some space, Lila knew.

'How's my girl?' Noah brushed his lips against hers. She leaned into his embrace.

'I wish I could say okay, Noah, but I think it's a ways off yet.'

'Yeah.' His lips on her temple now. God, she wanted him to take her to bed, to forget everything but the doctor had warned them off penetrative sex for a few weeks. She looked into Noah's eyes and knew he was thinking the same.

'How about a soak in the tub?' she murmured against his lips. Noah led her by the hand to the bathroom and they stripped each other slowly as the bathtub filled, kissing every piece of exposed flesh before climbing into the tub. Lila straddled him, coiling her arms around his neck and studying his face as if she'd never seen it before.

'I love you, Noah Applebaum.'

He smiled, his large hands stroking slowly up her back and around to cup her heavy breasts. He dipped his head to take each of her nipples into his mouth in turn, his tongue flicking around the nub. He slipped his hand gently between her legs. 'Does it hurt when I do this?'

He stroked her clit gently and she shook her head.

'No, that feels so good.' She reached down to stroke his cock, engorged and throbbing as she ran her hands along it, her finger gently teasing the tip, feeling it jerk, hearing Noah's moan. They kissed slowly, tasting each other, their tongues massaging, their breath mingling.

It was a slow, tender, beautiful release of tension, bringing each other to orgasm, Lila's back arching, her head dropping back as she came, Noah groaning her name as her hands stroked and caressed until he shot hot, white semen onto her belly.

Afterward, she lay back against his chest, and he splayed his large hands over her stomach, still swollen but noticeably slimmer. Lila sighed.

'One day, I hope that my belly will be swollen with your babies again. Lots of them. Boys and girls and the boys are as handsome as their daddy, and the girls are all as brilliant as you too.'

Noah kissed her temple. 'So the boys don't have to be brilliant?'

'No, they're boys; they just have to be pretty.' They both laughed, glad that they could still be silly together in the face of recent horrors.

'I meant to tell you,' Lila said, 'I got a lovely bouquet from a friend of yours...Joanne is it?'

Noah was surprised. 'That was nice of her.'

'I would like to meet her...and speaking of meeting people, I think it's time I met your parents.'

'Dad and step-mom, but yes.'

'Don't you like Molly?'

'I adore Molly and I guarantee so will you but she's always been very careful to say she's not replacing my mom, even though she loves me like I was her son.'

Lila felt a pang. 'That's really sweet. I wish I had known my mom but no, not a thing.'

Noah's arms tightened around her. 'Molly will mother you, I promise. And, look, I'll try and arrange something soon. Should we include Charlie and Tinsley?'

'It might keep the conversation lighter,' Lila said, trying to hide a grin.

'You just want Tinsley there as a shield.'

'Damn right. You know who I've been thinking about? Cora and Delphine.'

Noah sighed. 'I know. We really do need to go see them, clue them in.'

'Yes, I think we've been lucky none of this has gotten out and I haven't called to explain. I couldn't bear that.'

BUT, of course, it finally did get out – and in the worst way. Lila and Tinsley were shopping at the local farmer's market when Lila suddenly noticed people stopping to stare at her. She frowned at them but didn't say anything until they got into her car. She asked Tinsley if she had noticed.

'Yes, actually, all morning, even when we were having coffee,' Tinsley admitted. Lila shook her head.

'I don't get it – do I have a booger on my face or something?'

Tinsley laughed. 'Girl, don't you know me better than that? I would have told you.'

They laughed about that on the drive home but it wasn't until they were preparing lunch and Lila flicked the T.V. on in the kitchen that they discovered the horrible truth.

Lila, her stabbing, Richard Carnegie, his murder and her subsequent pregnancy by her own doctor. All over the news. And the angle? Lila was a gold-digger who drove an ex-lover to stab her just as she was about to ensnare billionaire Carnegie. Her subsequent disappearance and pregnancy by her doctor – another rich man, of course and the loss of that baby – *what would Lila do now that her meal ticket was slipping out of her grasp?*

Tinsley was enraged – but Lila felt sick. This was everything she hoped would not become public knowledge.

When Noah came home, furious, a couple of hours later, she merely looked at him calmly and said one word.

'The Carnegies.'

53

UPPER EAST SIDE, MANHATTAN

Delphine looked at her coolly. 'You look...well.'

Lila knew she didn't – in fact she looked like crap, flying on the red-eye from Seattle, having begged Delphine to see her. Her hair was a messy bun at the nape of her neck, her clothes hurriedly pulled on sweats.

'Delphine...I'm so sorry you had to find out like this. I was going to come see you but events over took me.'

'You had six months.'

Lila winced but nodded. 'I did. But I was a coward. I didn't know how to tell the mother of my murdered ex-fiancé that I was already pregnant with another man's baby. Would you have been able to do that?'

Delphine looked away. Lila took a deep breath in.

'Delphine...Richard and I...we should never even have been engaged, or even been a couple for a long time before I was attacked. We both knew it. We loved each other but as friends. We just didn't know how to get off the rollercoaster.'

Delphine studied her. 'When you went to see him that last time –

'

'We broke things off. We parted on good terms, I want you to know that.'

'Did you sleep with the good doctor before or after that conversation, Lila?' Delphine's voice was ice and Lila knew she already knew the answer.

'Before. And I am sorry; Delphine, but I don't regret anything. I fell in love with Noah long before I slept with him. He is everything to me and our child, although she didn't survive, she is still real to me. I still feel like a mother.'

Delphine's face softened. 'I'm sorry about the child, Lila, truly. But I thought we were close, that you trusted me enough that you would have known to come to me. When we lost Richard, it was agony but when you left too...a part of me died.'

Her words broke the dam that Lila had been building around her emotions and she gave a sob. 'I don't want to do this,' she said, 'I don't want to cry and have you think I'm crying so you'll be nice to me. What I did...I cannot take back, I don't want to take it back. But if I could save some of the hurt you felt...I know it's too late. I love you, Delphine, I loved Richard, I love Cora and Harry and Richard Sr. But I cannot be part of your family anymore.'

Delphine mouth quivered and she quickly covered it with her hand, looking away from Lila, breathing deeply to steady her nerves.

'Don't say that,' she whispered eventually. 'Please don't exile us from your life. Not permanently. If you need more time, fine but please, when you're stronger, come back to us. If not as our daughter, as our friend.'

Lila, trying to contain herself, closed her eyes. *Please let me go.* But a part of her didn't want that either. They had been her family. Lila just felt she didn't deserve to have both the Carnegies and her new life – it was too much.

'Hello.' A small voice behind her. Lila turned. Cora, red-haired, thin as a bird, stood behind her. Her eyes were dull, her features pinched but she gazed at Lila not with hatred but with sorrow. Lila could not help but hold out her arms to her and Cora went into them, hugging her tightly.

Delphine watched them for a moment then got up. For a long moment, she placed her hand on Lila's shoulder, looking down at her, then nodded and left the room.

54

MANHATTAN

Noah sat with Charlie in the precinct, watching the rest of the office as they went about their jobs. Charlie was on the phone but he ended the call.

'Sorry, man, another bad tip. Didn't think we'd get nothing on Riley, and I mean, nothing.'

'You talked to that brother you don't see eye to eye with?'

Charlie rolled his eyes. 'Multiple times. Look, is Lila freaking out about that news story? Because I guarantee no-one will remember it by next week.'

'Only that the Carnegies will be hurt but she's with them now.'

'Any idea who sold that story?'

Noah gave a humorless snort. 'Oh yes...Lauren Shannon. She's still sore at me; I really should have seen it coming.'

'Well, at least we know something then. I'm getting a little tired of being in the dark about these attacks.'

'Me too. I feel antsy about being here even, about Lila being in the city. You must feel that way about Tinsley.'

Charlie nodded. 'Man, the things men do to women.'

'The things we do.'

. . .

CORA FINALLY LET LILA GO. She sat back and wiped her eyes. 'Lila, I'm so sorry about everything. When I saw that story, I knew why you had left, and I didn't blame you. I heard what you said to Mom and you're right. You and Richard weren't destined to be happy ever after.'

Lila was a little thrown. 'Cora...I thought you'd be the angriest of all of them at me. You'd just buried your brother and now you find out, I was already pregnant with another man's baby at the funeral. I can't forgive myself for that part, even though I don't regret being pregnant.'

Cora stared at her with large blue eyes, struggling to find the words then said. 'We've all done bad things, Lila, all of us. I...*oh god...*'

She crumpled into tears again and Lila, really worried now about the young woman, hugged her tightly.

'Cora, what is it? What are you trying to tell me?'

Cora, through her tears, said something unintelligible. Lila stroked her hair back from her face. 'Cora, breathe. That's it, another one. Now, tell me slowly.'

Cora was trembling violently. 'It was *him,* you see. I fell in love with him and I thought....that night...I thought he wanted me but then he took me to her place and then I saw him kiss her.'

Lila shook her head. 'Cora, you're not making any sense.'

Cora was shaking her head back and forth. 'I paid someone. A guy I know, not a good guy. I paid him to scare her off....I paid him to get rid of her but I didn't know he would actually go through with it... I was so scared...'

Lila's blood went cold. 'Cora...are you telling me...'

'I was the one who sent that man to hurt Tinsley. Oh god, Lila, I was so in love with Charlie and it wasn't fair and I was crazy jealous and...'

Lila's head was in her hands, not wanting to hear anymore. 'No...no...'

'I sent him to hurt Tinsley, Lila...*I tried to kill Tinsley...*'

55

HOLD ONTO ME: SHATTERED BILLIONAIRE PART

Lila and Noah are recovering from the loss of their much-wanted child and the media frenzy which exposed their whereabouts to the world – and to whomever is hunting Lila down. Their friends Charlie and Tinsley have become irrevocably tied up in the mystery, and Lila is horrified to learn of a near fatal attack on Tinsley. When she discovers who was behind that attack, Lila is caught in the middle of jealousy, hatred and murder and it's not clear who will survive. Desperate to start making a happy, safe life with Noah, their world is destroyed by one act of such jealousy and as Lila struggles to hold on to the man she loves, the killer closes in...

56

MANHATTAN

Noah looked down at Lila, tucked into the crook of his arm as they watched TV. back at their hotel. She had been quiet ever since she'd been at the Carnegie's – although she said it had gone well – and now Noah was worried. He picked up the remote control and flicked off the TV. Lila barely reacted.

'Okay,' he said, 'there's something on your mind. Spill it.'

Lila hesitated then sighed. 'I was thinking of all the ways that love – or at least what we might think is love – is corrupted. Tainted.'

Noah smiled. 'That's deep for this late in the evening. What's really bothering you?'

Lila rubbed her eyes. 'Just between us?'

'Of course.'

She gazed at him for a long moment then... 'Cora hired a guy to kill Tinsley.'

Noah felt the blood drain from his face and he groaned. 'Oh, *fuck.*'

'Yeah.' Lila wrapped her arm around his waist for comfort. 'The upside is she's distraught about it. She's glad the guy didn't succeed.'

'Because of Charlie?'

Lila nodded. 'See what I mean? People do crazy things for love.

Or lust.' She swallowed hard and looked at him. 'Noah, I have something I want to tell you and, god, it's not easy. I have never told anyone this, not even Charlie.'

He frowned. 'What is it, love?'

'I slept with Riley. About fifteen months ago. Richard and I were going through a bad patch, he'd been cheating and I had tried to be blind to it but one night, Riley and I were at the bar late, after closing and I'd just had enough. It was only that one time but...'

'But what?' Noah kept his voice level. He didn't judge Lila – or Riley – for what they had done but he was still strangely jealous.

'He told me that he was in love with me, that if he were someone else, he would beg me not to marry Richard. He wasn't...I mean to say, he didn't come across as obsessive just a sad guy with a crush. I ached for him, felt guilty. '

Noah tightened his arms around her. 'We all make mistakes with other people's hearts, all of us. Doesn't make us bad people.'

Lila pulled away from him so she could face him. 'Exactly. Which is why I have a hard time thinking that Riley is behind all of this. It just doesn't make any sense.'

Noah was quiet for a moment, letting her think. 'The photos on the wall of his apartment, though.'

'Someone could have put them there...no, I know, it's ridiculous. Maybe it was his way of dealing with his crush.'

Noah was skeptical. 'Sweetheart, if you have a little crush, you maybe have one photo. Not thousands.'

'Where the hell did he get them from, that's what I want to know. Actually, scratch that. We weren't talking about Riley and me; this is about....do I tell Charlie and Tinsley what Cora did?'

Noah let a long breath hiss out from between his teeth. 'That's a hard one...'

'Isn't it just. What would you do?'

Noah considered. 'Maybe get Cora to talk to Tinsley in private. Tinsley deserves to know the truth – Charlie...well, that's up to Tinsley.'

Lila nodded slowly. 'That's a good idea, yeah, that is a good idea. I'll call Cora in the morning.' Noah saw her shoulders relax and a small smile play around her lips. 'Thank you, baby, you always know what to do for the best.'

She crawled back into his arms and pressed her lips against his. 'Why do I feel, despite everything, that things are going to be okay? I think it's *you*, Noah Applebaum. When I'm with you, I feel safe, loved.'

'You are both those things, Lila Belle.' He grinned then. 'I never did ask, is your middle name really Belle?'

Lila chuckled. 'No, it's just what Delphine used to call me. Cora is Cora Belle and somehow that translated to me as well. I liked it.'

'What *is* your middle name?'

'I don't have one. I don't even know what my real name is, or even if my birth mother gave me a name. Apparently, and I know this is weird, until I was three and put into the children's home, they called me Lily. It was Charlie who named me Lila, and gave me his mother's maiden name.' She smiled now, remembering and Noah stroked her face.

'Maybe, one day soon, I can give your my name – if you want it,' he smiled but his eyes were wary. Lila kissed him.

'Nothing would make me happier.' She pressed her lips against his neck. Noah buried his face in her hair.

'Then, when you're fully healed, we'll go away together. Somewhere only we know and I'll ask you properly.'

She looked up at him with shining eyes. 'I can't wait, my love. I can't wait.'

THE NEXT MORNING, Lila drove out to Westchester in the hire car Noah had arranged for her. She had pooh-poohed his suggestion being driven by a bodyguard. 'Who's going to get me travelling at speed on the Interstate?'

He had no argument and she kissed him gratefully. 'I'll call you when I get there, I promise.'

It was Richard Sr. who greeted her at the door. Never an effusive man, Lila was shocked when he pulled her into a bear-hug. 'We missed you around here, Lila Belle.'

His warm voice brought tears to her eyes and all she could think of then was how much she'd hurt all of them by disappearing.

Richard told her that Cora was waiting for her in her room and with a smile; he went back to his study.

Cora was sitting on her bed, her big eyes wide with nervousness and Lila couldn't help but feel for the young woman. Cora was fragile, vulnerable...but, Lila reminded herself sternly, that was no excuse for what Cora had done. And it was hardly a little thing either...

'Cora, darling, I've been doing a lot of thinking about what you told me.'

Cora frowned. 'What did I tell you?'

A small pang of dread hit Lila's stomach and she sighed. 'Cora, I think you know.'

'No idea what you're talking about.'

So this was how it was going to go, was it? Lila shook her head. 'Yes, you do, Cora and pretending otherwise is not going to help it go away.'

Cora stuck her nose in the air. 'You're really going to have to enlighten me.'

Lila had heard enough. 'Cora, what you did was despicable.' Enough with treading softly, Lila thought, and she saw Cora's face redden.

'Lila...'

'No, Cora, no. We are not doing this. You put me in the middle by telling me, and now you have to step up and face the consequences. I think you should talk to Tinsley, tell her what happened, why you did what you did.'

Cora laughed, a false high sound. 'I hardly know the woman, why should I talk to her?'

Lily's mood darkened. 'Trying to have someone killed, Cora, just because they're involved with a man you like – you don't think that's good reason?'

Cora looked away from Lila's gaze. 'I don't understand why you're saying this to me. It must be the hormones in your system; I know you must still be feeling strange after the baby and everything.'

Low blow. 'Cora, do you really want me to tell Tinsley? Charlie? Your parents?'

Cora looked at them, her blue gaze icy. Her mouth hitched up in a cruel smile. 'And who do you think they'll believe, Lila?'

Lila's temper flared and she clenched her fists, digging her nails into her palm. 'Fine. Let's see, shall we?'

She stalked out of the room and down the stairs. She slammed the front door on her way out and it was only when she was halfway up the drive that she let out a howl of frustration. Why couldn't this be simple? She'd had visions of taking Cora to Tinsley, a tearful admission, an instant pardon from Tinsley. And everyone lives happily ever after, she shook her head. You bloody fool, Tierney.

She drove back into the city and to her hotel, greeting Noah's security team. In the suite, she dumped her bag and slumped onto the couch. Jesus. What should she do? Who was her loyalty to?

She grabbed a pillow and stuck her face in it, screaming a loud 'Fuck!' deep into its softness.

No. If Cora was going to be a bitch about this, then there was only one thing to do. Tell Tinsley what she knew. Then it was up to Tinsley what action she took and Lila could take herself out of the equation.

She called Tinsley at the bar and asked her to meet her later then she went to shower, hoping the cool water would cool her hot temper. So much violence, she thought as she scrubbed at her body with the soap, so much damn violence. She looked down at the sill livid scars on her belly. Her body had quickly gone back to its pre-pregnancy shape, and now she could feel her ribs against the taut skin. Too skinny. She had hardly eaten since Matty had been stillborn, and she knew Noah was torn between insisting she eat and look after herself and not wanting to pressure her. God. She cranked the faucet off and leaned her forehead against the cool tile. She wanted to get away with him soon, go somewhere where it was the just the two of them, start rebuilding a life.

When she was dressed, she was gazing unenthusiastically in the fridge when the intercom buzzed. 'Hey, sweetcheeks, it's me.'

Charlie presented her with a bunch of flowers. 'Cheesy, I know, but what the hell?'

She grinned and kissed him. 'They're gorgeous, thanks, Charlie. You not working?'

He shrugged. 'Yeah, kinda, but I wanted to see you.

'Because?'

His grin was crooked. 'Do I need a reason?'

Lila relaxed and hugged him. 'Of course not. Just seems every time lately, there's been a reason. It's good that you just want to hang out with your oldest buddy.'

'Word, sister. Where's the good doc?'

'Meeting. He's thinking of quitting the hospital and setting up somewhere else, his own practice so he's meeting with some insiders, get some advice.'

Charlie made a face. 'God, business meetings.'

Lila nodded, grinning. 'Which is why you're a cop and I'm an artist. Not that you would know, I've been 'resting' for way too long.'

'Time to get back into it?'

'God, yes, I've been drifting for a few years now. So much for my independent woman stance; first Richard, now Noah – they both supported me financially whether I like it or not.' She sighed. 'I have to do something, Charlie. Maybe I could go back and retrain as an art teacher.' She suddenly looked excited. 'God, why didn't I think of that before?'

Charlie was watching her, a small smile on his face. 'You just keep making plans over there. You staying in Seattle?'

She nodded. 'I am. It's where Noah is, where I want to be. Only one thing missing and that's you.'

'Yeah.' Charlie's smile faded. 'Well, when things go bad here, I'll come home.'

Lila studied him. He looked tired and drawn. 'You okay?'

He nodded. 'Just a lot on my mind. They're going to partner me up with someone new next week and I don't know how I feel about the guy. Or the job. Or New York.'

'What about Tinsley?'

'The one good thing.'

Lila smiled. 'I'm glad.' She chewed her lip then sighed. 'Charlie, I have something to tell you and I don't want you to blow up and get crazy. This is me asking you as a friend, not a cop.'

'Go for it, shorty.'

'It's about the attack on Tinsley. I know who it was.'

Charlie sat up, his face hard. 'What the fuck?'

'It was Cora,' Lila hurried on, seeing the anger in his eyes. 'She admitted it to me a few days ago. I didn't know what to do so I talked things over with Noah and went back to see Cora yesterday to get her to go to Tinsley herself.'

'And?'

'She's denying she ever admitted it to me. You should have seen her, Charlie. She was stone-cold. I've never seen her like that before.'

Charlie dropped his head back and stared at the ceiling. 'You should have come to me,' he said in a low, angry voice and Lila flushed.

'I know, I'm sorry. But I was caught between...'

'Cora tried to have Tinsley killed. *Stabbed to* death, Lila. Does that sound familiar to you?'

The blood drained from Lila's face. 'No...no way, Charlie. Cora and I were so close before the wedding, she was excited about it.'

'Was she? Or is she just a better actress than we give her credit for? She's always been troubled, on a knife-edge – sorry, that was a bad metaphor. But, Lila, really...she was really close to Richard. Isn't it possible she got jealous, worried she'd lose her brother? If she knew who to go to hire a killer – why not Cora? Maybe it was the same guy who stabbed you. Jesus, Lila...'

He got up, pulling his phone out of his pocket and Lila knew he would swing into action now.

'What are you going to do?'

Charlie, phone to ear, looked down at her, his face set and grim. 'I'm going to arrest Cora Carnegie on suspicion of attempted murder,' he said, '*two* counts.'

Lila put her head in her hands and hoped she'd done the right thing.

57

HAWAIIAN ISLANDS

A *month later...*

LILA STRETCHED LUXURIOUSLY on the sun lounger on the terrace of their villa. In the distance, she could see the red gleam of the erupting volcanoes on the other islands. They had been here for a day, a villa borrowed from one of Noah's friends, and they'd walked along the beach, swam in the clear water and gorged themselves on the amazing food they'd bought in town; fresh fruit, cheese, bread and wine.

Lila looked up as Noah came out onto the terrace, a new bottle of champagne in his hand. He was wearing grey marl shorts and nothing else and she delighted in his firm body, broad shoulders, firm stomach and thick, muscled arms. Damn, it had been too long...

Noah, seeing her blatant lust, grinned...and dropped an ice cube on her bare belly. She shrieked with laughter. 'You ruined the moment, doofus,' she grumbled. Noah plucked the ice cube up with his mouth, and then ran it around the soft mound of her belly. Lila sighed happily. Noah, grinning, undid the halter neck of her bikini top, freeing her breasts, already faintly tanned – her olive skin soaked up the sun. She watched, smiling, as he took her nipple into his mouth and she gasped as the remnants of the ice cube touched her sensitive bud.

'Noah...'

His hand slipped up the inside of her thigh, stroking and kneading the soft flesh there, until his fingers crept under the cotton of her shorts and began to stroke her sex. Lila moaned softly, her own fingers knotting in his short dark curls. Noah moved to tease her other nipple as his long forefinger slipped inside her and began to seek the spot that made her groan and cry out.

His head came up and he grinned, kissing her mouth, his intentions clear. He slid her shorts down her long legs then stood to push his own shorts down. His cock, so big and thick, stood proudly against his belly and he fisted the root of it as he came to her again. She held out her arms to him and he went into them, both of them sighing at the feel of skin against skin.

'I love you, Noah Applebaum,' she whispered as she wrapped her legs around his waist and he smiled as he slid into her, groaning softly at the feel of her soft, wet cunt enveloping him as he filled her.

'God, Lila...'

They moved together, completely focused on each other, enjoying every sensation as they fucked for the first time in weeks. They loved and laughed, made each other come over and over long into the night then finally, exhausted and sated, lay together, limbs entwined, watching the distant light show of the volcanoes.

'This place is unreal,' Lila said, her head resting against his chest. 'Your friend's very generous to lend this place out to you.'

'He is,' Noah agreed, his hands gently stroking her bare skin. 'When we get back to Seattle, we should double date with Jakob and Quilla – you and she have a lot in common. A *lot*.'

'Do they have kids?'

'Twins, adopted. Girls, Maika and Nell, I think their names are.'

They lay in silence for a long time the Lila sighed. 'Do you think we'll have a lot of kids?'

'We already have one. Just because she's no longer here...I still feel like a father.'

She smiled up at him. 'I know, I feel like a mom. You think we'll have more?'

He pressed his lips to her forehead. 'I think so, I hope so. We have time though, baby. Let's just enjoy *us*, for now.'

'Agreed.' She snuggled closer, tracing a line down his chest with her finger. 'Noah?'

''Sup?'

'I'm thinking about going back to school, retraining as a teacher.'

Noah looked down at her in surprise. 'Really?'

'Yup. I haven't painted anything new for years now and I can't live off your goodwill forever.'

Noah hissed in frustration. 'Baby...I wish you'd stop worrying about that. It's just money. What's mine is yours; I thought you would have realized that by now.'

'Easy for you to say; you're not the one being called a gold-digger. Besides, I am realistic – even teaching, I'll never match your wealth but I can at least contribute. I need that.'

Noah sighed, clearly not satisfied. 'Fine.'

She nuzzled his chin. 'Don't be mad, Applebum.'

He chuckled, kissing her softly. 'I'm not mad, just...I want to look after you.'

'And you do. All the time. But money isn't a part of that, you care for me in far more important ways.'

'Mushy.'

She laughed. 'If you like.'

They held each other in silence for a while before Lila untangled herself from him. 'Where are you going?' Noah grumbled as she got up. She grinned.

'Just to pee, be right back.'

She padded barefoot and naked through the dark villa to the bathroom. God, she could happily live here forever, just the two of them. She had a slight headache and she leaned her hot forehead against the cool tile as she used the toilet.

Here, she could forget about the mess in New York. Cora had been arrested and bailed and the DA was considering the charges against her. She had confessed to hiring someone to kill Tinsley - during a psychotic break, Cora claimed, driven made by jealousy. Tinsley had been shocked to the core that Cora was behind the attack and hadn't taken the news that Lila had known and not told her well. Not well at all and for the past couple of weeks, before they had come to the island, Lila and Tinsley's relationship had cooled.

Cora, however, vehemently denied that she was behind Lila's attempted murder. Lila somehow believed her but Charlie was so convinced they had at last found the answers they were looking for that she kept her beliefs to herself. Charlie wasn't an irrational man, she figured, if he was so convinced, there must be a reason.

Lila, on Charlie's recommendation, hadn't contacted the Carnegies and it was killing her not to know how Delphine and Richard Sr. were doing. For so long, they had been her family and now...she couldn't ever imagine a way back for their relationship. That part of her life was over and if Cora really was responsible for the horrific stabbing Lila had endured and somehow survived, then the silver lining was that she could truly move on.

With Noah. She washed her hands and smiled to herself. God, she loved that man. Every time she saw him it was like the first time; her heart would race, her breath would catch in her throat. When he put his hands on her – god, his hands – her skin would vibrate with pleasure, the pulse between her legs would start to pound.

Thinking about that, she went back to the terrace to find him asleep. She grinned and straddled him, her hands slipping between his legs to cup his balls, stroke his cock into tumescence.

She chuckled as he pretended to be asleep then as a wide smile spread across his face and his eyes opened as she spread her labia and guided him into her slick cunt.

'Well, hello again to you,' he murmured, his hands splaying out over her bare back as she rode him gently. His lips found hers, his tongue teasing hers. 'God, you taste so good, Miss Lila.'

She smiled, her lips curving up against his. 'Glad you think so.' She slammed her hips hard against him, taking him in deep and he groaned. His fingers clamped onto the soft flesh of her waist, keeping her impaled on his cock. He looked up at her, his clear green eyes amused, loving, and intense.

'I love you, Miss Lila Tierney, more than anything else in this godforsaken world.'

'Glad to hear it.'

He grinned widely. 'Then, seeing as my cock is deep inside your beautiful cunt, I think this is the exact right time to say, Lila Tierney, would you do me the honor of marrying me?'

Lila thrust hard onto his cock as he reached down to rub her clit and she moaned with pleasure. 'Yes...yes, god, yes Noah...I will marry you....as long as you promise to keep doing...*that*...yes...*yes*...'

58

MANHATTAN

Tinsley rolled over in bed and sighed. Sleep was eluding her yet again and next to her, the bed was empty. Charlie was working a case that took him into Brooklyn most nights – at least that was the official story. Tinsley knew he was searching out any and every place that Riley might be. Now that Cora was on the hook for the attempted murders, Charlie had grown quiet and restless, wanting to find his partner and friend. Tinsley knew it was because he felt guilty about being convinced of Riley's guilt and not listening to any other theory than 'Riley tried to kill Lila'.

God, what a mess. When Lila had told her that Cora had confessed to Tinsley's attack, the shock had made her lash out at her friend, accuse of her of putting Cora first. Lila had taken her tongue-lashing stoically.

'I know it seems that way,' she had softly, 'after Tinsley had ranted at her, 'but it's not the truth. I love you so much and I wanted to be sure. I want Cora to come to you herself but she turned on me too.'

That last line haunted Tinsley. She turned on me too...*jesus*, if Tinsley thought she'd had it bad over the last few months, it was nothing to what Lila had endured. Tinsley remembered the pain of the knife slicing into her body and her cuts weren't even serious.

Imagine having a knife plunged deep in your belly, *repeatedly...* Tinsley shuddered. She couldn't fathom it.

SHE GOT out of bed to get some water. A cigar box sat on the kitchen counter, half-open. Tinsley couldn't resist. She sipped her water and flipped open the lid to the box. She saw, straight away, the photo of Charlie and Lila – god, how sweet, she though. They were teenagers; Charlie must have been about nineteen, twenty, Lila a little younger, maybe not even in her teens. Charlie had his heavy arm around her neck and they were both laughing as they play-wrestled.

Tinsley guiltily looked through the rest of the box. Receipts from movies – some really old, she noticed – tickets from the Staten Island ferries, from the Washington State ferries, museum leaflets, concert ticket stubs. A life, she thought, a whole life documented in memories. She had never thought that Charlie could be so sentimental.

She found the letter at the bottom and recognised Lila's handwriting immediately. The envelope was a heavy, expensive paper and Tinsley picked it up. She hesitated before sliding the notepaper out and opening it.

MY DEAREST, oldest friend,

I HAVE no words to say I'm sorry for leaving like this – just know I would not do so unless it was absolutely necessary.

Charlie, you are my brother, my friend, my guide and knowing I won't be able to see you, at least not in the near future, is killing me. I have to do this, Charlie, and please, please, don't come looking for me. Please. I really need to be alone in this.

If you can, or are willing, please give this other letter to the Carnegies and tell them I'm so sorry to do this so soon after Richard's death.

I'm sorry, Charlie. I'll miss you and I love you,
Lila.

. . .

TINSLEY FELT tears prick the backs of her eyes. God, what a shitstorm the whole thing was. She wasn't surprised that Charlie had kept this letter – the bond between them and the love that Lila felt for him was in every line.

'Enjoying that?'

Tinsley gasped and spun around, dropping the letter to the floor. Charlie, his face half in shadow, waited. She picked the letter up and put it back in the box.

'Charlie, I'm so sorry, I have no excuse.'

There was a long silence then he stepped forward into the light and she couldn't read his expression. 'Don't worry about it.'

She watched him pick the box up and shove it into a drawer before finally standing. The tension in the air was heavy.

'Shit, Charlie,' she went to him and tried to put her hand on his chest but he ducked away.

'I said, don't worry about it. I'm heading for a shower, I'm pretty gross.'

He walked away. 'I could join you,' she called out, hopefully, but when he didn't answer, she felt even worse. She debated following him but instead, went back to bed and waited.

He was toweling his hair dry roughly as he walked back into their bedroom. Their bedroom. *Huh.* They'd been living here less than two weeks and Tinsley couldn't get used to the fact she was living with a guy. It just wasn't her and now she found herself wondering if it had been worth the risk. This right here was why she needed her own space, needed somewhere she could absolutely relax. She hated confrontation at the best of times but when it was with the person you were sharing a bed with...

Charlie got into bed and pulled her into his arms. He smelled of shower gel and fresh laundry. Tinsley snuggled up to him gratefully, felt his erection against her thigh and wrapped a leg around him.

'Forgive me?'

He kissed her roughly. 'Nothing to forgive.' he took her, thrusting deep inside her, pressing her back onto the bed as he fucked her. Tinsley, her hands pinned by his, stared up at him as he moved. Something wasn't right, something was off, she realized sadly.

She didn't come although she pretended to and when he was in the bathroom afterward, she tried to figure out why. It was only later, when he was snoring gently beside her that she realized what it was. He hadn't looked directly at her the whole time they'd made love.

The next day she got home to find all his possessions gone, a note on the table.

I can't do this. I'm sorry. Tinsley re-read the note and then crumpled it in her hand.

She felt strangely relieved.

59

SEATTLE

M r. *Halston Applebaum would like to announce the engagement of his son, Dr. Noah Alexander Applebaum of King County, Seattle, Washington State to Miss Lila Tierney of San Juan Island, Washington State.*

LILA NODDED APPROVINGLY. 'Nice. Short and sweet.'

Noah grinned. 'Only my Dad would insist on placing an engagement notice nowadays.'

'Meh,' Lila shrugged. 'There's no harm in it. I'm just glad he likes me, is all.'

On return from the island, Noah and Lila had been busy, out with his father and his step-mother, getting to know some of his friends. She especially liked Jakob and Quilla Mallory and she and Quilla had met up a few times on their own since. She liked the other woman a great deal; she was sassy, and funny and beautiful and more than anything, a survivor. Quilla had been raped and stabbed by a vengeful ex-colleague of Jakob's and still carried the scars of that attack. Her two young sons, she told Lila, made everything worthwhile.

'Even though they are exhausting,' she grinned at Lila. Lila adored the two boys; their mischievous grins and rambunctious personalities were encouraged by their mother – much to Jakob's chagrin.

'You'd think she would want them quiet at the end of the day but no,' he grinned fondly at his wife, 'I get home and there they are, all three of them, yelling at me, singing at me.'

Lila could picture the scene now and felt a pang of sadness. Would she and Matty have been as bonded as Quilla and her boys? She hoped so.

Quilla nudged her, seeing her contemplation. 'I know what you're thinking,' she said, 'and yes, I think you and Matty would have had a great time together.'

Lila smiled at her, tears in her eyes. 'Thank you. I miss her. I know that sounds strange, but I do.'

'Of course you do.'

Lila sighed. 'I keep thinking maybe the stabbing did something to me, made it so I couldn't carry to full term.'

Quilla's eyes were kind. 'I can't tell you the answer to that, only that when it happened to me, it destroyed my uterus. Hence…'

'God, I'm sorry.'

'Don't be. It's just one of those things. We didn't ask for that, did we? We have to make the best of the fact we survived, Lila. We *survived*.'

LILA WAS STILL THINKING of Quilla's words later when she and Noah were alone. 'Quilla told me that the arts foundation she runs is thinking about branching out to help survivors of violence get back on their feet. She asked me if I would be interested in leading some groups and doing some work around that. I'm not sure what…maybe art therapy?'

She was excited by the prospect and Noah grinned. 'Look at you, all excited. You look like a kid with a new toy.'

'Whatever, Grandpa.' She giggled at his face then. Noah tugged on a lock of her hair.

'So, I'm thinking we should mark our engagement somehow?'

Lila gave him a look. 'I told you, I don't do rings. Wedding yes, engagement...'

'You wore an engagement ring for Richard.'

Lila swallowed. 'Noah...this time's it's different. Richard kept on and on and on at me to wear one; in the end I just gave in. You know me better than he *ever* did. You get me.'

Noah sat back in his chair, grinning. 'Nicely done, Tierney.'

Lila was going to protest but then thought the better of it. 'Thank you.' She yawned and crawled into his lap. 'If you want me tonight, you'll have to be quick.'

Noah burst out laughing. 'My god, has the romance gone already?' He tickled her until she begged him to stop. They made love slowly and leisurely then fell asleep wrapped around each other.

The phone woke them at four in the morning. Noah scrambled for his cell phone and checked it. 'Yours,' he said, somewhat smugly and Lila groaned, not even bothering to open her eyes as she groped for her phone on the nightstand.

'Yeah?' Her voice was muffled but then her head shot up, her eyes opened. 'Charlie? Is everything okay?'

Noah was watching her now, his brow creased. Lila looked at him, and then said into the phone. 'Okay. Okay then. Let me know. Yeah, you too, bub.'

She ended the call and looked at Noah for a long minute, her eyes full of confusion and sadness. 'What? What is it, Lila?'

She shook her head in disbelief. 'It's all over,' she said in stunned voice, 'Riley's body has been found.'

60

MANHATTAN

Woods Kinsayle was white-faced and trembling as he sat beside Charlie in the police cruiser. Charlie, to his credit, had insisted on going to tell the Kinsayles the news himself and Woods had volunteered to help identify the body.

Charlie looked over at him now. 'Woods...I have to warn you. We pulled him out of the East River – and it looks like he's been there for some time. There's...god, Woods, are you sure?'

'I'll know if it's my brother,' Woods said stiffly. 'I'll know.'

Charlie sighed. The body had been discovered by kids who were no doubt telling the story of how they pulled the gross dead guy out of the water. They wouldn't have to exaggerate much. Riley – if it *was* him – was bloated, half missing and naked. What they could tell was that there was a bullet hole in what was left of his skull, at the temple. Fish had been eating him, the elements not helping either; there wasn't much left to identify.

At the mortuary, Woods gagged when he saw the remains. Charlie didn't blame him. It was hard to think this had once been Riley – fun-loving Riley Kinsayle, with the charm and cuteness women adored. Riley Kinsayle who may or may not have been obsessed with Lila.

'It's him,' Woods said eventually, his eyes locked on the bloated head. He pointed at it. 'Behind that ear, he had a small '*K*' tattooed. If it's there, it's him.'

The mortician looked at Charlie who nodded once and the mortician, gloved hands, lifted the ear gently. A part of it came away in his hands and Woods whirled around and threw up in the nearest trash can. The mortician – who had seen it all in his day – looked up and nodded. 'A '*K*' behind the left ear – confirmed.'

'Fuck.' Charlie hissed the word and Woods gave a strangled sob, pushing open the door and slamming out of the room. Charlie thanked the technician and went to find him.

Woods was outside, breathing in deep lungfuls of air to try and not throw up again. Charlie stood at his side and waited.

'I knew it,' said Woods eventually, wiping his mouth. 'I knew he was dead. I could feel it.'

Charlie tried to keep the skepticism out of his tone. 'Yeah?'

Woods nodded. 'Okay, so we didn't get along a lot of the time but he was my brother, you know?'

Charlie nodded, staying quiet. If Woods thought he could kid the world that he and Riley had been close...

'I know what you're thinking,' Woods suddenly said, his expression fierce. 'Yeah, I busted his chops. Yeah I kicked his ass. That's what we did.'

Charlie couldn't stop himself. 'No, Woods, that's what *you* did.'

The other man's expression became sly then. 'Have you considered that Riley might have killed himself when he found out the guy he trusted with his life every day was trying to lock him up? That you breaking into his apartment and going through his personal stuff was a violation of that trust? That you thinking he could have stabbed Lila in cold blood might have been the straw that broke the camel's back?'

Charlie looked at him steadily. 'Riley wasn't suicidal. And having a wall plastered with photos that the subject didn't know were being taken isn't just 'personal stuff', Woods, it's stalking. It's obsession. Lila had no idea.'

Woods laughed then. 'God, you poor deluded asshole. You don't think Lila knew how Riley felt about her? They fucked, for Christ sakes.'

Charlie went very still. 'You don't know what the hell you're talking about.'

Woods' smile was snaky. 'Your precious little Lila screwed my brother on the floor of the bar. He told me as much himself. See, you can take the girl out of the trailer park but...'

Charlie slammed his fist into Woods' jaw and the other man went down hard. He tried to defend himself but Charlie whaled on him with his fists, unrelenting until Woods was beaten bloody and two men from the mortuary were pulling Charlie off him.

HIS CAPTAIN just shook his head. 'I'm sorry, Charlie. Badge and gun. I wouldn't be surprised if Woods presses charges. He'd just identified his brother's for Christ's sake. Now, look, I can talk to the powers that be, tell them you were distraught over Riley....you listening to me, Sherman?'

Charlie was staring out of the window at the white sky over Manhattan. He shifted his attention to his captain and stared at him, his face set. 'Don't bother,' he said calmly. He stood, placed his gun and badge on the desk. 'I quit.'

His captain sighed. 'Sherman, don't be an idiot.'

'I'm not. Truly I'm not. I've been thinking about it for a while. Now Riley's gone and Tinsley and I have called it quits, there's nothing left for me here. My family is in Seattle. Lila is in Seattle and I want to be with my family.'

His captain stared at him. 'Well, you can't leave until we know about Wood's condition or whether charges will be brought.'

'That's fine. You know where to get a hold of me.'

CHARLIE WALKED out into the street and took a deep breath. Yeah, this was what he wanted. He'd had enough of this city; too many damn people. It was time.

He pulled out his cell phone and dialed. When Lila answered, he smiled. 'Hey kiddo, guess what? I'm coming home.'

61

SEATTLE

L ila was only half listening to Quilla as she showed her around the QCM Foundation's offices. She couldn't stop thinking about Riley, his merry face, his smile. His body the night they had made love. He had been exactly what she needed that night and now he was dead. Maybe because of her, because she used him. No, no, that night had been so...she had wanted him and he had wanted her. That was it; purely natural, purely instinctual.

But the men in her life kept winding up dead. God.

'Lila?' Quilla's lovely face was concerned. 'Are you okay?'

If anyone were to understand, it would be this woman but Lila couldn't bring herself to talk about it. Shame. She felt ashamed. She tried to smile at Quilla. 'No, sorry, bit of a headache. Where were we?'

'This is where we interview the people who apply to the fund. It's very informal but because we just can't give money out left and right, it is quite stringent. I do confess, it's mostly gut instinct. If someone's passionate about art, you can tell. If they love pastel chalk under their fingernails or smudged on their cheek, if they talk about a particular shade of a color, you know that person is genuine. If they're in it for fame or just to impress, sorry, there's the door.'

Lila considered. 'I like that. College is great but it depends so much on results, on almost reducing artists to tick-lists instead of who they really are. '

Quilla smiled. 'You get it.'

Lila nodded. 'I do. What I don't get is what you want me to do.'

'Come with me,' Quilla smiled. She led Lila down to a small office. A young blonde woman was talking to a small of group of females.

'That's Nan, she's a teacher and helped set up this group. This group is for survivors of domestic violence. They can come here, to these offices and downstairs we have studios that they can use whenever they like to just express themselves. We also have some rooms with cots and facilities so that they can stay if they want to. It's a safe space. Nan runs this workshop twice a week where they can discuss their work and get critiqued.'

Lila looked through the window to watch the women talking and laughing. 'What a great idea.'

'We're very proud. Now, let's go grab some coffee and I'll tell you what I have in mind.'

IN THE SPACIOUS, clean cafeteria on the top floor, they sat in comfortable chairs with steaming cups of hot chocolate. Quilla sipped hers.

'What I have in mind is a new group, for survivors like you and me. Woman – or men, but we may need to do separate groups to avoid triggering – people who have survived non-domestic violent crime. Rape, muggings, attempted murders, serious physical and mental harm. I am a huge believer in art therapy.'

'Me too,' Lila was getting excited now. 'Wow. Wow.'

Quilla grinned. 'That's the spirit. What do you say? Want to come run it for us?'

Lila nodded enthusiastically. 'Hell, yes. God, Quilla, I can't thank you enough.'

'No need for thanks, I know you'll be perfect.'

Lila laughed. 'You're very confident in my ability.'

Quilla shrugged, chuckling. 'Noah has been singing your praises since even before he reconnected with you.'

Lila flushed with pleasure. 'He has?'

'Oh yes. I'm probably breaking some sort of 'bro-code' here but there were many night of him talking about how he'd met the most perfect woman in the world and how he wished you hadn't disappeared on him.'

'There were?'

'Lila Tierney, are you getting emotional?'

'No,' Lila protested but her eyes had teared up and she blinked them rapidly. Quilla laughed.

'Well, he was a lost cause, Lila. That man is crazy about you.'

Lila grabbed a tissue from her bag. 'And I about him. We're getting married, you know.'

'I do know, and I'm so happy for you.'

'You'll come to the wedding?'

'Try and kept me away. Although I warn you, I'm a terrible drunk.'

Lila laughed. 'Excellent, then there'll be two of us.'

AFTER SAYING GOODBYE TO QUILLA – who she was forming a little bit of a girl crush on – she went to a coffeehouse nearby. Even though she hated to admit it, the fact that Cora was practically under house arrest and poor Riley was dead at least gave her the freedom of knowing that whoever tried to kill her was out of action. She didn't have to have Noah's hired security following her around, scoping the place out. She could just be in the world, do whatever she wanted, go wherever she liked without checking in.

She ordered a tea and sat at a table in the window. It was late fall and already cold. Christmas decorations were starting to go up. Lila loved this time of year and for the first time in months, she felt content, safe, happy. She was marrying a wonderful man and now with this job...she called Noah, too excited to wait.

'Hey sweetcheeks.'

'Hey buddy – why do you sound all echoey?'

'On speakerphone, so no dirty talk.'

'I really love your huge, throbbing...'

'Really *am* on speakerphone, babe,' Noah said to a roomful of laughter and Lila chuckled.

'Drill, I was going to say but that still sounds dirty.'

'Yes, yes it does. Lila, I do have my hands inside a patient, so...' But he was laughing too.

'Okay, sorry, I just called to say I have a job and I want to take you out to dinner later, when you get off work.'

'Sold, well done baby. Where you taking me?'

Lila thought quickly. 'The Maison Rouge?'

'Sounds perfect. I'll come home first and we'll go together.'

'I'll book a table.'

'Splendid. See you later, then, love you.'

'Love you too,' Lila suppressed another laugh, 'and your enormous cock.'

'Oh dear God, woman,' now there were cheers as Noah laughed and said goodbye.

Lila put her phone away and laughed to herself. She loved that she could be as cheeky and silly with him as she liked and he didn't care. Even in front of his peers and subordinates, he had a sense of humor and total lack of arrogance because he was the best at his job so he didn't feel the need to impress anyone else.

'I love you so much Noah Applebaum,' she uttered to herself as she finished her tea and gathered her stuff. She walked out into the cold, crisp air and hailed a cab to take her home.

62

MANHATTAN

Tinsley felt she was sitting with a complete stranger. Charlie looked...odd. Almost gleeful, which for him and his classic 'resting bitch face', was very strange. She grinned at him. She had expected this meeting – the first since he'd left her – to be awkward; in fact it was almost jovial.

'What's up with you? You look weird. Why is your face making that shape?'

Charlie grinned. 'What shape?'

'That weird smiling thing. You're freaking me out.'

Charlie shrugged good-naturedly. 'I'm going home, Tins. I'm a west coast boy, I belong there.'

'Is Lila excited?'

'Think so. She's scouting places for me and I'm staying with her and Noah until I get settled.'

Tinsley drank some beer. 'So this is it, then?'

He took her hand. 'Not forever, I hope.'

She smiled but pulled her hand away. 'I hope not too. When do you leave?'

'Saturday.'

She nodded, thinking how quickly life moved on. 'Well, I hope you find your peace there, Charlie.'

'You too, kiddo. Got any plans?'

Tinsley laughed softly. 'Not a one.'

'Will you come out to Seattle sometime?'

'Of course. I'll be there for the wedding, of course, whenever that is.'

Charlie smiled, relaxing back in his seat. 'I'm glad you and Lila have made up. She really didn't know what to do about Cora.'

Tinsley nodded. 'I know. Speaking of whom, any news?'

'Last I heard, D.A. pushing for the attempted murder of Lila to be dropped but to press ahead with your case.'

'God, what a fucking mess,' she muttered. 'Look, Cora's a messed up kid who needs proper mental health care and a stint away from the ivory tower. I don't want her in prison.'

Charlie shrugged. 'Sorry, I have no sympathy.'

'Cold.'

'In this case, yes.'

Tinsley blew out her cheeks. 'Okay then. But I might go talk to someone, I really think...'

'Stay out of it, Tinsley,' Charlie said vehemently. 'The girl tried to have you killed. End of story, she goes to jail.'

Tinsley found her palms were sweating, that her chest was tight. 'Okay, if it'll make you happy.' She didn't like the malicious gleam she suddenly saw in his eyes and she suddenly realized that it wasn't *her* welfare he was concerned with.

'You still think she had Lila stabbed?'

'I think she's more than capable.'

THE REST of the evening passed quickly and Charlie, never one for long goodbyes, left early. Tinsley was relieved again – she had been feeling that around him for a while now, as if something was wrong, off kilter. God. She hoped Charlie didn't intrude on Lila and Noah's life too much. She went back to the bar and helped Mikey to close up even thought it was her night off.

Mikey looked at her amused. 'You sure you wanna be doing this?'

'I need to keep occupied or I'm going to come up with mad conspiracy theories about my ex.'

'Which one?'

She grinned slightly. 'The moody one.'

Mikey rolled his eyes. He'd never taken to Charlie. 'Good riddance, if you ask me. There's something off about that guy. I know Lila always said he's a teddy bear...well, I reckon less teddy, more bear.'

Tinsley tried and failed to give her partner a disapproving look. 'He's okay, just...'

'A douche?'

Tinsley laughed. 'Oh come on now, he's always looked after Lila.'

'I'll give him that, but I always thought –' He stopped when he saw Tinsley's stricken face. She was staring at the TV. above the bar.

'Mikey, turn the sound up. Turn the sound up now....oh god....oh god...'

63

SEATTLE

Lila was in the shower when Noah got home and he grinned as he pulled his clothes off and stepped into the cubicle with her. She started slightly as he touched her then turned, shampoo suds on her face. He laughed, brushing them away and kissed her. 'You, Miss Tierney, are a very, very bad girl.'

With one swift movement, he turned her and pushed her against the cool tiles. Lila giggled, knowing what was coming next and as she spread her legs, he thrust into her. Gasping as his engorged cock plunged deep into her cunt, Lila moaned, leaning her head back on his shoulder as he fucked her, his hands pressing hers to the tile. His teeth nipped at her earlobe as he took her, releasing one hand so he could reach down to her clit and stroke it.

Lila gave a long gasp, tensed and came; moments later he followed, groaning and murmuring her name over and over as his cum pumped deep into her.

As THEY DRESSED HE GRINNED. Lila smirked back. 'What?'

'I love the fact that you're going to dinner with my seed still deep inside you.'

She laughed, half-shocked. 'Well...yes. It makes me feel kind of sexy to know that, carrying a little bit of you with me.'

'Actually, quite a lot...'

'Don't be gross,' she was giggling furiously now, lobbing a towel at him. 'God, how did you get the position you are being such a goofball?'

Noah slid his tie around his neck. 'I blame you. I used to be so serious...'

'Yeah, right. How do I look?'

She was wearing a white silk slip which hugged her curves and had cut outs at the waist, showing off her creamy olive skin. She pulled her hair into a messy ponytail on one side, and skipped all but the lightest make-up. Noah's obvious admiration made her feel even sexier.

'Are we going to make it to dinner?' She said with an eyebrow raised. Noah grinned.

'We'd better go now or we definitely won't.'

AT THE RESTAURANT, she told him all about the Quilla Chen Mallory Foundation and the role Quilla envisioned her playing. Noah was impressed.

'I gotta say,' he said, 'that sounds amazing.'

Lila nodded. 'Doesn't it? And as much as I do not want to be defined by what happened to me, I think this is a positive thing. I can't wait to get started.'

They chatted about it for a while then Noah reached into his pocket. 'Now, before you give me a lecture, this is not an engagement ring. It's not big or ostentatious but something to celebrate you and me. I had the idea a while back but it took me some time to design it and have it made, so...'

He opened the ring box and there was a small, delicate silver ring, with three interlocking rings on top of the band. It was beautiful and Lila's chest got tight.

'Oh Noah, it's perfect...' She touched the three tiny rings with her fingertip.

'You, me and Matty,' Noah said in a gruff voice. Lila covered her mouth, tears dripping down her cheeks.

'Noah...' She leaned over the table to kiss him. 'Thank you. Thank you.'

He smiled, obviously as moved at her reaction as she was by his gift. 'Do you want to try it on?'

Smiling she shook her head and he looked stung but she put her hand on his. 'I would like to wear it as my wedding band...if that's okay with you.'

His relief – and joy – was palpable. 'Of course...god, of course, I never even thought of that.'

They both laughed, their fingers interlocking. Lila gazed at him then back at the ring and she grinned. 'I suppose I ought to try it, you know, because of the fit.'

Noah laughed. 'Oh, absolutely.' He slid it onto her ring finger. 'Wow'.

'Wow is right. What an incredible man you are, Noah Applebaum. How the hell was I so lucky to meet you?'

She asked the question then they both remembered the circumstances. Lila gave a soft laugh. 'If it meant not meeting you, I would happily take that knife over and over.'

Noah flinched. 'Don't say that.'

'You know what I mean. My life began when I met you, Noah.'

Their food got cold and other diners kept casting amused glances in their direction but neither of them cared. Tonight was about them.

AT A QUARTER OF MIDNIGHT, Noah helped her into her coat. She put her hands on his chest and gazed up at him, with soft eyes. 'Noah, I want you to know...'

Noah pressed his lips to hers. 'What, Lila?'

'I want you to know...that I'm going to do very naughty things to you when we get back home.'

Noah chuckled. 'Then let's get there quicker.'

The Seattle night was cold and steam blew out of their mouths when they breathed. Lila hugged her coat closer and Noah grinned down at her.

Then all hell broke loose. Into Lila's eye line stumbled a woman, long dirty blonde strewn across her face. Something glinted in her hand and then there was a loud popping sound. Screaming.

Noah staggered back and as Lila turned to look at him, her eyes widened in horror as blood started to bloom across the front of his shirt. He looked back at her confused, reached out and then collapsed.

All Lila could hear was the frantic beat of her heart. She didn't care if the next bullet came her way, all she could think about was Noah, his big frame sprawled on the sidewalk. She dropped to her knees beside him, every sane thought in her head gone as she screamed his name over and over...

And he didn't answer.

TINSLEY YANKED her suitcase from the luggage wheel and practically ran through SeaTac airport. She hailed a cab, jabbering the name of the hospital to the driver, who took one look at her stricken face and broke every speed limit in the city to get her there.

At the desk, she lied and said she was Lila's cousin and they directed up to the emergency room waiting area.

Lila was pale, shaken, her white dress covered in blood. She sat with another woman Tinsley didn't recognize, and a tall, handsome man who was taking to Charlie. When Charlie saw her, he came over.

'How is he?' Tinsley whispered and Charlie shook his head.

'We won't know for hours. He was shot in the chest, just once, but it's bad.'

Tinsley peeked around Charlie to see Lila, her head down. 'How's Lila?'

'In shock. She hasn't said a word.'

Tinsley looked at Charlie's closed face, and then ducked around him to go to her friend. 'Lila?'

Lila looked up and the raw pain in her eyes was almost more than Tinsley could bear to look at. She frowned as if trying to place Tinsley and Tinsley crouched down in front of her.

'Darling, I'm here for whatever you need.' She took Lila's hands and smiled at the woman next to her. 'Hey, there, I'm Tinsley.'

The other woman smiled, touched her arm. 'Quilla Mallory. It's...' She broke off and looked away and Tinsley nodded.

'Yeah, I know.' She got up and took the seat on the opposite side to Lila. Charlie was right, Lila was almost catatonic. She had a small black velvet box in her hand that she kept turning and turning around. She bent her head and Tinsley heard her whispering something over and over.

Pleasepleasepleasepleasepleasepleaseplease....

Tinsley ached for her friend. *So much pain, so much loss. Not Noah. Please let him live.* She found herself echoing the mantra of her friend. She looked at Quilla over her friend's head and the other woman looked as devastated as she did. They must be friends of Noah's, she thought.

As if reading her mind, Quilla spoke. 'This is my husband, Jakob. We're old friend of Noah's.'

Tinsley nodded to the other man, who spoke in a low voice. 'It was Lauren, Noah's ex. She was arrested, didn't even put up a struggle. Said she wanted to kill them both but she never got off more than one shot before a passerby tackled her.'

'God,' Tinsley spoke before she could catch herself, 'what the fuck is wrong with people?'

She leaned her head against Lila's, felt her friend stiffen then Lila's hand crept into hers.

'Why can't they just let us be?' Her voice was gruff, broken. 'All we want is to be happy, be together. What possible good comes of this?'

'I know, sweetheart.'

The depths of Lila's despair were searing. Tinsley felt tears coming and got up, not wanting Lila to see them. She went to Charlie who was staring out of the window. It was early morning but the city was still dark. Charlie didn't turn to her, just kept his gaze fixed in front of him. It took Tinsley a moment to realize he was staring at Lila's reflection in the glass. Her heart went out to him and she touched his arm. He started and turned to her, his eyes flat and cold.

'Charlie, I'm here for whatever you two need...'

He jerked his head towards the corridor and she followed him out. He closed the door, before turning to her. 'We're fine. She's fine, I'm here now.'

Tinsley was stung. 'She's my friend too, Charlie.'

'We don't need you here. Thank you for coming but we're fine.'

Tinsley's hands clenched into fists and her temper swelled. 'Why are you being like this? Lila needs all the friends she can get right now.'

Charlie had stopped even looking at her directly. 'You should go.'

'I'm not going anywhere, asshole,' she hissed at him. She took a deep breath in, trying to calm herself. Anger and confusion was giving way to something else now, something more tangible. Fear. Was Charlie losing it? Tinsley studied the man she had been so intimate with and saw nothing there that she recognized. Was he just in shock? No...it was something else.

'Charlie, I am here for Lila and believe it or not, I don't need your permission to stay with my friend.' She tried to push past him to go back into the waiting area but he grabbed her wrist. Hard. She winced and pulled away just as she heard someone say Lila's name. She turned to see an elderly, distinguished looking gentleman, his face etched in pain hurrying towards them. Noah's father. The gentle looking woman to his right had tears flooding down her cheeks.

'Charles,' Mr. Applebaum looked at Charlie, 'We came as soon as we could.'

'We drove from Portland,' the woman said, presumably Mrs. Applebaum.

Charlie greeted them warmly, much to Tinsley's shock. He showed them into the waiting room and she heard them comforting Lila. Charlie stood at the door and looked at her icily.

'Go back to New York, Tinsley, we're fine here.'

Tinsley stood her ground. 'No fucking way, Sherman. I'm here for Lila, not you.'

He stepped towards her and smiled. It did not reach his eyes. 'Don't be a little cunt. Get out of here.' And he was gone, into the waiting room, closing the door firmly behind him.

Tinsley could barely believe what had happened. She stumbled down the corridor blindly and out into the frigid morning air. She stood there for a while then realized she had left her suitcase upstairs. God, she didn't want to go back to that room now...for the first time, she was afraid of Charlie Sherman.

She sat on a small wall outside of the front entrance and tried to stop the trembling that wracked her body. 'What the hell is going on?' she whispered to herself then jumped as a voice behind her said, 'Excuse me, are you Tinsley Chang?'

A young orderly was standing behind her – her suitcase at his side. She nodded and, smiling awkwardly, the orderly handed her the case and disappeared back into the hospital.

She had been banished. She took the case and wheeled it to where the cabs waited but before she got in, she looked up to the fourth floor where the waiting room was.

Charlie Sherman looked down at her – and straight through her as if she didn't exist.

Lila sat at Noah's bedside, her hand in his, watching the machines breathe for him. He had been out of surgery for just a couple of hours now but he looked so still, so pale that she couldn't believe he was actually still alive.

The surgeon had come to find her just after ten am. and told her that they'd stabilized Noah but the bullet had destroyed one lung and clipped his heart. 'I don't want to give you false hope,' he'd said.

Hope. That seemed like a ridiculous notion now and Lila was at her breaking point. Richard, Matty, Riley...now Noah. She put her head down onto the bed and sobbed silently, her fingers twisting in

Noah's. She cried all of her despair out and eventually fell asleep next to him.

There was someone stroking her hair and her head shot up eagerly – was he awake? Her heart thudded with disappointment when she saw Noah was still unconscious. Charlie was sitting beside her, his arm around her shoulders. She sat up and he pulled her into a hug. Lila, drained and exhausted, didn't much feel like being held – by anyone other than Noah – and she pulled away after a second.

'How long have you been here?' She tubbed her face.

'Long enough,' Charlie said. 'Any change?'

'No.' Lila sighed, stroking Noah's hand. 'Hey,' she said looking back at Charlie. 'Where did Tinsley go? She was there one minute, gone the next.'

Charlie smiled coolly. 'She's in town somewhere, I don't know. I thought you had too many people around you last night so I sent her back to the hotel.'

Lila sighed. 'You didn't need to do that, Charlie, she could have stayed.'

'Too many people.'

Lila couldn't be bothered to argue but Charlie's attitude was irritating her. Ever since she'd called him, hysterical, after Noah had been shot, he'd taken over, speaking to the doctors on her behalf without her consent, talking to Noah's parents as if he'd known them for years. It shouldn't irk her, she knew, he was only doing what was best but his attitude that she couldn't handle things for herself was annoying.

It wasn't just that...his entire manner was that of a consoling husband – not a friend. He was dismissive of any positive news about Noah's condition – not that there was much – and he seemed to be 'preparing' her for the worst, as if it were a foregone conclusion that Noah would die.

Lila shook off Charlie's hand on her shoulder. 'Please, Charlie, I just want to be alone, right now.'

'I'm not sure that's a good idea.'

'I wasn't asking for your opinion.' She snapped back at him.

Charlie stared at her, and she looked away. 'Please, Charlie, I want to be with Noah.'

Charlie said no more but the door to Noah's room slammed after him. Lila sighed. *Forget him, Noah is what's important.* She moved her chair closer and stroked his face. Already lean, he seemed to have lost even more weight overnight, his cheeks were hollow, his skin looked pinched.

He was still the most beautiful sight in the world to Lila though and she stood and bent over him, kissed him where she could. 'I love you so much,' she whispered, 'Please come home to me.'

She imagined she felt a slight pressure on her hand from his fingers but it was so slight she knew she imagined it. There was a small tap on the door and Quilla Mallory poked her head around the door. Lila felt relieved, glad to see her friend. Quilla tiptoed in. 'How is he?'

Her lovely dark eyes were full of sorrow and compassion. 'The same,' Lila said, 'Which I'm looking at as good at the moment. His body needs to heal, rest. I'd rather he sleep and....well, we both know how it is, don't we?'

'We do,' Quilla nodded. 'May I stay with you a while?'

Lila nodded, smiling. 'I would like that.' She needed her friend's gentle presence here; not only that, but she knew Quilla really understood what being a victim of violence meant to both the sufferer and their loved ones.

Quilla took the chair vacated by Charlie and placed her hand on Lila's back gently. 'I want you to know, you are not alone in this. Whatever you need, just ask, please.'

Lila felt tears spring up in her eyes. 'Thank you, Quilla.'

'I hope you don't mind; I spoke to the staff and they're going to bring a cot in here for you to sleep on. You need to rest as well.'

See, Charlie? This is the way to care for someone. 'I will, I promise and thank you, Quilla.'

Quilla smiled at her, and then nodded at Noah. 'I think he looks a little brighter, don't you?'

Lila was grateful for her friend's attempt to make Noah seem better but they both knew his life was hanging in the balance.

Lila thought about Lauren, about what she'd stolen from Lila – her child and now possibly her love – for what reason? Was she any different from Cora and her jealousy of Tinsley? Nope.

So much hatred, so much fucking entitlement, she thought angrily. *Who the fuck do these people think they are?*

She said as much to Quilla now and her friend nodded. 'I know. It's twisted and disgusting and sadly all too prevalent.' Quilla sighed. 'Gregor Fisk decided that I was his to decide who I fucked and when I died. But I survived, barely, but I'm still here. You're still here, Lila, and Noah will get better.'

Lila looked her with hopeful eyes. 'You promise?'

Quilla smiled. 'Lila, this is a man who can run a half-marathon and not even break a sweat. Hell, even if he runs a marathon, he just says 'woo, that was a tough one' and jogs to the water stand.'

Lila laughed softly. 'You're right.' She looked back at Noah. 'It's going to be okay.

He's going to come back to me.'

TINSLEY HOLED up in the motel for a couple of days. Because of the prominence of Noah's family, the local news ran reports on his condition on every bulletin – critical but stable.

God. Tinsley, even forty-eight hours after the event was still seething about Charlie's treatment of her. Angry and confused. Had their relationship deteriorated that much or was it because Charlie was stressed out?

Don't be a little cunt.

Every time she thought of that and the look on Charlie's face, she would stop, take in a sharp breath. It was so vicious, so spiteful, and so full of rage. When had they got to this?

The letter. It all began when I read that letter that night. It had been the catalyst she was sure but thinking back to its contents, she couldn't figure out why he would take exception to her reading it. It was a simple goodbye letter from one friend to another.

Please don't try to find me.

Well, Charlie had ignored that and...Tinsley sat up. Charlie had ignored Lila's plea for privacy. He had found her. *So what?* Tinsley told herself, *he's a cop, he had connections and he was probably worried about her.* Except...would he have been able to find her? He hardly had the cash to hire someone to do it for him, but if he had been watching her. An insane theory began to form in Tinsley's head and she closed her eyes trying to sort through the melee.

Why was Charlie upset about the letter? Because it proved Lila had asked him to stay away. So what? He was a friend anxious about another friend. Charlie had disliked Richard. Maybe he knew Rich cheated on Lila – Lila may well have confided in her oldest friend. Except she knew Lila hadn't...

Jesus, Chang, what mad theory are you trying to come up with? Tinsley got up and went to grab a shower. She would go back to the hospital today and whether Charlie Sherman liked it or not, she would see Lila.

As QUILLA HAD TOLD HER, the staff had brought in a cot for Lila to sleep on and she crawled gratefully into it when she could barely keep her eyes open. It was still afternoon and there was some noise from the other parts of the hospital but she soon fell into a deep but troubled sleep, wracked by nightmares...

THEY WERE on the island again, making love slowly in the huge king sized bed. Noah was kissing her as he drove his huge cock into her harder and deeper with every stroke. Lila was gasping, moaning with pleasure and when she came, a thousand stars exploded in her vision.

But then things turned darker as Noah, turning his head, seemed to say something to someone behind him. Are you ready? She's yours...

What? Noah pulled out from her and stood to the side of the bed and then a figure stood before her....she couldn't make out the face. She looked at Noah who smiled. It's okay, baby, this is what I want. The figure had a knife and as Lila began to scream, he raised it above his head and brought to down...

LILA SHUDDERED and half-opened her eyes. 'Ssh, ssh, it's okay baby, go back to sleep.' Someone was stroking her hair, her face and she was so dog-tired she couldn't be bothered to process what was happening. She gave in to the darkness again.

TINSLEY WALKED DOWN THE CORRIDOR, her heart thudding heavily against her ribs. Despite her bravado she was nervous – Charlie was bound to be here and if he treated her like he did the first time...she didn't know that she could keep her temper. She found Noah's room by repeating her lie about being Lila's cousin and as she approached the door, she could see the lighting was low. The door was open a crack and she peered in to see Noah still unconscious and hooked up to the machines. She bit her lip; she knew it had been ridiculous to hope for some sort of miraculous recovery. She stepped into the room a little and stopped.

At the far end of the room, Lila slept on a cot, Charlie crouched beside her. He was stroking her face and Tinsley couldn't tear her eyes away from the tender way he was touching her friend. Jesus...

'Lila?' Charlie's voice was a whisper, 'Can you hear me, baby?'

Lila gave no reaction and to her horror, Tinsley watched Charlie run his hand gently down Lila's body, cup her breast. He slid his hand under her sweater and stroked her belly. Tinsley couldn't believe it. Charlie leaned in and kissed Lila's mouth.

'I'm so sorry, baby...I'll take your pain away...' His voice was a whisper. Tinsley couldn't help the squeak of horror that escaped her and as his head shot up, she ran.

She stumbled down the hallway to the nearest exit and almost fell down the stairs. God, what the fuck was that? She staggered down two flights then stopped, breathing hard.

Above her the exit door crashed open. Tinsley looked up – she was hidden in shadow but she could clearly see Charlie, his face a mask of rage, descending the stairs at a pace. She ran, down, down, down, hearing him in pursuit, her chest tight, little sobs as her terror overtook her. She crashed out into the reception...people.

God. As she collapsed with relief into the arms of a security guard, she turned, expecting Charlie to crash out behind her.

Nothing. No-one. Ignoring the frantic questions of the security guard, she glanced around – had he come out another door? Was he waiting for her outside? Oh god...

Eventually she calmed herself enough to tell the security guard that someone had been chasing her but she could tell he didn't believe her. She managed to persuade him to stay with her until she caught a cab and on the drive back to the motel, she had the cab driver stop at an ATM so she could withdraw some cash. She needed to change motels, she realized, now, tonight and perhaps every night as long as she was in Seattle.

Because she had no intention of leaving Lila at the mercy of Charlie. Her mad conspiracies didn't seem so crazy now. If she was convinced more than ever of one thing, it was this.

Charlie was in love with Lila and Tinsley didn't think there was anything that could stop him from taking what he wanted from her.

Even if it was her life.

LILA SHOWERED AT THE HOSPITAL – quickly, she didn't want to miss a moment in case Noah woke and when she got back to the room, Charlie was waiting for her.

'Hey, beauty.'

She half-smiled back at him. For the last two days, he hadn't left her alone for a moment and as much as she appreciated the support, she wanted to be with Noah, wanted that moment of reunion when – not if, she told herself constantly – he woke up.

'He's looking better,' Charlie said, picking up on her mood. She nodded, dumping her wash bag – hurriedly put together for her by Quilla in the hospital's pharmacy. She combed out her wet hair, never taking her eyes from her love, so still in the bed. She felt strange, almost as if the other man in the room, the man she'd known since she was a child, was a stranger to her. An unwanted interloper. She supposed she should feel guilty but she didn't.

'Charlie, it's good of you to come here every day but there's no need. I'm okay. It might be days, weeks or...' Her voice broke and Charlie moved to hug her but she stepped out of his way, smiling to ease the snub. 'I'm sorry; I just don't want to be touched. You understand, right?'

'Of course.'

She went to sit by Noah's bed and took his hand. 'I was saying, maybe you should go home, get back to finding a place to live. When Noah comes home, I'd like it to be the two of us. You get that, right?'

Charlie nodded, smiled but it didn't reach his eyes and she couldn't read his expression. Hurt? Anger? 'Lila, don't worry. It'll all work out for the best.'

She didn't really know what he meant by that but she couldn't be bothered to figure it out. Go away, go away. 'I wonder when Tinsley will come visit again?'

She turned to look at Charlie then and saw, to her shock, his face crease with annoyance. 'Charlie, what the hell is going on between the two of you?'

Charlie sighed. 'Baby, she's no friend of yours believe me. When we were in New York, she was obsessed with the fact that we ever were...intimate. I wish I had never told her.'

Lila shifted uncomfortably. 'Charlie – that was one night, a hundred years ago. Why would you tell her?'

He shrugged. 'We were having the talk, you know? When we cashed in our v-cards, who with. I didn't think she'd take it so badly.'

'I don't believe it,' Lila retorted. 'Tinsley isn't the jealous type.'

'You don't know her as well as you think.'

Lila sighed. 'I don't want to argue with you, Charlie; I just want to be with Noah. Alone.'

He left the room and she felt relieved. She didn't need to hear about Charlie and Tinsley right now. Fuck, she felt alone. Quilla had told her to call when she needed a break and she was seriously considering it. She'd been living on snacks from the machine for the last four days and her gut felt heavy and sore from junk food. She stroked Noah's hair. 'Will you be okay for a while, my love? I need some hot food in me, so I can look after you properly.'

IN THE CAFETERIA, she sat alone in a corner, not wanting to speak to anyone. The vegetable soup made her feel much better, more awake and she ate some fruit, squirreling away some in her bag along with a couple of bottles of water. Before she went back up to Noah, she stepped outside to breath in some fresh air. She sat on the wall outside the hospital. It was cold but she didn't mind that; the hospital rooms were always too warm for her. She closed her eyes, letting the fresh air swirl around her. It was nearly Christmas, she thought, and once again, her life was in turmoil. God, Noah, please fight this, please come back to me.

Lila knew that if Noah died, she wouldn't survive it. No way. He was her soulmate, her reason to smile. She could not imagine life without him; it was unthinkable.

She opened her eyes and a movement caught her eye. Across the parking lot, a thicket of trees and now as she watched she saw something moving in them. Someone. Whoever it was stopped and she suddenly felt as if they were looking straight at her, watching her. Paranoia. She got up and walked quickly back into the hospital. Freaking out about nothing, she said to herself, as she jabbed the button for the elevator then changed her mind. She ran up the floor flights of stairs – four days of sitting and her muscles were about to atrophy. She felt the slight burn of her muscles as she pulled open the door to Noah's floor and skidded to a stop. Doctors, nurses were rushing into his room, a loud alarm was sounding.

Code Blue....Code Blue...

TINSLEY GRABBED her bag and dumped it into the rental car. She had figured if she was going to be moving around a lot then it would be cheaper and easier. The motel she was at was cheap but clean and she was regretting having to leave but it was just safer. She wouldn't put it past Charlie Sherman to come after her, shut her up. Now, more than ever, she was convinced that Charlie was at the root of everything, and she meant everything, that had happened over the last year or so.

She knew it would sound crazy to the cops if she went to them and she couldn't risk discussing it with Lila - Charlie was her oldest friend. Shit, she thought now as she drove, what the hell am I going to do?

The answer came as she was unpacking at the next motel. Her cell phone buzzed and she was amazed when she saw who it was.

'Harrison Carnegie?'

Harry laughed. 'The same. Hey Tins, how's it hanging?'

He sounded remarkably casual, she thought but she knew him better. 'Harry....about Cora...'

'I'm so sorry, Tins,' Harry dropped the act immediately, 'I should have called weeks ago. Look, on behalf of my whole family, I wanted to say...there's no excuse for what Cora did and I for one am so, so happy that it...that you...' He faltered and she smiled, glad of hearing a friendly voice.

'Harry, it's okay...really. That's in the past...look, I know the D.A. wants to charge Cora but when I get back to New York, I'm going to the police and asking them to drop the charges.'

'You don't have to do that, Tinsley, she knows she did wrong.'

Tinsley smiled down the phone. God it was good to hear his voice. 'I want to, truly. On the condition she gets some major psychiatric help.'

Harry gave a soft laugh. 'I think Mom's got you covered there. Where are you?'

'Huh?'

'You said 'when I get back'?'

Tinsley hesitated for a moment. 'Seattle. Have you heard about Noah Applebaum?'

'Yeah, it's all the news. How's Lila?'

'I wish I knew.'

It was Harry's turn to be confused. 'What?'

It all poured out of her then, the way Charlie had treated her, her suspicions. Harry listened to her in silence and as she came to a halt, she suddenly realized how mad she must sound. 'Harry?'

'What motel are you in?'

She told him. 'Why?'

'I'm coming to Seattle. I don't want you there alone.'

She honestly wanted to tell him no...but she couldn't.

HALSTON AND MOLLY APPLEBAUM, quickly followed by Quilla and Jakob Mallory, found Lila in the hallway outside Noah's room. Tears were flooding down her face but she was smiling. 'He's awake.'

WHEN SHE'D GOTTEN BACK and heard the code blue, it had been as bad as it sounded. Noah had coded and during the fight to get him back, she was kept out of the room, listening to them fighting to get him back and when they did, Noah had opened his eyes and cursed loudly.

Lila, hearing this, had dissolved into tearful laughter and he'd heard her. 'Lila Tierney, get your ass in here.'

The doctors were shaking their head in disbelief but Lila didn't pay attention, just flew into Noah's outstretched arms.

She kissed him with tears rolling down her cheeks, laughing. 'Only you could make such a dramatic entrance to the land of the living.'

When they were alone, they talked about what had happened. The doctor examined him. 'You've stabilized better than a guy an inch from death a few hours ago should have, superman, but take it easy. No sexy shenanigans.'

'Come on, Will,' Noah grinned at the doctor – a friend and colleague. 'Have you seen my fiancé?'

Lila flushed and stuck her tongue out at him. As soon as the doctor left, Noah beckoned her over to him again and wrapped his arms around her, wincing a little.

'Don't strain yourself,' Lila frowned at him. 'Last thing we need is you ripping open your stitches.'

'Yes, Mom.'

'Oh god, I need to call your parents,' she started to stand up but he pulled her back.

'In a while. For now, I just need it to be you and me for a minute.'

She cupped his cheek with her palm and smiled as she kissed him. 'That's all I ever want from now on,' she said softly, 'all I ever want.'

THE SIGHT of Harry's face made Tinsley want to break down and cry and as soon as he wrapped his arms around her, that's exactly what she did. Harry just held her close, his lips at her temple as people looked curiously at them as they hurried past.

He drove her rental car out to a diner he knew outside the city and they ate breakfast together, Harry gently asking her to go over everything again. He held her hand the whole time she was speaking, his thumb stroking a rhythm across her skin. Tinsley felt safe for the first time in.... 'Months,' she said with a half-smile. 'I've been on edge ever since the - well, you know.'

Harry nodded somberly. 'Again, I – '

'Don't apologize any more,' she said, 'you're here now and I've never been so glad to see anyone in my life.'

Harry smiled. 'When I went back to Oz, I couldn't stop thinking about you. I know what we said, no strings, no commitment and I respected that. So I didn't call, didn't get in touch often. But I never stopped thinking about you. I did hear you were back with Charlie Sherman.'

Tinsley met his gaze. 'This isn't some mad ex-girlfriend thing I've got going on, Harry, I swear to god it isn't. I was relieved when he left. He seemed to change on a dime.'

Harry put his hands up. 'Hey, hey. I believe every word. Never liked the guy.' He drained his coffee and signaled to the waitress for a refill, thanking her with a smile.

'Tins, let's get this out in the open. What's your maddest, most wild theory about all this?'

So she told him everything she suspected, in minute detail and Harry listened to it. When she was finished, his eyes were fixed on hers. 'First thing we're going to do is go get your stuff and you're coming to stay with me at the Four Seasons. I'll get extra security.'

Tinsley didn't protest. 'Thank you, Harry, I mean it.'

'Don't mention it, it's the least I can do. Then, we're going to go see Lauren Shannon.'

Tinsley's eyebrows shot up. 'Why?'

Harry looked grim. 'Because if your theory is right, I think she wasn't the only one involved in the shooting of Noah Applebaum.'

HALSTON PUT his arm around Lila's shoulders. 'Lila, I'm sure you're the reason my boy fought so hard to recover.'

Lila blushed red but Noah grinned. 'You bet she is.'

Hal's smile faded. 'Now, what are we going to do about Lauren? I assume you're pressing charges.'

'Yes, we are,' Lila's tone was hard. 'I want that bitch locked up for good.' She clenched her hands into fists and Molly hugged her.

'My daughter will pay for what she has done.' They all turned around. Lila had never met Derek Shannon before but the look of sorrow and guilt on his face said it all. Derek looked at Noah.

'Noah, I'm so happy to see you alive. May I please speak to you for a moment, I promise, I won't stay long.'

Noah half-smiled. 'Of course.' He gave a sharp look at his father who was about to protest. Derek introduced himself to all of them then sat down by Noah's bed.

'Lauren will spend the rest of her life in prison. She will have to rely on the county's charity for her defense because in my eyes, she has no defense. I came here to apologize on her behalf, and to tell you that I am no longer in contact with her. She has gone too far this time.'

Lila couldn't help give a cynical laugh. 'Yep, because killing an unborn child wasn't *'far enough'*.' She left the room, disgusted, having heard enough. Molly and Quilla followed her out and took her down to the cafeteria. Molly shooed her into a seat while Quilla brought over a tray heaving with food. 'Eat,' she ordered Lila, 'and then Jakob is going to take you to our place and you're going to get some sleep. We'll all sit with Noah.'

Lila had to admit it was tempting, although she was loath to leave Noah now he was awake. She was aware, however, that she looked atrocious. Quilla and Molly chatted easily to her as she scarfed down the meal gratefully, knowing they were distracting her from what must be going on upstairs.

LATER, she kissed Noah goodbye, and left with Jakob. He drove her back to his and Quilla's home on Bainbridge Island. 'God, this place is beautiful,' Lila gaped at the stunning house, all white and Zen. Jakob, who she had discovered, wasn't nearly as stern as he looked, grinned at her.

'All Quilla's doing,' he said proudly, 'would you like a drink?'

'Love one, something cold would be nice.'

'Iced tea?'

'Perfect.' She followed him into a vast kitchen – from the homely mess of it, she guessed it was the heart of their home. Out of the French windows she saw a large garden where a tall, blonde girl was playing with two small boys. Jakob stuck his head out of the door. 'Hey guys, we're back.'

'Daddy!' As the two boys greeted him, he swept them up into his arms and kissed them. Lila grinned as they shrieked with joy. 'Come and say hello to our friend Lila.'

The two boys weren't shy at all, climbing onto Lila's lap and studying her closely. They were gorgeous, and she couldn't help but hug them. The blonde girl grinned merrily at her.

'Hey there, I'm Hayley, these two monster's aunt. Well, actually, technically, I'm their cousin. It's complicated. It's nice to see you, Quilla talks about you all the time.'

Lila relaxed in their company, enjoying the tea and playing with the boys. God, it felt good to do something normal but she had to admit, seeing the two boys playing and enjoying the company of their father and cousin, she ached for little Matty. She had never thought she would be a mother until she'd actually gotten pregnant and now she couldn't imagine not being one.

Hayley showed her to the guest room as Lila began to flag and Lila sank gratefully into a dreamless sleep.

When she woke it was dark and she saw that someone, possibly Hayley, had put a few clothes on the end of the bed, new underwear. In the en-suite bathroom, she found toiletries and a new toothbrush laid out. She smiled; the thoughtfulness and kindness of these people was unlimited; Noah knew how to pick his friends. Her thoughts flashed to Charlie and her stomach clenched. Would they ever get back to how it had been? She hoped so, but a small part of her also considered that life without him, with these friends, with Noah, might not be such a bad thing. Maybe they had been wrapped around each other's lives long enough.

Showered and dressed in jeans and a sweater that fit her perfectly, she went downstairs to find Quilla was cooking. Her friend waved a wooden spoon at her in greeting. 'Hey, how did you sleep?'

'Wonderfully, thank you, and thanks for the clothes and things, it was very kind and much appreciated.'

Quilla grinned, her lovely face lit up. 'Noah threw me out, said I should come home and feed you. His dad and step-mom are with him but I think he was hoping for some peace to get some sleep. He did look exhausted when I left but unbelievably good.'

Lila sat down at the huge kitchen table, watching Quilla cook an enormous pan of chili. Quilla crushed some garlic and put it into the pan with chopped onions. 'I thought I'd make just a ton of comfort food,' she said, 'I've sent Jakob and the boys out to get some ice cream for dessert, so we can girl-talk if we want.'

'The boys are adorable,' Lila grinned, 'and I know they're adopted but they look so much like Jakob.'

Quilla laughed. 'I know. When we went to the children's home to meet all the kids, I took one look at them and said '*they* are our children'. Jakob agreed and that was that. Well, not quite but you know what I mean.'

Lila smiled. 'I do. I spent my whole childhood in a home. I would have loved for some people like you and Jakob to come along.'

'We could always adopted you now,' Quilla joked and Lila liked it that she didn't say 'oh poor thing'. Lila had never felt that loneliness... because of Charlie, she thought and she suddenly felt bad for how she had been treating him lately.

She would call him, she decided, now Noah was out of immediate danger, and try and get their friendship back on track, albeit with new boundaries. Decided, she went to help Quilla prepare the dinner and they chatted easily until Jakob and the boys returned.

TINSLEY AND HARRY were in his hotel suite, planning their visit to the prison where Lauren Shannon was being held. 'Do we do good cop/bad cop?' She asked Harry who grinned.

'No we just offer her the thing she loves the most – money. Money to get the best lawyer possible.'

'Surely her dad would have given her that?'

Harry shook his head. 'I did some digging. Daddy Shannon has disowned her; she has to rely on the state.'

'Woah,' Tinsley's eyes were wide, 'that's cold.'

Harry shrugged. 'From what I've found out, it's long overdue. I don't blame the man; even familial love can only go so far when someone behaves like that.'

Tinsley nodded. 'How do we stop her hiring the best lawyers with our money and getting off?'

Harry grinned wickedly. 'Easy. By hiring them first ourselves but she doesn't need to know that does she?'

'Harry...this all takes money and I know how generous you are but really, this isn't your fight?'

'Isn't it? Just because Noah Applebaum isn't my family, all of this leads back to Lila's stabbing and Richard's murder. It is my fight. Plus, anyone who tries to hurt you immediately makes my shit list.'

She smiled and touched his cheek. He covered her hand with his, holding her to his skin, his eyes on her. 'Remind me again how I could have been so dumb as to go back to Australia without you?'

Tinsley flushed with pleasure. 'It wasn't the right time for us.'

He nodded and they gazed at each other in silence for a long moment. 'And now?' He said softly then without waiting for a reply, leaned forward and brushed her lips with his. Tinsley's hands came up automatically and slid into his short hair. As they kissed, Harry pulled her onto his lap, his mouth hungry on hers, and his hands under her t-shirt, sliding it over her head.

Soon naked, they tumbled onto the floor and Tinsley moved down his body to take him into her mouth, sweeping her lips over the wide crest of his pulsing cock. The silky skin felt so good on her tongue as she traced the blue veins, and she tasted the salty tang of his pre-cum. Harry moaned as she teased him, and soon he was pulling her upwards so he could thrust inside her. Tinsley straddled him, his hands on her breasts as they moved together, both smiling and loving. This was so different to the dead serious sex that she and Charlie had and even though it was good, this was love-making, not just sex. She and Harry bonded as friends first then lovers and the combination left her feeling complete.

Afterward they ordered room service and ate it in front of the TV., chatting idly about Australia. 'Do you think you'll go back, ever? Long term, I mean.' Harry asked her as he scooped some apple pie into his mouth.

'Ask me that a few months ago and I would have said no. But now?

I can see it.' She hoped she wasn't blushing too much but Harry grinned at her.

'That is very good to know, Miss Chang. That is very good to know.' And he kissed her again and they started where they had left off.

NOAH WAITED FOR THE DOCTOR – his colleague Doug Halpern – to check him over. Doug was a cardio-god, one of the best in the world. He nodded at Noah now. 'If all my patients were in as good physical condition as you, Applebaum, my life would be easier. Don't get me wrong, you have a long way to go yet, but your wounds are healing, your heart trace showed no problems and even with one lung, you'll be able to function pretty much the same. Maybe not too many marathons anymore, but even that isn't out of the realms of possibility.'

Noah grinned. 'You know me, Doug, I get antsy if I don't exercise.'

'Yup, he's weird like that, me, I prefer sloth,' Lila walked into the room and smiled at them both. She studied Noah. 'You do look good, baby.'

She went to kiss his cheek and sit by him. Doug nodded at them.

'Well, just be careful you two. Don't put too much stress on his heart by being too gorgeous, Lila.'

'Dude, are you hitting on my fiancée?' Noah was laughing as Lila flushed.

Doug grinned. 'Hell yes. Perks of having saved your damn life.'

Noah nodded. 'Fair enough.'

'When you two have stopped objectifying me...' but Lila laughed along with them. It felt so good to be relaxed again, to know that they would be okay after everything. Doug left them alone and Lila snuggled into Noah's side.

'Hey handsome.'

'You look refreshed,' he noted, brushing his lips against her. 'That's good, I was worried.'

'You were worried about me?' Lila rolled her eyes. 'Quilla and

Jakob spoiled me. I really do have to commend you on your choice of friends, I adore them, and their kids. So cute.'

'Making you broody?'

'Oh yes but we need to get you back to fighting fit before we even consider that again.'

She kissed his jawbone, smoothed the hair at his temples. 'Thank god you're okay.'

'Between us we have nine lives, we must have,' he nodded, twirling a lock of her hair – freshly washed that morning – between his finger and thumb.

She studied him. 'Do you have this feeling of what's next? I mean, we've been through the mill these last eighteen months but I still feel, there's more to come. Am I being pessimistic?'

Noah considered. 'No...and I think it's that we still don't know for sure who kicked this whole thing off. Who it was who stabbed you – or hired someone to do it. We've – you've – had no closure on that.'

'I think you're right but it could be we'll never know.' She sighed. 'Is it wrong I want to lock you away somewhere safe where no-one can touch you?'

'Nope, that's exactly how I feel about you.'

'It sucks.'

'Yep.'

She nuzzled closer to him, careful not to tug on any of the tubes and wires which stuck of out him. 'A day at a time.'

'A day at a time,' he agreed and held her close.

TINSLEY HADN'T STEPPED two feet inside the prison when she decided she never, ever wanted to do it again. The sense of hopelessness was palpable. She slipped her hand into Harry's feeling him squeeze her fingers reassuringly. The Carnegie name had gotten them in to interview Lauren Shannon, they had sent their offer of money in advance. As expected, Lauren had jumped at the chance and Tinsley felt no guilt about the way they were fooling her.

Lauren's hair was shoved into a greasy ponytail and she barely made eye cotact with them both as she was led into the interview room. She flicked her eyes dismissively at Tinsley and Tinsley glared back.

Harry did all the talking and he got straight to the point. 'Lauren, did someone tell you, or pay you to shoot Noah Applebaum?'

Lauren smirked. 'You don't think a woman could come up with and execute – so to speak – a plan like that?'

'Oh I do...I just don't believe it in this case. So, tell me, did someone hire you? Or perhaps a better description would be 'encourage'?'

Lauren looked out of the window. 'I called a lawyer, one of my dad's friends, told him you were stumping up the money to hire me good representation. He told me no.'

'Not my problem. Answer the question.'

Lauren smiled. 'Perhaps. Perhaps someone with a vested interest in seeing Noah dead was...supportive. Perhaps they found the gun for me.'

Tinsley was getting irritated. 'Was it Charlie Sherman?'

Harry cleared his throat – a warning and Tinsley got his meaning – leading the witness.

Lauren's eyes were twinkling – she was enjoying the game. 'He didn't give me his name.'

Progress. Harry glanced at Tinsley. 'Lauren, are you able to describe this man?'

'I never met him. He called me.'

Tinsley made a disgusted sound. 'Motherfucker.'

Lauren laughed softly. 'So you see...I can't even use that as a defense. Who's going to believe that? A man told me to do it.'

Harry too was frustrated. 'Is there anything, anything distinguishing about his voice, the way he spoke, accent?'

She shook her head. 'I got the impression he was disguising his voice.'

'Fuck,' Tinsley hissed then looked back at Lauren. 'Just tell us what he said, his exact words.'

'He asked me if I wanted to get back at Noah and told me he could help me. He said he'd pay two-hundred grand to shoot Noah but I had to do it in public and in front of his girlfriend.'

'Did the man ask you to shoot Lila as well?'

Lauren shook her head. 'No, that was just something I said to the cops when I was arrested. He was very specific – I was only to kill Noah.'

'Did he give a reason for that?'

'Yes.' She smiled nastily. 'He told me that he wanted to be the one to kill Lila – said he'd tried before but next time, he would take his time and make sure she was dead.'

Tinsley felt sick and she felt Harry slip his arm around her waist. 'Is there anything else you can tell us?' She asked Lauren, who chuckled darkly.

'Yeah. I wouldn't want to be Lila Tierney when he gets hold of her.'

'SHE TOLD US NOTHING,' Tinsley groaned as they got back into the car and Harry looked at her in amazement.

'Are you kidding? She told us so much.'

'Like what?'

'For one thing....Lila's attacker is still out there. Another – we know now it can't have been Riley – which means Riley was probably killed and framed. Another – if the killer was able to manipulate Lauren, what makes us think he won't have done it to others. There's one more person I think we have to see before we really double-down on this and go to Lila and Noah.'

'Who?'

Harry smiled grimly. 'The one person we know can be manipulated easily – especially as she was in love with the man we suspect. My sister. We're going to see Cora.'

. . .

THE CAB STOPPED outside of the hospital entrance and Lila thanked the driver and tipped him well. 'Could you come back about ten-thirty?'

The driver smiled. 'Of course, Miss, see you then.'

Lila walked towards the entrance of the hospital. She'd spent the night at home. Getting things ready for Noah's homecoming. Now he was out of bed and into a chair, the doctors had told him he could be released to rest at home in as few as two weeks. Lila couldn't quite believe it. She grinned to herself now and her pace quickened.

'Lila.'

She started violently and whirled around. Charlie smiled at her. 'Sorry.'

'Charlie...*jesus*.' She put a hand on her chest to still her thumping heart. 'Where have you been? I've been trying to call you.'

'I know, honey, I'm sorry, had things I was doing. Found a place.'

'Good. Look I was just going in to see Noah.'

'How is he?'

She smiled. 'Doing really well. Come in and say hello.'

Charlie looked up at the well-lit hospital. 'I won't today, I don't want to intrude. I'll come back another day.'

'You sure?'

He nodded. 'I would like us to sit and talk soon. Very soon. I think we need to get some stuff resolved.'

Lila nodded. 'I think we do. Call me tomorrow, okay? And we'll talk.'

'Promise.' And he was gone. Lila frowned after him. She wasn't imagining it, their friendship had change drastically. There was awkwardness there.

Tomorrow. Tomorrow they would see if they could salvage anything from the mire of recent events and rejuvenate their friendship.

. . .

TINSLEY HAD ELECTED to stay in Seattle while Harry went to see his sister in New York. Harry had understood; whatever she had done, Cora had still instigated a ferocious attack on Tinsley.

'I don't think it's a good idea for us to be in the same room,' she had told him and he agreed. Nothing good would come of that.

Harry had told her he would fly straight back to Seattle after speaking to Cora and so Tinsley was holed up at his hotel, mindlessly ordering room service and watching TV. to take her mind off what they were finding out. It didn't work and she ended up with a yellow legal pad and pen making charts and flow diagrams and writing everything down. It didn't take her long to make the connection and now she wondered how they hadn't seen it months ago. Of course, if she was right, it meant she herself had fucked the killer – unwittingly of course – and that their whole relationship had been a lie. If Charlie was as dangerously obsessed with Lila as they thought...

'He'll never stop.' God, she needed to warn Lila now. She would risk Lila not believing her, even if it lodged a tiny suspicion of doubt in her mind, it might protect her. Tinsley considered what to do next. Harry had asked her to stay in the room, keep safe, but if Lila was still in danger...

She could get a cab straight to the hospital and speak to Lila there; it would safe right? Probably safer than going to her home...

Mind made up, she grabbed her purse and head out of the door.

As far as she was concerned, there wasn't a moment to lose.

IT DIDN'T TAKE LONG for Harry to extract a confession from Cora, who broke down in tears. 'It wasn't like that, he didn't ask me to kill her but just said...while she was in the picture, we could never be together.'

'Fucking asshole,' Harry raged. His mother, Delphine sat on Cora's other side, looked devastated but resigned.

'Do you think Lila is in danger?'

Harry nodded. 'The worst kind – and I don't think we can wait any longer to tell her. I have to go back to Seattle. Right now.'

· · ·

LILA AND NOAH were laughing together when Tinsley knocked softly at the door. Lila's eyes widened when she saw her friend and she jumped up and pulled her into a hug.

'Where the hell have you been?'

Tinsley realized her friend was crying and she hugged her back tightly. 'I need to talk to you, alone,' she whispered. 'Meet me at the bottom of the stairs, the exit is next door.'

She pulled away from Lila's curious stare and kissed Noah. 'I'm so glad you're looking so well.'

'Thanks Tins...what's going on?'

'Nothing you should worry about. I'm sorry, I only have a few minutes, I have to go pick Harry up at the airport.'

'Harry...Carnegie?' Lila was shocked but Tinsley smiled.

'The very one. He would like to come see you if you don't mind.'

She stayed for another five minutes then nodded for Lila to follow her out. 'Give me five minutes then come down.'

'What's with all the intrigue?'

'I want to make sure I wasn't followed.'

Lila stared at her. 'You're scaring me.'

Tinsley tried to smile. 'I don't mean to. Remember, five minutes.'

And she disappeared in to the stairwell. Lila shook her head – what the hell was going on?

Noah asked the same question and she shook her head. 'I don't know, I really don't.'

Five minutes later, she stuck her cell phone in her pocket. 'Be back in a few.' She kissed him but he held onto her hand.

'Lila...I'm worried.'

'Let me just go find out what's on Tinsley's mind. Get some rest, I love you.'

He didn't look happy. 'Come back soon. Love you too.'

Lila smiled and went out into the corridor pushing open the door. It was pretty poorly lit and she walked down carefully so she didn't trip.

'Tins?'

No reply. Lila's heart began to beat a little faster. She peered into the dark as she descended the final flight. 'Tins.'

Her foot hit something soft and she heard a moan. Lila snagged her phone from her pocket and switched on the light. Tinsley lay on her back, her face contorted in such pain Lila gasped. Tinsley was covered in blood and the hilt of a knife protruded from her stomach.

'Oh god, no, no, no...' Lila dropped to her knees and Tinsley looked up at her with wide eyes.

'Lila...no...he's...'

A gloved hand was clamped over Lila's face, and as she struggled, her attacker slammed her head against the wall and she was dumped, dazed to the floor. As she began to pass out, she saw the attacker rip the knife from Tinsley's body and begin to stab her again as Tinsley, her voice weakening, cried '*No, no, please, no...*

Charlie, please no...'

NOAH STARTED TO GET PANICKY. Surely Lila should be back by now? He eased out of bed, thankful he no longer had wires and tubes attached, and shuffled to the door. All was quiet in the corridor but the nurse at the station looked up and smiled.

'Look who's out of bed.'

He tried to smile. 'Have you see Lila?'

The nurse shook her head. 'Not since earlier. Why?'

Noah just shook his head. 'She as supposed to be back by – '

He turned sharp as the door to the stairwell opened and a breathless, panicked young man almost fell out of the door. 'Please, I need help...there's a girl down there...I think she's been stabbed.'

'No, no, no...' The adrenaline coursed through Noah and he lurched towards the door just as the nurse, alarmed, both called for assistance and yelled at Noah to stop.

'Noah, you're not well enough...stop...'

He didn't listening. He grabbed the rail and climb down the stairs as best as he could, desperate to get to her...not again, please, not again...

The lights flooded on and he heard people shouting behind him. As he made it to the top of the last flight, he saw her.

Tinsley. She was prone on the floor, in a pool of blood, her clothes soaked red. Noah's heart began to pound out of his chest as he rushed down to her. 'Tinsley, oh my god...'

Tinsley opened her eyes and looked up at him. 'Noah...' He could barely hear her. 'Noah, he has Lila....Charlie has Lila...'

Everything in Noah's world stopped. 'Did Charlie do this to you?'

She nodded, gasping for air. 'I'm sorry, Noah...I'm sorry...' As the medics rushed in to help her, to help him, Tinsley's head fell back and her last breath sighed from her lungs.

A medic listened to her chest and started to perform CPR but Noah knew it was too late. There was so much blood. Tinsley was dead.

And Lila was gone...

SHE HAD WATCHED him stab her friend to death and now, as she started to regain consciousness, she wondered why she wasn't dead too.

Charlie. She opened her eyes. She was laying on her back on the back seat of a moving car, her hands and feet bound. She turned her head to see him driving, his face set and grim. It was Charlie. It was Charlie. It didn't take a genius to figure it all out now. As far as Charlie was concerned, Lila belonged to him. He'd stopped her wedding by stabbing her, framed Riley – had he known she and Riley had slept together? – and probably killed him, arranged Richard's murder. Had he coerced Lauren into shooting Noah?

God. You should have finished me in that changing room, she thought angrily, then at least the others could have been saved. You bastard. You cowardly fucker.

Now she thought about it, it was so obvious. He'd called her that day....

. . .

CHARLIE SHERMAN SMILED GRIMLY to himself. *She was at the bridal boutique. So easy...he'd checked it out a while back when she told him about the place. Security was minimal – yeah, they set an alarm at night, but during the day... The fire exit he could jimmy open in seconds...wasit really going to be this easy?*

He could hardly wait. He'd dreamed of this day for years, ever since that night that she'd given her virginity to him. God the feel of her skin, her silky tight cunt as he'd thrust into her. She'd been so drunk that any inhibitions had fled and she'd enjoyed herself as much as he had. Then...nothing. 'Let's keep that one night special, I don't want to ruin our friendship because of sex.'

Bitch. He'd agreed, of course, how else was he going to keep her close and he'd waited, and watched as her beauty, her warmth, her quick wit had brought the men flocking. His Lila wasn't a whore though, she chose her lovers carefully. And then she'd met the billionaire and it had all gone to hell. Richard fucking Carnegie. When he'd found out that Carnegie had cheated on Lila, he was sure that she'd end it. She even knew about the cheating and stayed with him and then promised to marry the motherfucker.

But it was the night, a few days before the wedding when he'd known what he had to do. He'd gone to meet her at the bar, a little later than normal. The door was locked but he'd gone around the back and sure enough, the back door was open. He walked into the bar – and saw them. Lila and Riley. Fucking, right there on the floor. He watched them silently – well, he watched her, her face when she came, when Riley's face was buried in her sex.

Bitch.

Slipping in the back door of the bridal boutique was easy. A quick check of the other fitting room and then he was there. She pulled back the curtain and he drove the knife into her soft belly. So easy, so beautiful. She barely had time to gasp; he stabbed her quickly, brutally, blood spattering then gushing from her wounds.

Afterward he made his escape but the adrenaline inside was raging what a rush, what a thrill...

.   .   .

CHARLIE LOOKED BACK at Lila and smiled. 'You're awake. Good.' His voice was almost tender.

Lila's eyes filled with tears. 'You murdered Tinsley.'

Charlie shrugged. 'She got in my way.'

'She used to be your girlfriend...I thought you loved her.'

Charlie laughed. 'For a bright woman, Lila, you can be dense. The only woman I've ever loved is you.'

Hearing him say it out loud in such a matter of fact manner was terrifying. 'You were the one who stabbed me.'

Charlie steered the car to a stop and turned to her. 'Yes.'

'Why?'

'Richard.'

She shook her head. 'What about him?'

'Riley. And then Noah. And every other man you've fucked. Every one of them took something from me. And the only way I can think of to right that wrong is to take you.'

She stared at him and didn't know the monster in front of her. 'You're going to kill me.'

'Yes, Lila, of course I am.'

She felt strangely relieved. 'And you won't hurt anyone else?'

He smiled, a strange rictus. 'No, Lila. I won't be able to, because you and I will die together. Once I stab you, I'll cut my own throat. I don't want to live in a world without you.'

She closed her eyes. 'You're insane.'

'And you're going to die today. Now, lie still and quiet and it'll all be over soon.' Charlie started the car again and pulled out onto the highway.

HARRY CARNEGIE STARED at the police in disbelief. 'No. No, she can't be...*oh god...*' He covered his mouth as if he were about to throw up. Tinsley dead? No, they must be mistaken.

When he'd got to the airport and she hadn't met him, he'd called the suite and one of his security men had told him Tinsley had insisted on going to the hospital. He'd taken a cab there only to be greeted by reception full of police and shocked faces. He heard a whisper. Someone was murdered in the hospital. His chest had clenched tight but he brushed it away. He'd asked for Noah's room at the desk which is when they'd called a policeman over and he'd been taken into a private room.

There, the detective in charge had told him gently that a Miss Tinsley Chang had been stabbed to death in a stairwell, and that a Miss Tierney had been abducted.

Tinsley was dead.

Harry turned away from the other men so they couldn't see the raw grief in his face. I just found you again, baby. Why didn't you wait for me to come here? 'Can I see Mr Applebaum now, please?'

'Of course...he wanted to tell you himself but we thought you two might be too close...'

Harry gave a humorless laugh. 'We've never even met.' And yet they were bonded in blood.

Noah Applebaum looked haunted. As Harry stepped into his hospital room, Noah turned and saw him. The two men stared at each other for a long moment then Noah unsteadily moved towards him. These two men, who had never met, embraced, hugged each other tightly.

'I'm so sorry, Harry, I'm so sorry.'

'Me too, Noah. There's still hope, right?'

Noah pulled out of the hug and tried to smile. 'You bet there is, Lila's a fighter. If I wasn't in this damn hospital, I'd be out hunting that son-of-a-bitch down, but they're watching me like a hawk.'

Harry nodded. He studied Noah's movement. 'So you feel okay? You can walk?'

Noah half-smiled, knowing something else was coming. 'Yeah, why?'

'I can distract anyone that needs to be distracted.'

'They took my clothes so I couldn't sneak out.'

Harry sized him up. 'Okay, so I'm about two inches shorter but we're a similar build.'

Noah did grin then. 'You sure?'

Harry nodded. 'If the roles were reversed?'

'You betcha, buddy. You could come if you want.'

'I don't want to leave Tinsley,' Harry said simply, as he began to undress. Noah nodded, understanding.

'Man, when this is over and Lila's safe...'

'Go,' Harry brushed his gratitude away. 'We'll have all the time to talk after. You got any idea where he would take her?'

Noah shook his head. 'But I know her history and I know how obsessed people think. If he's going to kill her, he'll want to do it somewhere significant. I'll start where they first met – at the old children's home in Puget Ridge.'

Harry nodded. 'Good. Then I'll give you a one hour start before I go to the police. Back up, you understand?'

Noah shook Harry's hand gratefully. 'I owe you big.'

Harry gripped his hand tightly. 'If you can, kill the fucker. Please. For Lila. For Tinsley. For my brother.'

Noah sneaked out of the hospital easier than he expected. Everyone was just wrapped up in Tinsley's murder. When he'd been trying to guess where Charlie would take her, he'd had to think back to the times he and Lila had talked about her childhood. That was back in the early days, when she was in rehab, before they'd even kissed, before that dream of a day when they'd made love – and made Matty. God, he wanted the chance to make babies with Lila, to build a house, a family with her. She was his heart and now his heart was being ripped from him and it was a million times more painful than the bullet Lauren had fired into him.

In spite of his bravado, his assurances to Harry, Noah's body was screaming at him. His chest burned, his one remaining lung working overtime. Despite his calm exterior, Noah was in the worst agony of his life – physically and emotionally but the adrenaline, the need to get to Lila was all-encompassing.

Just be alive, sweetheart, please. Fight, Lila, fight...I'm coming for you.

. . .

CHARLIE PARKED the car behind the old children's home and pulled Lila from the back seat. He'd taped her mouth so she couldn't scream. After he'd taken her in and laid her on the floor of an empty room, he took the tape off.

'Scream all you want, no-one will get to you before I kill you. There's no point, there's no hope now, Lila.'

He grabbed his backpack and pulled out a gun and a knife. The knife was stained with blood. 'Whoops,' he said, grinning nastily. 'Better wipe Tinsley off of this before you get it.'

Lila's temper exploded then. 'You killed innocent people Charlie, and my whole life I've been defending you from people saying that you're bad news, that you're bad and mean and scary. I defended you!' She started to cry now. 'I loved you, Charlie, not as a lover, but as a friend, as a brother. You were my *person*.'

She was sobbing and to her amazement, he scooped her up and held her. 'That's all I've ever wanted to be, Lila, is yours. Yours alone.'

'You stabbed me,' she whispered and he nodded.

'I did. And I'm going to again, Lila, you understand that now, right?'

Lila drew in a breath and when she pulled away and met his gaze, she smiled. 'I know. I know, baby, it has to be this way.'

Charlie's smile spread across his face. 'It does.' He wiped her tears from her cheeks.

You fucking deluded psycho...'Charlie, if we're going to die today...then surely we should celebrate us before you cut me open.'

A frown crossed his face. 'What do you mean?'

She smiled and leaned forward brushing her lips against his. *Would he fall for this?* Her heart was thudding madly. She looked up at him from beneath her lashes. 'Fuck me, Charlie...let's go out on a high. Fuck me good and then I promise, I won't fight you.'

He stared at her and she couldn't tell if he would go for it but then he reached for the knife. She held her breath then he severed the tape around her feet, around her hands. He tore open her dress and placed the tip of the knife against her belly.

'I swear, if you're messing with me, Lila, I'll stab you so many times they won't bother to count them...and then I'll do the same to your fucking Doctor.'

Slowly, Lila lay back and spread her legs. 'Fuck me, Charlie...please....'

With a growl he yanked the zipper on his jeans down and shoving her legs further apart. Playing along, she reached for his face. 'Kiss me, baby.'

He ground his mouth down on hers and Lila kissed him back... and then clamped her teeth down on his tongue hard. Charlie screamed and rocked back, and Lila jammed her foot hard into his exposed groin, then kicked him in the face and rolled out of his way. She scrambled to her feet and went for his gun but he grabbed her leg and dragged her back toward him.

'You fucking little bitch! I warned you, I warned you.'

God, he was strong but Lila, fear and anger raging through her, managed to fight him off again as he swiped at her with his knife. The tip of the blade caught the soft skin of her belly and she cried out.

'You'll scream for me again and again before I'm done, you whore,' Charlie was getting the upper hand again as he grasped both of her wrists but she twisted away from him and ran through the old derelict house. The back door hung open and she headed toward that, would have made it too but she didn't see the hole in the floorboards and her foot disappeared into it, her ankle snapping with a loud crack. Lila did scream then as loud as she could because she couldn't move and Charlie was advancing on her, the knife glinting in his hand.

The pain in her ankle was making her light-headed but as Charlie dropped to his knees beside her, she tried to move. Charlie just laughed and to her horror, he pressed his face to the cut on her abdomen and lapped at the blood with his tongue.

'Does your cunt taste as sweet as your blood, Lila?'

'Fuck you, Charlie.'

'My pleasure...' He reached under her dress and yanked her delicate panties off with one motion. Lila rammed her legs together but he just grinned, his hand burrowing between them. Lila screamed as loud as she could, more out of desperation than hope.

The door, the front door, was kicked in and a whirlwind of fury threw himself at Charlie, knocking them both flying.

Noah. 'Oh my god,' Lila whispered as her lover wrestled and fought with Charlie. Charlie punched him hard against the chest, against the wound and Noah was winded. Lila dragged herself up on one foot and dived to help Noah, throwing herself bodily at Charlie while Noah recovered his composure. Noah roared as Charlie grabbed Lila by the throat and raised the knife to kill her; Noah grabbed Charlie by the back of the head and dragged him away. Lila scrambled for the knife Charlie had dropped and swiped at the man as he got away from Noah and went after her. Lila and Charlie tumbled to the floor and for a second, it looked all over.

The knife in Charlie's hand was driven hard at her – just as Charlie's throat exploded and covered Lila in blood. The knife dropped from his hand and he slumped, very, very dead to the floor, his eyes bulging from his head, staring straight into Lila's.

Noah lowered the gun – the gun that Charlie had forgotten about – and dropped it to the floor. He came to Lila immediately and they held each other.

'It's over now, my darling Lila. It's all over.'

And for once, she was glad to hear those words...

Noah kissed her tenderly and grinned as they moved together. 'Well, Miss Tierney...what's next?...

THE END.

❀ Created with Vellum

Lightning Source UK Ltd.
Milton Keynes UK
UKHW022019110822
407199UK00003B/81